Business is Business

The troll rubbed his belly, disappointed. He so wanted to tell Martes of his rough journey over the western ocean, his trek through the New World forest, his perfect choice of where to place the child. "But I . . ."

"Oberon's ovaries!" Martes barked. "Don't you realize? When he finds his son gone, Lord Douglas will sing me again. And when he sings someone, he knows all they know. No secret stays buried, no sin unrevealed."

Scratching his protruding brow, the troll asked, "Won't he come to me next then?"

"Yes."

"And won't I know where his son is?" He knew he was missing something. He just couldn't figure it out.

"Of course." Martes smiled. It was not a comforting sight. "But you won't tell him anything."

"I won't?" The troll's eyebrows reached for each other in an expression of pure confusion.

"Of course not," Martes said, pulling a pennywhistle from his coat pocket and putting it to his lips. He covered all the holes with his small fingers and, with the other end pointed straight at the troll, blew one short, shrill note.

"Oh," said the troll, looking down at the tiny dart that had just sprouted from his throat. Suddenly it was all very clear.

TOR BOOKS BY ADAM STEMPLE

• • •

Singer of Souls
Steward of Song

STEWARD
OF SONG

• • •

ADAM STEMPLE

A TOM DOHERTY ASSOCIATES BOOK

NEW YORK

This is a work of fiction. All of the characters, organizations, and events portrayed in this novel are either products of the author's imagination or are used fictitiously.

STEWARD OF SONG

Copyright © 2008 by Adam Stemple

All rights reserved.

A Tor Book
Published by Tom Doherty Associates, LLC
175 Fifth Avenue
New York, NY 10010

www.tor-forge.com

Tor® is a registered trademark of Tom Doherty Associates, LLC.

ISBN-13: 978-0-7653-5538-6
ISBN-10: 0-7653-5538-8

First Edition: March 2008
First Mass Market Edition: December 2008

Printed in the United States of America

0 9 8 7 6 5 4 3 2 1

FOR HEIDI, AN INSPIRATION TO US ALL

Hard names at first, and threatening words,
that are but noisy breath,
may grow to clubs and naked swords,
to murder and to death.
—Isaac Watts, *Songs Divine and Moral, Song XVII*
"Love Between Brothers and Sisters"

STEWARD
OF SONG

· · · · prologue · · · ·

The troll leaned against the streetlight, trying to look nonchalant. He was a little nervous. Working with Martes was a chancy business to begin with, and this latest job had been even chancier than most.

It wasn't every day that you kidnapped your liege lord's only child.

"What news?" came a voice from right behind him. He nearly jumped out of his stone skin. Turning, he saw Martes.

"It is done," said the troll, surprising himself with his even tone.

"Excellent," Martes said, black rat-eyes gleaming. Martes was only a third the troll's height, with a hump and a limp and a giant grotesque nose, but the troll knew that no fey that crossed the little bogie had ever survived for more than a day or two.

"I left him with . . ."

"Shut it!" Martes had to reach up, but he landed a solid shot to the troll's stomach. It hurt more than the troll would have thought, coming from a creature so much smaller than he was. "Don't tell me where you took him."

The troll rubbed his belly, disappointed. He so wanted to tell Martes of his rough journey over the western ocean, his trek through the New World forest, his perfect choice of where to place the child. "But I . . ."

"Oberon's ovaries!" Martes barked. "Don't you realize? When he finds his son gone, Lord Douglas will sing me again. And when he sings someone, he knows all that they know. No secret stays buried, no sin unrevealed."

Scratching his protruding brow, the troll asked, "Won't he come to me next then?"

"Yes."

"And won't I know where his son is?" He knew he was missing something. He just couldn't figure it out.

"Of course." Martes smiled. It was not a comforting sight. "But you won't tell him anything."

"I won't?" The troll's eyebrows reached for each other in an expression of pure confusion.

"Of course not," Martes said, pulling a pennywhistle from his coat pocket and putting it to his lips. He covered all the holes with his small fingers and, with the other end pointed straight at the troll, blew one short, shrill note.

"Oh," the troll said, looking down at the tiny dart that had just sprouted from his throat. Suddenly it was all very clear. "Of course not. I'll be . . ." His eyes rolled back and he toppled over, hitting the pavement with a solid *thunk*.

"You'll be dead," said Martes. Then he tucked the assassin's flute back into his moleskin cloak and skipped off. He was whistling.

• • • one • • •

It was still dark when Scott Stewart woke up. He wasn't sure where he was. But he knew what time it was. He always knew what time it was.

Four-twelve A.M., he thought. *Why am I awake?*

He went to roll out of his cot, but ran into more bed than he expected.

Oh yeah, they let me out. He fumbled around until he found a bedside lamp. Light flooded the room. His room. Much bigger than he was used to, but still sparsely decorated: ratty dresser, a few posters of pastoral scenes tacked to the walls, a bedside table holding an unplugged alarm clock and a tear-away calendar with cartoons he didn't get that always seemed to feature a lot of poorly drawn chickens. His sister, Bridie, had helped him, pulled some strings, got him out of the halfway house early and into this nice little cottage in Leverett. Out in the woods, away from the lights and the people. She knew he couldn't take living with other people.

How long have I been here? His sense of time was screwy. He always knew what time it was, but couldn't seem to remember how much had passed. *Couple of weeks maybe?* He tore a page off the calendar. It claimed to be early September and showed the chickens hijacking two cows and a farm cat for some nefarious purpose Scott couldn't quite comprehend.

Spotting a pack of smokes, he went for them hungrily. *Oughta take my pills. Promised Bridie I would. But I feel pretty good today. Might skip them.*

He thought maybe he'd said that to himself a lot since leaving the halfway house. He may not have taken his pills in some time.

"Doesn't matter," he said aloud. "Nothing bad's going to happen today."

He knew this. Just like he always knew the time. Because if something bad was going to happen to him, Scott would know. He could sense it, see it coming. He might be as crazy as they said. But he was never wrong. Not about the bad things anyway.

"Now, let's see what woke me up." He stood and worked himself into some jeans that lay next to the bed. Grabbed a T-shirt from the floor, as well. Thought about a jacket but didn't look for one. It might be early September, but it still felt quite warm. Fall would come to the western Massachusetts hills, but it would do so at its own leisurely pace.

Lit cigarette now dangling from his mouth, Scott pushed open the door to his bedroom. Outside the bedroom, there wasn't much more to his house. It was one story, one bedroom, the bathroom a stall, the kitchen little more than a sink and a stove tucked in the corner. But the openness of the main living area appealed to him and the rent was cheap enough that he could pay for it with his disability checks. And there were no neighbors to bug him, no electric lights shining in his windows to keep him awake. A nice quiet little hut in the country.

Except tonight, something had woken him.

"Hello?" Scott called to the empty living room. "Anybody

there?" to the lonely Salvation Army couch. "Hello?" again to the tiny TV and its three static-filled channels.

He tried to think back to what had disturbed his sleep. *A sound? A feeling?* He couldn't discount the fact that a fair number of doctors considered him crazy—it may have been the whirring of his own mind jarring him awake. Certainly wouldn't have been the first time. But he was pretty sure he'd heard something. Something that didn't belong.

A cursory check of the bathroom turned up nothing. One small closet, the same. Scott made himself look out the windows, but couldn't really see anything. Maybe some amorphous shapes moving ominously among the trees, or floating darker black against the night sky. But that was hardly an unusual sight for him. He pushed the curtains back in place and sat down on his one ragged couch.

"Guess I'd better check outside."

But he didn't move from his seat. He sat and smoked and picked at the fraying edges of the plaid upholstery. Took the pulse in his neck. It seemed fast.

He thought, *Four twenty-one A.M. Not so long till daylight. I'll check outside then.*

That thought calmed him, and he took his pulse again. His heartbeat was slowing.

Until he heard the noise.

It was a wild screeching, like he'd heard the local farm cats making when they fought. Or fucked. It was hard to tell with them sometimes.

But this was no cat. He knew. He knew because suddenly, he could see all the bad things that would happen if he didn't go outside. Not to him. But to the thing screaming.

Crushing his cigarette out in a full ashtray by his right hand, Scott stood. He didn't understand it. He'd never sensed anything about anyone but himself. And he'd never had so many visions, either. He'd always seen just one bad thing after another. Unavoidable bad things. He'd told a number of therapists about his visions since coming back from the desert, but they'd called them self-fulfilling prophecies. Tried to teach him "positive visualization." He'd made the attempt. He was always willing to make the attempt. But it was only ever the bad visions that came to pass. Eventually, he'd come to welcome them. He couldn't avoid anything, but at least he was never surprised.

Not this time though. Starvation, disease, chills, coyotes, bobcats, bears, great horned owls—all could be warded off by the simple expedient of opening his front door. He knew this.

Because there was a baby out there. And it was screaming its head off.

THE BABY LAY in a basket woven out of twigs. It was wearing only a large cloth diaper, tied at the sides—no pins. Small, it couldn't have been more than a week or two old, but already sported a thick head of curly black hair. Scott couldn't tell what color its eyes were—they were screwed shut for better screaming.

"Um . . . there, there?" said Scott, stooping to pick the baby up. This had very little effect, and the baby redoubled its howling as he grabbed it. Still, Scott smiled.

The visions were fading.

Let's see . . . hand under head? Yes, that's right. Now, let's check the diaper. Ah, a little boy.

"Settle down, little fella. Uncle Scott's got you." Scott carried the baby inside, cooing to him softly. "Course, I don't know what I'm going to do with you."

Child services, he thought. *I bet Bridie knows someone . . .*

As soon as he thought this, new visions hit him: the baby—but maybe a year old, now—covered in its own excrement, staring blankly at the wall of a dingy closet while a police officer hand-cuffed a bearded man in the background; a woman with greasy hair and wild eyes, shaking the baby till its head flopped back and forth loosely; the baby sleeping peacefully in a crib, while a teenage boy crept into the room pawing at his crotch . . .

"Jesus!" Scott staggered at the horrific scenes in his head. "All right, I'll keep him!"

And once again, the visions faded.

The screaming didn't, however. Scott cooed some more, and tickled the baby's little feet, to no avail.

"What's wrong, little fella?"

What had Bridie always said about babies? Bridie was eight years older than Scott, and ten years older than Douglas. She'd helped raise both of them, and never let them forget it. But she had summed up the caring of babies into one succinct sentence. *Oh yeah, "feed them, change them, and don't drop them."*

Scott peeked into the diaper. Clean. "So far, so good. Since I haven't dropped you." He carried the screaming infant into his tiny kitchen. "But what do we have to eat?"

He toed open the fridge and peered inside. Hot dogs, cheap beer, government cheese. It didn't look good. He was going to need supplies. Lots of supplies.

Four thirty-nine A.M. But I can't wait for daylight.

Scott was going to have drive through the hills in the dark.

Boo-yah.

BALANCING THE SQUALLING baby in his left arm, Scott fiddled his keys out of his pocket with the other. It was tough to work the lock. His hand was shaking pretty bad, and he kept glancing up at the dark forest.

Things come out of the night. If you don't watch the treeline, the horizon, the windows . . .

Eventually he got the door open and plopped into the front seat of his ancient Honda Prelude. The dim interior light was comforting. Keeping the baby in his lap, he stretched the seatbelt across both of them, trying to ignore the baby's protests. Surprisingly, the car turned over on the first try. He put it in gear and moved slowly out of the driveway, gravel crunching beneath the tires. Stopped at the end of the short drive for nearly two minutes, waiting for visions of violent crashes to come and checking and rechecking each direction, making sure no cars were coming. No visions came, and no cars either—not unusual for this two-mile stretch of cracked pavement Scott shared with only two other homes. Eventually he pulled out of the driveway and onto the road. He'd only gone ten yards when he slammed on the brakes.

There was someone in the road.

The someone stood only about three feet high, and for a moment Scott thought it was a child.

"Is everyone dropping their kids off with me today?" he said, though it was barely audible over the baby's cries.

Then he saw the beard. The beard started at the small man's chin and stretched, curly and dark, all the way to his waist, where it was wrapped into an impromptu loincloth. He wore nothing else. Shading his eyes from the light, the small man took a step closer, and his face curled into a malicious grin as he squinted into the car at Scott.

No, he's not looking at me.

"Hey!" Scott shouted. "Stop looking at my baby!" And he leaned on the horn.

The small man jerked at the noise, looked rapidly left and right, then took three running steps into the woods and was gone.

Scott sat in the car and shook. He looked down at the screaming baby.

"Well," he said. "That was one of my more lucid ones. Remind me to take my medication when we get home."

The baby didn't answer.

As soon as his hands were steady, Scott stomped on the gas and the old car chugged toward town.

HE DROVE DOWN Chestnut Hill then up over Cave Hill, the darkness seeming to press against the windows of the car, trying to find a way in. As he passed Leverett Pond, premorning fog was lifting from its waters and creeping toward the road. There was no moon, no streetlights, and the thin beam of the Prelude's only working headlight barely pierced the darkness, let alone the fog. Not for the first time, Scott wished the roads had lines painted on them out here in the boondocks.

"White lines would give me something to aim at," he said. He could actually hear himself speak now; the baby had quieted some. Scott didn't believe the baby was calmer, though. Just out of breath. He tried to think of some comforting words to say, but all that came out was, "something to aim at," again.

Scott glanced down. The baby did not look reassured. In fact, it looked about ready to start screaming again.

"Never mind," Scott said quickly. "Nothing's bad going to happen. Really." The baby sniffled. "I know it. I just don't like driving at night. I see things. They aren't really there. They just . . ." He was babbling. He hated when he did that. But the baby seemed to like it when he talked, so he kept going. "It's tough, little guy. 'Cause some stuff comes true and some stuff isn't there, and no one believes either one, and sometimes I'm not so sure myself." He checked all his mirrors reflexively. Rear, side, side, then rear again. "I guess I'm crazy," he said, smiling down at the baby, "but that doesn't mean they're not out to get me, right?"

The baby didn't smile back. But it didn't cry either. Scott put one hand on its tiny belly and drove on.

Several harrowing minutes later and Scott was turning onto the well-lit and aptly named Pleasant Street, and heading right into Amherst proper. Scott sighed. He'd made it through the hills and darkness. He was in civilization.

TWENTY-FOUR-HOUR SHOPPING CHOICES in the town of Amherst were few and far between. There was a Cumberland Farms convenience store nearby, or Scott could go through town and hit the Stop and Shop on Route 9. The Stop and Shop was a big grocery store, but was only open all night from Monday to Friday. Scott wasn't sure what day it was, and he didn't want to go all the way there and find it closed. The Cumberland Farms might not have what he needed, but at least it was nearby.

"And what do I need?" Scott asked the baby as he pulled into the Cumberland Farms parking lot. Scooping the baby up with one hand, he bumped the door shut with his hip. He didn't bother locking it. Figured someone could go ahead and steal it if they could start it. He had a hard enough time—and he had the keys.

The girl behind the counter looked at him suspiciously as he came in. She had the pale unhealthy complexion of most night-shift workers and hair that had obviously been permed at the nearby mall.

"Can I help you?" she asked, not sounding like she meant it.

Scott held the baby up. Surprisingly, he didn't scream, just burped softly at the girl. Her face immediately softened.

"Need supplies," Scott mumbled.

"Oh, isn't he a cute one!" She leaned over the counter to get a better look. Her shirt came open a little and Scott blushed. If she was out of high school, she hadn't been for long. He forced himself to look at her name tag. Traci. With an 'I.'

"Yeah." *Maybe I should put a whole sentence together.*

Traci wrinkled her forehead as she peered at the baby. "What's he wearing?"

"Cloth."

"Yeesh. Mom out of town?"

"She died." *Oh, perfect,* Scott thought. *Why did I say that?* He knew how he looked, what most people thought of him. *Crazy. Now she's going to think I killed my wife.* "In childbirth," he added, hoping the baby was young enough for that to seem plausible.

Luckily, Traci looked at him kindly, told him, "You poor thing," and came out from behind the counter. "Let me see him."

Scott stood transfixed as she pulled the baby expertly from his grasp.

"I have four younger brothers," she said, as if that explained everything. "Follow me."

He did and she loaded his arms with supplies: diapers, bottles, formula— "Baby this young should really still be on the boob. But that isn't possible in your case"—diaper rash creams, a pacifier—"Go ahead and use it; I don't believe in nipple confusion."

Scott nodded as if he knew exactly what nipple confusion was.

"Oh, sorry." Traci blushed. "I guess that won't be a problem for you anyway."

Scott just kept nodding, pretty much completely lost now.

"Let's see . . ." Traci stood with the baby on one hip and her hand on the other, surveying the store. "What else?"

"Um," Scott said, "How does it all work?"

Traci frowned, but not unpleasantly. "You better sit down. We may be a while."

Scott crossed his legs and sat right there on the floor. Reached his arms up for the baby. Traci peered at him oddly for a second then shrugged and handed him the baby. Scott looked at the little thing's scrunched-up face and traced a small line through its thick black hair. Then he looked up at Traci.

"I'm ready."

• • • TWO • • •

*C*hrist, Bridie Stewart thought. *I hate Edinburgh.*

She stood outside a run-down chip shop staring at the wet mass of dough and newspaper that the Pakistani behind the counter had just sold her.

Next person who tells me I'm named after a pastry goes home with less teeth than they woke up with. Sighing, she tossed her lunch into a nearby bin and started walking. *It's an Irish name. Means strong. Now, where's this fucking cop shop?*

The directions from the train station were pretty straightforward. But the streets changed names so many times, Bridie had maybe gotten a little confused. Okay, a lot confused. All right, she was completely lost, and although she supposedly shared the same language with these people, she was beginning to suspect they didn't share the same sense of direction. Every time she asked a local for help, she got sent farther off course, ending up deeper in the drab gray bowels of this stone city than she'd started that morning.

And it seems like I've been walking uphill forever, she thought, cursing her choice of footwear. *Tomorrow, I pull the sensible shoes out of the luggage.*

She'd wanted to make a favorable impression on the police. Cops were the same everywhere. If she looked hot, maybe show a little leg, a little cleavage, they'd never suspect she was pumping them for information.

But now she was pissed off and tired and her feet hurt, and she knew if she ever did find the station, there was no way she was going to pull off charming. No, she'd just end up being herself: uber-bitch. And piss off everyone within a half-mile radius.

Bridie looked up as a fat wet raindrop hit her forehead.

"Oh, for God's sake," she said to the sky. "Why don't you rain on me now?"

And as the requested deluge started, she thought again, *Christ, I hate Edinburgh.*

MAYBE A HALF hour later, and Bridie had finally figured out that the street names were printed on white iron signs attached to buildings instead of on something sensible like a signpost near the road. Using this hard-won knowledge, she determined that she was on Leith Road, a four-lane street that seemed to appear out of nowhere. Big-block gray stone buildings housed shops and bars and restaurants, the stone invariably painted bright white if the restaurant was Italian. She stomped along till a giant roundabout interrupted her progress, then stopped to consider her options.

The main road continued out the opposite end of the roundabout and seemed to fall away to the sea, the buildings lining it growing to four and five stories. The smaller side exits looked to disappear altogether. Bridie wished she had a coin with eight sides so she could flip it to decide which unpromising route to follow. But then she spotted a tiny blue sign—on a post, no less!—with the single word 'Police' on it. It pointed vaguely left.

Bridie wasn't confident enough of which way the cars were

coming from yet to jaywalk, so she waited for the green walk light to come on before hiking her purse up on her shoulder a little more and crossing to Gayfield Square. Since she was looking for the Gayfield Police Station, this was greatly encouraging.

The square was more of a rectangle, a one-way cobblestone street that ran around a block-long park then right back out to the Leith Road roundabout. Across from the park was a misshapen building of stone and cement and 1960's design that looked completely out of place with the surrounding architecture. An odd wing came off the second floor to teeter precariously over a parking lot full of Vauxhalls and Astras painted the white, yellow, and black of the Edinburgh City Police.

Bridie was there. Finally.

IF SHE'D BEEN expecting the inside of a Scottish police station to look different from the ones she was used to in America, Bridie would have been disappointed. All the essential pieces were there: the out-of-date computers, the cheap fluorescent lighting, the overflowing case files, the stink of sweat and old beverages, the air of desperation. And the cops. Big, piggy bastards, with close-cropped skulls and suspicious eyes, all crowding around to get a look at the slim wet woman who had just charged through the door.

"Can I help ye, ma'am?"

Yeah, Bridie thought. *You can stop staring at my nipples.*

"Bridie Stewart," was what she said out loud. "Here to see Detective Inspector Hamilton." *Had to wear white today, didn't I?*

"Ah, Ms. Stewart," called a man from the back of the room. He was tall and muscular and young, and he leaned insolently against the frame of a doorway leading to a private office. Possibly his own.

Well, hello there, tall, dark, and official.

He looked more like a model than a cop, with his black wavy hair a little longer than maybe regulations allowed, and his skin clear and healthy even in the poor lighting. Pushing himself upright, he marched forward to shake Bridie's hand.

"Detective Inspector Hamilton, CID."

"Pleased to meet . . ."

"Follow me, missy." This from behind her. The speaker was taller than Inspector Hamilton and broader in the shoulders. He was also older. Gray hair had been allowed to sprout only a millimeter off his skull before being brutally sheared. Stern eyes peered out from underneath pronounced eye ridges, and his mouth seemed stuck somewhere between a frown and a sneer. Possibly permanently stuck, as a thick scar ran nearly the length of his face, reaching from just below his right eye to the opposite side of his chin.

"Um . . . okay."

The older man turned without speaking and hulked away. Bridie followed, Inspector Hamilton close on her heels. They marched a short ways down a drab hallway, and the older man kicked open a door, leading them all inside.

The room they stepped into held only a small table, two chairs facing each other across it, a third slightly askew. Even as lightly furnished as it was it was still cramped. The monotony of the sickly yellow walls—made even uglier by the ever-present fluorescent lights—was broken only by the occasional informational poster espousing the dangers of methamphetamines or the benefits of community service. Bridie had seen rooms like this before.

"Sit down," said the older man, his voice low and guttural. "And tell us what you know about Douglas Stewart."

As she sat down, Bridie glanced at the older man fearfully, then back up at Hamilton. "I . . . um . . ."

Hamilton's face softened. "C'mon, Fraser, give her a break. She just found out her grandma died. And that it was her brother who killed her."

"I dinnae care about any of that," Fraser growled. "She's his blood. And I seen wha he did to that wee old woman. I want some answers!" He slammed a meaty fist down on the table in front of Bridie.

The two men looked surprised when Bridie gave a short bark of laughter. "You've got to be fucking kidding me."

Fraser froze with his fist down on the table. He turned his head to look at Hamilton, who shrugged and asked, "What do you mean?"

Bridie stood. Adjusted her wet shirt as best she could. "I was on the job for eight years. And you're going to pull good cop/bad cop on me?" She pointed at Fraser. "Where'd you get this guy? The set of a Frankenstein movie? And you . . ." Hamilton took an almost imperceptible step back when she turned her gaze back to him. "Am I supposed to go all weak in the knees when you turn those baby blues on me? I hate to break it to you, but you're not my type."

"You were a cop?" asked Fraser, his voice softer and just a touch more refined than it had been a minute ago.

"Springfield, Mass., PD."

"The information we got said you were a . . ." Hamilton scratched his head. "A 'roving bartender.'"

Bridie nodded. "For about a year now."

Fraser straightened up. "What's that?"

"I wear a short skirt and a cowboy hat. Carry a holster full of shot glasses and sell drinks to stupid frat boys. Beats getting shot at." She shrugged. "Pays better, too." Bridie sat back down. Crossed her legs carefully. "Now, how about you boys stop screwing around and tell me what you think happened. 'Cause I know you're wrong."

Hamilton hooked the chair across from her with his foot, spinning it around to face him, before plopping down in it backward. Folding his arms, he rested his chin on them, big blue eyes boring into Bridie's.

"How do you know we're wrong?"

"Well, don't misunderstand me. Douglas is a worthless drug addict. A thief and a liar. A canker sore on the ass of society. But . . ." Bridie paused, and her eyes shone. But only for a second. "But he's my little brother and I love him. And there's no way he killed Grandma McLaren."

IT HAD ONLY been a week since her death, but already Grandma McLaren's house looked run-down. The windows were dingy and unwashed, the flowers in their hanging baskets wilted, the walkway cracked and worn. It was as if the house was heartbroken, and wanted to die to be with her.

"Watch yer step, luv," Fraser said.

"Thanks," Bridie replied. "I've never seen a front step before."

Hamilton chuckled. "Best watch yours, Fraser. She'll cut something off with that tongue of hers."

Bridie turned and glared at him, but he just smiled and raised his hands. "Don't shoot, Officer. I'm unarmed."

She turned so he couldn't see her in case she smiled, and followed Fraser into the house. It had been cleaned after the lab techs had tagged and bagged and photographed everything. But Bridie had been to enough crime scenes that she imagined she could still smell the death and despair that had filled the house a week earlier.

"They found most of her on that," Fraser said, pointing to a stained couch against the back wall. "The rest of her was spread over the walls and stairway."

"Get any prints?" Bridie asked.

"Buckets of 'em. Bloody fingerprints all over the place."

"They match my brother's?" Bridie glanced at the walls, looking for signs of the blood that had been washed away days ago.

"Dinnae know. Your brother's never been printed."

"Tell her about the finger," Hamilton interjected.

"The finger?" Bridie asked.

"They did find a match for the prints. A pinkie finger on top of Calton Hill. Found it lying next to a priest with his head blown off."

Bride furrowed her eyebrows. "You guys run into this kind of stuff a lot in this country?"

Hamilton shook his head. Fraser said, "Twenty-five years I've worked in this city. Never seen anything like it."

Bridie paced around the small living room. Peered down at the dark stains on the couch. "Who else you looked at for this?"

Hamilton and Fraser glanced at each other. Neither spoke.

"No one, huh?" Bridie wanted to spit on the floor. "You lazy bastards."

Hamilton held up his hands again. "Look, Ms. Stewart. You were a cop. You know how it is. There's no coincidences, no special circumstances, no surprise endings. Ninety-nine times out of a hundred it's the guy you thought it was all along. And if you waste your time chasing down all the other leads, your guy gets away."

Fraser added, "And the guys in the other dozen cases you're supposed to be working, as well."

"And that one guy out of a hundred who didn't do it?" Bridie asked.

"Well," Hamilton shrugged. "It's a tough world and make no mistake. But we all have to live in it just the same."

Bridie fixed him with a hard stare.

Hamilton spoke softly. "He's a known drug addict, in the

country illegally. He lived with your grandmother. He was spotted leaving here the morning of the murder, and the Calton Hill guard places him on the hilltop with that dead priest, too."

Bridie shook her head. "He couldn't have . . ."

"He did it, Ms. Stewart. He killed your grandmother and the priest, and then he ran." Hamilton took a step closer. "But he's lucky he did it in this country. We have no guns. There's no death penalty here, Ms. Stewart." He was close enough that she could feel the warmth of him now, and he put his hands on her shoulders. "You help me find him, Ms. Stewart. You help me find your brother, and I'll bring him in safe."

Bridie let out a long breath. *It'd be easy to just collapse into those strong arms and cry for a week or so.* "Okay," she said aloud. "I'll help you. But I'll need everything you got."

"What do you mean?"

"Crime scene photos, known associates, witness list, interview transcripts. Everything." She shrugged out of Hamilton's grip and made for the door. "You give me access, and I'll get you your man."

The man who killed Grandma McLaren, that is. Not my little brother.

"And call me Bridie." She smiled. "It means 'strong,' you know."

THE CRIME SCENE photos were tough to look at. Shot after shot of blood-spattered walls and random body parts, close-ups of particularly grisly pieces of flesh that were apparently of special interest to the photographer. Grandma McLaren's severed head. Even if the victim hadn't been her grandmother, Bridie suspected she'd have still said the same thing to Hamilton.

"I'm going to need a drink when we're through here." She had her feet up on Hamilton's desk, a pile of photos in her hands.

Hamilton nodded. "I'll buy you one. Bridie." As if he was trying the name out in his mouth. Checking the taste of it.

"Didn't find the murder weapon, right?"

"No."

"Figure out what it was, though?"

"I believe the pathologist's official verdict was, 'a big-ass knife.'"

Bridie shuffled a photo to the back of the pile. "Sounds about right."

"I've got the interview transcripts for you, too."

Bridie tossed the photos on the desk and took the stack of papers Hamilton was holding out.

"Thanks." *Why was he being so helpful? It can't be just because he wants to sleep with me.* She glanced up at Hamilton where he stood, reading over her shoulder, tip of his tongue just protruding out of his mouth as he concentrated. *Only one way to find out, I suppose.* "Why are you being so helpful?"

Hamilton blinked and his tongue disappeared. "What?"

"I said, why are you being so helpful? It can't just be professional courtesy. What's up?"

He looked at the ceiling. "Because it's so gruesome, Bridie. Edinburgh doesn't see stuff like this. People are calling for blood. And your brother has vanished off the face of the earth."

"So I'm the latest straw you're grasping at?"

"You're the only straw. We've got nothing."

Bridie nodded, looking back down at the transcripts. Started skimming. The neighbors all told the same story: Douglas was seen leaving the house at approximately 7:45 A.M. on August 27. He was wearing a leather jacket and carried a guitar. He may have been limping. At any rate, he looked sick or wounded or shaken. Maybe all three. He drove off in Grandma McLaren's Peugeot. Which was later found on top of Calton Hill.

Bridie had to admit it looked bad.

There wasn't much else. Douglas's only friend seemed to be his grandmother. Hamilton and Fraser had tracked down a store owner who'd had a business arrangement with Douglas for the summer. But he didn't claim to have spoken more than a dozen words or so to Douglas during that time, and their association had ended when the Fringe started. They'd also found a girl at the Braemar Gathering who'd worked next to Douglas during the Fringe.

"This Sandra Matheson. She didn't know anything?"

Hamilton shook his head. "Nope. Interviewed her myself."

Men, Bridie thought, *shouldn't be allowed to interrogate women.* She made a mental note to track this Sandra down herself. *They have no fucking clue how we think.*

"Shit. What time is it?"

Hamilton checked his watch. "Three-thirty. Why?"

"I should call my brother," Bridie said. Hamilton raised an eyebrow. "My *other* brother."

· · · martes · · ·

Martes wasn't frightened. He knew he'd be punished. Hurt. But he deserved it. If not for the kidnappings, then for any number of transgressions over the centuries. He stared out the tower window and shivered in anticipation.

"Where's my son, Martes?"

Lord Douglas had slipped into Martes's chambers unnoticed. *For a man that big,* Martes thought, *he can sure move quietly.*

Without turning to face his master, Martes said, "I do not know, my lord."

That much was true.

"But you were the one who took him, no?"

Martes nodded, still looking out the window. A red river snaked across the horizon. "I'm pledged to protect you and yours, Boss. You were going to kill him. The prophecies . . ."

"And I may still." Douglas hummed a few seemingly random notes, and Martes felt himself turn around. He'd made no effort to move. "When I find him."

"Boss, I . . ."

"Shhh. Don't speak. I'll get the answers myself." He hummed a deep note while whistling a sharp one simultaneously. Martes's eyes went wide as searing pain took him in the base of his crooked spine. "This may hurt a bit."

I'm certain it will. If he'd been able to move, Martes would have smiled. *I'm certain it will.*

• • • Three • • •

For the second time that day, Scott was awakened. This time, it was by the phone ringing.

Ten thirty-seven A.M., he thought. He looked down at the baby in his lap, still sleeping with a bottle in its mouth. *Won't stay that way for long, though, if I don't stop that phone.*

He sidled over on the couch till he could reach the phone.

"Hello?" he whispered.

"Scott? Scotty, is that you? I can barely hear you."

"That's 'cause I'm whispering, Bridie."

"Um . . . okay. You all right?"

"Yeah. Fine. You?"

"Why are you whisper . . . oh, never mind. Listen, Scotty, I've got a lot of work to do over here."

"You gonna save Douglas?" There was no answer. "Bridie?"

"Yes, Scotty. I'm going to save him. You going to be okay for a week or two?"

"Yeah, Bridie. Don't worry about me."

"You taking your meds?"

"Yeah." He'd gulped a handful of pills when he'd got back from the store. Hadn't seen any little bearded men since.

"Okay. Listen, Scotty. You have my cell number if you need anything. Anything. I can be back home in twelve hours if things get bad."

"Okay, Bridie. I'll call you."

"Promise?"

"I promise."

"I love you, Scotty-dog."

"Okay, Bridie. Bye."

Scott hung up. Looked at the baby in his lap. Fished a cigarette out of a pack on the table and flipped it into his mouth. Looked at the baby again. Heaved a big sigh and put the cigarette down in the ashtray. The baby wriggled a little in its sleep, and Scott smiled down at it.

"There, there."

It felt good holding a baby. Felt right. Like it was his own child. Not that Scott had ever had a child. Hadn't even had that many girlfriends, truth be told. He was kind of awkward as a boy, had a few dates during high school, even got laid a couple times, but nothing serious came of it. And then 9/11 hit, and he joined the Marines the next day. Threw himself into training in a patriotic frenzy, never taking leave, spending the time instead out on the range, or in hand-to-hand instruction, or disassembling his weapons and putting them back together. He turned himself into a genuine, all-American, killing machine.

And then, thousands of miles from home, an RPG blew his messmate's arm into his lap. And as his buddy bled out into the sand, Scott felt something click in his head. A connection was made that hadn't been there before and he began seeing things before they happened. Firefights, ambushes, IED's—he saw them all coming. He tried to tell people, warn them of the approaching dangers. But no one believed him, no one dared. And even if they did, what could they do? They were Marines; they were supposed to get shot at.

Scott didn't last long. "Went crazy in the desert," they said and shipped him home. Full psych disability. Some time in lockup, few months at the halfway house, then here. His new home.

The baby opened its eyes. Its face turned bright red as it looked up at Scott.

"What? What's the matter, little fella?"

There was a long rumbling sound, and the baby's face relaxed. Then came the smell.

"Ah," Scott said. *Feed them, change them, don't drop them.* "Time for number two?"

The baby's little mouth screwed up on one side. Might have been a smile.

THE ODIOUS TASK done, Scott washed up, leaving the baby face up on a blanket he'd laid down on the living room floor. He watched the baby for a while to make sure it couldn't roll away. Didn't seem likely.

"I suppose we should give you a name," Scott said as he came back into the room. The baby looked up at him, and immediately started to cry again. "And another bottle, too?"

Without waiting for an answer, Scott rushed back into the kitchen to heat a bottle.

What had Traci at the store said again? One scoop per ounce. Check. Heat it on the stove—no microwaving. That's okay, I don't own one. Test it on your wrist. Check. Good to go.

Scott curled up next to the baby on the floor, and fed it a bottle as it lay there. The baby quieted, and was soon fast asleep again. Scott lay next to it, watching it, afraid to move and wake it, and eventually he drifted off as well.

Feeding, changing, and napping took up the rest of the day. As night fell, Scott looked around his small house. Dirty bottles lined the table, diaper packages torn open in haste lay where he'd tossed them, white cream spattered the floor from a tube of diaper cream he'd stepped on. The place was trashed. But Scott was too exhausted to clean. He hadn't been this tired since the Marines.

Hell, I wasn't this tired when I was in *the Marines.*

He crawled into bed and passed out, swearing he'd make some time to clean tomorrow. He hadn't counted on the baby needing to be fed three more times during the night. By the time morning peeked into his bedroom, Scott was even more spent than he'd been the night before.

And, of course, the baby was crying.

Scott thought blearily about taking the baby to child services again. But only for a second. The visions returned and shocked him fully awake.

"Coming, little fella!" he called. He was halfway to the kitchen before he realized something was terribly out of place.

The house was clean. Spotless. Dusted, even. It didn't make any sense. Scott was sure he hadn't cleaned up. And even if he had, he never would have done such a good job.

"Hello? Anybody there?" *That's getting to be my morning greeting to the house.* "Anyone besides you," he said to the crying baby.

Putting a bottle on the stove, Scott thought, *Did Bridie change her mind and come home? Sneak in and clean for me?*

But that didn't seem her style. Scott had visited her house; it was a sty. He kept his cleaner. A lot cleaner.

Must have been me then. I better take my pills today. He took one last look around at the sparkling countertops, the shiny fix-tures, the speck-free carpets. Shook his head. *Must have been me.*

Then he went to feed his baby.

SEVERAL FEEDINGS LATER, Scott remembered he still hadn't named the little fella.

"It'll have to be something Scottish," he said, tickling the baby's feet while it sucked on a bottle. "We're descended from Scottish kings, you know."

The baby didn't seem overly impressed.

"Could name you after Douglas. He's my little brother. He's in some trouble, though. Might be bad luck." Scott looked at the ceiling for a moment, thinking. "How about Angus? It doesn't get much more Scottish than that." He looked at the baby. "No, I don't think you look like an Angus."

Scott wasn't sure, but he thought the baby seemed relieved to not be named Angus.

"I could name you after me."

The baby glanced up at this. Scott decided it was in fear.

"Yeah, my name doesn't seem too lucky either, does it?" He looked back at the ceiling, then longingly at his pack of cigarettes. "Give me a little bit. I'll come up with something."

The baby kept looking at Scott. He didn't think babies this young could focus on anything yet, but this one seemed to be staring him right in the eye. As if he wanted to tell him something.

"Yes?" Scott said, then felt stupid. He shrugged. "Told you to give me a minute."

The baby seemed satisfied with that answer and looked away. Scott stared down at his little burden, trying to think of a good name, when suddenly one popped into his head. He didn't know for sure if it was Scottish, but he was certain, just like he knew the time (*11:18 A.M.*) that it was the baby's name.

"Fletcher," he said, and the baby looked up. "Fletcher Stewart."

The baby twisted its mouth up again. Scott was sure it was a smile this time.

"Wait till Bridie gets back. She'll tell us what it means."

The baby held his smile. Then his face turned red. And a low rumbling sound came from below.

"Fletcher!"

The baby giggled and Scott laughed, too, laying him down on the blanket to go get his changing supplies.

• • • Four • • •

The Braemar Gathering, Sandra Matheson's last known location, had only run for one day. The local constabulary assured Bridie that all the itinerant merchants had moved on swiftly when it ended.

"Probably up ta Aberfeldy for the Heart of Scotland," the officer on the phone said. "Or maybe doon ta the Forest of Ae for the Hairth o' Knokrach."

"Um . . . thanks." Bridie hung up. "You get any of that, Hamilton?" He'd been listening on an extension, elbow resting on his leg, other arm beside it, like Rodin's *Thinker* in a phone ad.

"Oh, aye," he said, his accent now broader in imitation of the cop on the phone. "The Heart o' Scotland and the Hairth o' Knokrach." He shrugged. "Nae clue, derlin'."

She chuckled. "What good are you then?"

He gave a brief leer before saying, "I can call the Tayside Police and have them watch Aberfeldy for someone of Sandra Matheson's description. Tell them to pick her up and hold her for us. Fraser!" he called out over his shoulder. "Where's the Forest of Ae?"

"Near Dumfries, I think," came the reply after a moment.

"I'll call Dumfries and Galloway for that one then."

"We better check for other festivals in the area," Bridie said. "Call them, too."

Hamilton nodded. "It'll keep till morning, though."

Bridie looked down at the pile of photos and transcripts still on the desk before her. The stuff had probably kept till a lot of mornings by now. There was never enough time in a cop's day to do everything. Bridie knew that as well as anyone. And she was tired. "All right. How about that drink then?"

"Oh, aye," he said. "I could murder a pint about now." He stood like a much older man, unfolding and stretching slowly. "Fraser! I'm knocking off. You need anything before I go?"

The older man waved from his desk without looking up. "Away with ye. Ye need yer beauty sleep."

THERE WAS A pub just up the street from the station. *There always is,* thought Bridie. As they entered, she was surprised by how quietly elegant the place seemed. Then she noticed that the marble bar was fake, the dark wood was actually painted brown, and the quiet was because the few balding men inhabiting the place were too busy nursing their beers alone to make conversation. It was a drinker's bar, a place to make the pains of the day disappear and the night pass as quickly as possible.

Hamilton stepped up to the bar and ordered "two pints of 80," then took Bridie and the beers to a table in back.

Against the wall, good view of the entrance. Bridie smiled. *Cop seat all the way.*

Hamilton peered at Bridie over his pint of ale. "So, you were a cop. Why'd you stop?"

In answer, Bridie pulled her shirt off her right shoulder a touch, revealing a long scar running over the top of her trapezius muscle. "Got called to a bar to help remove a drunk. I imagine you get a fair amount of those calls here."

"Oh, aye."

"Of course, here the drunks probably don't carry MAC-10s."

"Ah, MAC-10s," Hamilton sighed, sounding nostalgic.

"You're familiar with them?" Bridie peered at him. "I wouldn't think—"

He interrupted her with a wink. "Aye, a fine highland clan the McTens."

"Oh for Christ's sake, it's a machine gun."

"Not a family of kilt-wearing drunkards?"

Bridie studiously ignored him. "Anyway, the drunk pulled out a MAC-10 and opened up on us. The weapon has a tendency to pull up and left. If he hadn't started so high, he would've cut me in half."

Hamilton said nothing for a moment. "I imagine a lot of people retire after a close call like that. It sounds a dangerous business, law enforcement in the States."

"No, that's not it. The wound wasn't that bad, and I was the only one hit. It's that . . ." She didn't know why she was telling him this. She hadn't even told the shrink they assigned to her. Maybe it was just that it was a year or two later, she had some distance. From the event, as well as the country it happened in. And after a week or two, she'd probably never see this guy again, anyway. "Even hit, I managed to pull my piece. Double taps. First the body, then . . . Well, like they say, 'Two in the head, and you know he's dead.'" She took a long pull of her beer. *Bitter. Bitter and warm. Fucking Scotland.* "Ever kill anyone, Hamilton?"

"Hasn't come up, no." He shook his head. "But it sounds like you were justified. They give you time off after a shooting, don't they? Counseling?" He spun his glass idly watching the bubbles rise. "Didn't the remorse fade?"

"Remorse?" It was a very British way of asking. An American cop would have just asked, 'Ya feel better?' Bridie laughed. There wasn't much humor in it. "That's not why I quit. No, everyone agreed he had it coming. And if I'd felt bad, or even felt nothing, I'd have stayed a cop." She drained her beer, warm or not, it contained alcohol. "Nope, I liked it. Liked it more than I've ever liked anything before or since. The moment his head exploded, I felt like a God. I wanted to open up on the rest of the bar, see all the people scream and run. Watch them die. By my hand."

Hamilton stared. "I . . ." His voice trailed off. What could he say to that anyway?

A stout barmaid in black T-shirt and matching apron looked their way. Bridie waved to her. Held up two fingers.

"I unloaded my weapon. Broke it down. Left it on the bar. Haven't touched so much as a kitchen knife since."

"Em . . ."

"But that's how I know Douglas didn't kill anyone. I know my brother, and he couldn't have done it." She closed her eyes for just longer than a blink. "I could have. But not Douglas."

"Where were you when the murder occurred?"

"Roughly three thousand miles away, serving drinks to two hundred witnesses."

Shrugging, Hamilton said, "You're off the hook then."

"Forget about it, Hamilton." She made a shooing motion. "Don't know why I told you."

"Me, either." He shuddered almost imperceptibly. "You're a hard woman, aren't you, Bridie?"

She peered at him. "Oh, aye."

He smiled at that. Reached into his pocket as the drinks arrived. "My shout again. You're a guest in my country."

"Okay, I'll let you buy me another drink. But you have to tell me your first name."

Hamilton's clear skin blushed rosy. "Do I have to?"

Bridie smiled. "That bad?"

"It's Ogilvie."

"Ogilvie?" Bridie said nothing more for a moment. "I'll call you Hamilton if you don't mind."

Hamilton took a small sip of his beer. "Would you, please?"

OVER THE NEXT few hours and the next several beers, Bridie and Hamilton exchanged stories. She told him of the time she had to subdue a naked man who thought his penis was trying to kill him. Hamilton countered with the tale of a scantily clad young woman's attempts to lift the kilts of the armed guards at the castle.

"Had to stop her from showing the pride of Scotland's willies to the world! They go full regiment, you know."

Bridie told of the only other time she'd had to pull her weapon. It was to kill a dog.

"Only I couldn't get a clear shot. It was a pit bull with its teeth firmly clenched on this poor bastard's ass. And the guy's jumping around so much, I couldn't shoot without hitting him."

Hamilton lifted his glass, and peered blurrily around the side. "What happened next?"

"Well, I shot him, of course!"

They burst out laughing and ordered another round. By the time Hamilton offered her a ride back to her hotel, they were roaring drunk.

"Oh, I don't think you're in any shape to drive, Officer."

Hamilton drew himself up, looking haughty. "I'll have you know . . ." he began. "That you are absolutely correct." And he collapsed back into his chair, laughing. "I better call Fraser."

"I better call a cab."

"Damn. I was hoping . . ."

"I know what you were hoping," Bridie said, sounding surprisingly sober all of a sudden. "But I told you this morning: you're not my type."

Hamilton blinked. He didn't look like he heard that often.

Bridie's voice softened. "Come on, Officer. On your feet. We've got some phone calls to make."

"Okay," Hamilton said, wanly. "Bridie?"

"Yes?"

"You're a hard woman."

"Oh, aye." Bridie chuckled. "I get it from my grandma."

Suddenly, Bridie remembered the crime scene photo of Grandma McLaren's severed head, and the smile slipped off her face.

And I owe someone for her. I owe someone big time.

• • • oobel • • •

Squatting in the thick center of a leafy bush, the little man with the long beard peered at the house.

"Brownies and hobs," he muttered. "Brownies and hobs. How will Oobel ever eat . . ." He sniffed loudly through his nose. "The little fleshie, oh, so sweet? When it's protected by the brownies and the hobs?"

For the brownies watched the house, and the hobs watched the bairn. And a closer watch, Oobel had never seen. He sniffed and snarfed and plotted, eyeing the hobs with their sharp knives on guard, the brownies with their servant's tools waiting for the man-thing to sleep.

The man-thing. He looked large and dangerous. And he had seen Oobel. Oobel didn't know how. The man-thing also had machines that moved fast and made noise.

Oobel didn't like noise.

"The brownies must be bought. The hobs must be caught. And the man-thing made to go."

Oh, how Oobel wanted to gnaw on that tasty morsel, feel it squirm and cry. It was more than the usual hunger. This was no ordinary little fleshie. Oobel could tell. There was something more. Something deliciously . . . magic about it.

Yes, magic. Magic and blood, flesh and bone. All flowing and gushing and breaking under Oobel's sharp teeth.

"Then Oobel will feed. Oh yes, he will indeed! He will eat the little fleshie on the morrow."

An unfortunate field mouse wandered too close, and Oobel reached out, lightning fast, with a clawlike hand. And as he pulled the mouse's tiny legs off, one by one, he said again, "He will eat the little fleshie on the morrow."

· · · **Five** · · ·

Scott was exhausted. Again. It was amazing how much energy it took to take care of something that didn't move much or speak at all. Lying in bed with Fletcher curled up next to him, he wondered how long the little guy would let him sleep this time.

One hour? Two? Scott closed his eyes. However long it was going to be, he figured he might as well use every minute of it. Like most soldiers, he could be asleep in seconds. But not this time. Just before he drifted off, he heard a sonorous voice from right beside the bed.

"There are those who toil for you freely . . ."

What the . . .

Scott sat upright and looked around. The bedroom was empty.

"But you must still," the Voice continued, "give them what they are due. *Cowautam?*" Scott thought it still sounded like it was right beside him, though there was very clearly nobody there. It also had some sort of accent. Sounded vaguely . . .

Canadian? Scott thought. *Things couldn't get any weirder.*

"Great." He sighed. "I wasn't crazy enough? Now I've got to hear voices?"

Lying back down, he shut his eyes firmly, determined to ignore the Voice.

Every serial killer I ever heard of said they heard voices that told them what to do. Why not just tell the voices no?

"You hear that?" Scott whispered. "I won't do it. I'm not killing anybody."

There was silence for a moment. Then the Voice spoke again.

"A bowl of milk."

Now I know I'm crazy, Scott thought. *Course, I knew that before.*

"What?" he said, feeling stupid asking questions of the empty room. But the emptiness answered immediately.

"Place a bowl of milk on the floor of your kitchen. Then rest easy. You are watched over this night."

"A bowl of milk?"

"Yes."

"I don't have to kill anyone?" Scott opened his eyes.

"No."

A bowl of milk. Okay, that I can do.

Scott got up, careful not to disturb Fletcher, and padded on bare feet into the kitchen, muttering, "Crazy. Voices. Got to sleep. Fletcher will be up soon."

The house was dark, but his eyes were adjusted. He saw no one. Grabbing a bowl from the cupboard—it was one Bridie had given him, a souvenir from the Basketball Hall of Fame in Springfield—he filled it half full with milk. Still muttering—"Milk. Crazy. Voices."—he placed it on the floor and went back to bed. The Voice spoke no more. Even an old soldier couldn't fall asleep immediately after that experience. It took Scott a full five minutes to drift off.

HE SLEEPWALKED THROUGH two late-night feedings without hearing any more voices, and by the time morning came around he had almost convinced himself that the Voice had been a dream.

But the house was sparkling clean again, and the bowl of milk was gone. No, not gone, but cleaned to shining, and placed back in the cupboard.

Scott sighed and sat down on his couch. He thought desperately about a cigarette, but didn't want to see what his Fletcher-Vision would show him if he lit up.

"Why milk?" he asked the empty room. He wasn't particularly surprised when he got an answer.

"Because there are those who . . ." the voice from last night began.

"Toil for me freely. Yeah, I got that part." Standing, Scott scanned the room. Nothing but peeling paint and bad decor. Fletcher was still asleep in the bedroom. Scott was alone. "And who are you?"

"Come." The Voice was low and stilted, as if uncomfortable with English. "*Paspisha*. The sun rises. Your protectors need assistance."

"Not a chance. Fletcher will wake soon and . . ."

"When he wakes, you will know?"

Scott paused in his protest. "I suppose I will." The visions would alert him when Fletcher was hungry.

"And bring your weapon."

Scott thought about the standard Marine-issue M9 Beretta packed away in his closet. The Marines hadn't issued him that one, of course. But an ex-Marine in rural America can always find someone to sell him a gun.

"Absolutely not." He still wasn't convinced the Voice wasn't his own brain getting ready to tell him to climb a clock tower and start firing.

"Bring a knife at least. You may have to do some cutting."

Scott had a British Commando knife under his mattress. A genuine Fairburn-Sykes. It hadn't been used since WWII, but

Scott kept it oiled up and sharp, and it was still probably one of the best killing knives around.

Stomping into the kitchen, he rummaged around in a drawer, eventually coming out with an old, dull steak knife.

Be tough to go on much of a spree with this thing.

He fancied he could hear the Voice sighing.

"All right," Scott said. "I'm ready." Just then, Fletcher began wailing from the bedroom. "But he's not." Tossing the knife into the sink, Scott made for the baby.

"Bring the child," the Voice intoned. "We must hurry. Your protectors' enemy does not like the day. But he can hunt in the light if he so chooses."

Scott had no idea what the Voice was talking about. And he wasn't really listening, anyway. His baby was crying, and he had to feed him, or change him, or somehow make him happy. He hoisted the little guy off the floor, thinking, *I gotta get a crib,* then went to the kitchen to start a bottle.

But when Scott reached for the formula, Fletcher redoubled his screaming and Scott was suddenly hit with a terrible vision: The baby lay on a pile of dry pine needles screaming, his stomach flayed open, his skin peeled back, a shadow approaching . . .

This was the worst vision yet. It was like he was there, seeing the baby—*his baby!*—sliced open. He could hear the screams, smell the blood, almost feel the pain of it. He staggered against the sink, slapping at his eyes with his free hand, trying to make the vision stop. He almost dropped the baby.

"Come," said the Voice.

"Fuck you," Scott replied, his eyes squeezed shut, tears starting to leak around the edges.

"Come," the Voice repeated, louder this time.

The baby in his vision screamed louder now, too, and Scott banged on the sink with his fist, trying to drown out the imaginary sound with clanging metal. It wasn't enough. The shadow in his vision became a figure silhouetted by moonlight. The shape of it was somehow familiar.

It reached into the baby and pulled out something. Began eating.

Scott turned and vomited into the sink. His knees went weak, and he struggled to stand, putting his hand inside the sink for balance. As his knuckles brushed the steak knife he had thrown there, the vision disappeared.

But only for a moment. As his hand moved away from the knife, the bloody scene reappeared in his mind. Like a drowning man reaching for a safety line, Scott grabbed the knife. His sight cleared.

"Oh God," he gasped and turned on the cold water. He splashed his face with his one hand—still holding the knife. Cupped his hand under the flow and took a little sip, careful not to cut his lip. Took another, swished it around in his mouth before spitting it out. He looked at the steak knife. Then at Fletcher.

The baby stared up at him with a peaceful half-smile.

"You want me to go with the Voice?" Scott asked.

The baby didn't answer. Scott straightened up, grabbed the steak knife, and tucked it into his belt. The vision didn't return.

He looked at Fletcher tucked in the crook of his arm one more time, then turned to the door and addressed the empty air.

"I'm ready."

"Come," said the Voice.

As he made for the door, Scott whispered to Fletcher, "Maybe you could just tell me next time." Then he tickled the baby's feet and got a pleased giggle as a reward.

THE MORNING SUN slanted through a gap in the forest's pine canopy and made Scott squint as he stepped outside. Fletcher squeezed his eyes tight, too.

"Not a morning person, are you?" Scott said. He shaded the baby's eyes with his free hand. "Where to?"

The Voice responded in its deep tones. "Ten steps North and then face the rising sun."

Scott turned left and paced along the side of the house. Ten steps took him a little ways into the woods. When he turned east, the Voice said, "Look down."

Scott did as the Voice said, but saw nothing out of the ordinary. Typical New England ground cover of dead leaves and pine needles, couple of odd plants and bushes poking through.

"Do you see the holly?" asked the Voice.

"Um . . . no." Scott wouldn't know holly if she jumped up and bit him.

"The bush with the crimson berries."

Scott saw it then, a squat bush, maybe a foot and a half high, red berries peeking out from behind thin spiky leaves. He nodded.

"The far branch that is twisted into a knot. *Aumpanimmin.* Undo it."

Scott didn't see any knot. Kneeling down next to the bush, he gently pushed aside its branches with his free hand. The berries were so red they almost glowed, the leaves just beginning to yellow in anticipation of fall.

There. "I see it."

The branch was indeed knotted, though Scott didn't think he would have noticed if the Voice hadn't pointed it out. It looked more like a burl or some other parasite grown into the small tree's branch. But when looked at closely, it was definitely a knot. Scott was a Marine, not a sailor, so he didn't know what kind. But it looked complicated.

"I'll have to cut it."

"Ask permission."

"Um . . . okay," Scott said. "Can I cut it?"

"Not my permission," the Voice said. "The plant's."

"Um . . ." *What if it answers me?* Scott thought. *Would that be the craziest thing that's happened to me? Not even close,* he decided. "Can I cut you, plant?"

The plant didn't answer, so Scott pulled the steak knife out of his belt and made to hack at the woody knot.

"Careful!" the Voice roared.

Scott froze, his ears ringing from the shout. Then he chuckled. "I think that's the first time you've raised yourself."

The Voice didn't answer. Fletcher burped.

Scott eased the knife forward and laid the serrated edge against the Holly's knotted branch.

"Gonna need to saw a bit, Cap'n."

Again, the Voice said nothing.

Shrugging, Scott began working at the knot. It was tough going holding the baby in one arm and sawing with the other, and the old knife appeared entirely inadequate to the task. But after a few minutes of sweaty work, he cut through the last shredded strip. The branch whipped back, catching him across the cheek, and he jumped to his feet in surprise.

"Damn!"

Scott dropped the knife and put his hand to his face, feeling along the hot line the branch had marked on his cheek. His fingers came away bloodier than he was expecting.

"Damn," he said again, softer this time.

"We must hurry. Your wound will need tending."

"Nah, it's just a scratch." *Though it is bleeding a bit much for one.* "But why'd it spring back like that? It didn't look like it was going to."

"It was an *apé hana*."

"A what?"

"A trap. And you have sprung it. Your injury is worse than you think."

"Nah. I've been hurt worse." Scott pressed his shirtsleeve to his cheek. *Sure is bleeding something fierce, though.*

"*Hub, hub, hub.* We must hurry," the Voice said. "There are more traps to spring and your wound will need tending."

"Yeah, you mentioned that." Scott sighed and stooped to pick up the knife. Fletcher gurgled contentedly.

"Enjoying yourself?" Scott asked.

The baby didn't answer. The Voice said, "West to the rock with the flat top, then downhill and across the stream."

Scott began walking and the Voice added, "We must hurry."

"Just like in boot camp," Scott grumbled, breaking into a military jog. He thought he knew the stream the Voice meant; it was too wide to jump across holding a baby. *Keep your feet wet and your rifle dry,* he thought. "Yep, just like fucking boot camp."

He jogged on and the bouncing movement made Fletcher giggle. Scott couldn't help but smile at the little guy's chortling and before long he was laughing out loud. And he forgot about his tiredness and his insanity and the blood dripping from his cheek as he loped past the flat-topped rock and downhill to the stream, charging across it with Fletcher held high over his head.

Keep your feet wet and your baby *dry.*

• • • six • • •

Bridie stood in front of the savories cart on top of Calton Hill and eyed its motley collection of meat pies, breaded fish, doughnuts, chips, crisps, and soft drinks.

"What'll ye have, luv?" asked the moon-faced woman behind the counter.

Bridie sighed before answering, "Bottle of water." She turned to Hamilton. "What I wouldn't give for a pizza about now." She took her water from the counter and popped it open. Took a sip.

"You wouldnae want one of ours, I imagine." Hamilton frowned. "Unless you like tuna and corn. Those are quite tasty."

Bridie almost choked on her water. "Tuna and corn pizza? Jesus, and you call yourselves a civilized country."

Hamilton led her across the parking lot and into the shade of what for all the world looked like half of the Acropolis. Bridie stared at the giant pillars as they walked around it and said, "I don't even want to know."

Hamilton marched to where the middle of the monument would have been if it had been finished and said, "They found the priest here." Here was an unremarkable patch of grass.

"And the finger?"

"Right next to him. Priest's car was in the lot, keys in the ignition. Your grandmother's car was right next to it. No keys found."

Bridie knew all this—it was in the reports she'd read. But she wanted to get a feel for where everything had happened. *There's no replacement for first-person investigation.* She couldn't remember who had told her that. Maybe a teacher at the academy.

Standing next to Hamilton, she let herself take in the whole scene. Before her, Calton Hill dropped steadily away, revealing a scenic view of Edinburgh, its stone towers and churches looking like something out of a fairy tale. The pillars of the unfinished monument loomed in her peripheral vision. The sky was gray. The grass was trampled, but still a lush green, and showed no sign that a man had died here, his head blown violently apart, and someone's pinky—possibly her brother's—had been severed and left beside the corpse.

"Walk me through it," Bridie said.

"Ah, but you've already read the . . ."

"Walk me through it."

They tromped back to the parking lot and Hamilton gestured down the hill. "The late shift guard waves Douglas, in Mrs. McLaren's Peugeot, past the gate. He thinks he looks rougher than the usual early-morning patrons—though maybe not for the late-night revelers—and he jots down the time and plate number."

Bridie glanced at Hamilton. "What goes on up here at night?"

"Calton Hill's the north end of the 'Gay Triangle,'" he said. "They meet up here at night. Some anonymous sex, maybe a little rough trade, then it's back home to the wife and kiddies." Hamilton grinned. "They leave messages in the rocks to set up their assignations. The guards switch them around. We go in every once in a while to clean it out, but we don't usually make any arrests. Too many council members."

Bridie didn't say anything for a few moments, absorbing this new information. "Douglas isn't gay."

"Didnae say he was." Hamilton didn't look at Bridie, seeming to talk to a monument that looked like a wilting birthday cake. "But maybe he was. And maybe his grandmother found out, and they argued."

"No," Bridie said simply.

"Maybe he killed her so she couldn't reveal his secret. And maybe he came up here to meet his boyfriend, the priest, and in his homicidal state, killed him, too."

"Douglas isn't gay."

"So you say." Hamilton's voice was raised, now. "You said he's not a killer, either. And, yet he was meeting a priest—who *never* fuck young boys—in a spot known for homosexual activities, covered in the blood of his murdered grandmother!"

Bridie's face was suddenly scorching hot. "Listen, you Scotch dickhead! If Douglas was gay, it wouldn't have mattered. We live in a country that accepts that, not some backwater shithole where you still call them fags and queers and make them meet on lonely hilltops in the dead of night." Bridie turned and walked two paces to her left. "The priest's car was here?" she asked, her voice suddenly normal again.

But Hamilton wasn't ready to drop it, yet. "It fits all the facts, Bridie."

"It doesn't fit any of the facts." She ticked them off on her fingers. "He isn't gay, he didn't kill Grandma McLaren, and he wasn't meeting the priest."

"Bridie . . ."

"Walk me through it. The priest's car was here."

"It's Scottish, you know," Hamilton said, a bit peevishly.

"What is?" Bridie asked, glancing over her shoulder.

"Scottish dickhead. Not Scotch. That's a drink, not a person."

"Oh, for Christ's sa . . . You're beeping."

"What? Oh, my phone." Hamilton unhooked a small cell phone from his belt. "DI Hamilton," he said. Then, "They're waiting in Aberfeldy? They can't bring her down to at least Perth? I know Tayside has better things to . . . Aye. But that's a bit of a hike from—" He made a face and held the phone away from his ear, flicking two fingers in the shape of a peace sign at it. There wasn't anything peaceful about the gesture however. "Aye, all right," he said when he put the phone back up to his ear. "I'm going to send someone to question her." Shutting the phone angrily, he added, "You bloody provincial bastards."

"What's up?" Bridie asked.

"Tayside Police picked up Sandra Matheson. But they have better things to do than transport our prisoners for us, so they're holding her in their car all the way up in Aberfeldy." He sighed. "You're going up to talk to her."

"All right."

"We're quite progressive, you know," Hamilton said quietly. "We even have a gay police association."

Bridie didn't hear. She was already walking toward the car.

HAMILTON ASSIGNED AN acne-riddled young constable named Harris to drive Bridie to Aberfeldy.

"You wanted to handle the Q&A," he said, "and like I said before, I *do* have other cases to work."

That was all right by Bridie; she looked forward to a bit of quiet time to think about the case and plan her interrogation of Ms. Matheson. She didn't get it.

"It's great to work with DI Hamilton. He's quite a detective, you know. Solved some rather large cases for us. That's how he got to be Detective Inspector so young. 'An up and comer' the Chief Constable said when he promoted him. Don't know about the Chief, though. Bit too much the politician for my tastes; too ca' canny with the Council and the like."

Seemed Police Constable Harris was a bit of a talker.

Bridie sighed and leaned her head against the window, watching the M90 stream past as they headed north. They crossed the long bridge over the Firth of Forth, and the suburbs of the city turned into the rolling hills and soft green fields of Fife. Bridie didn't see the change, however. She was fast asleep.

"OH, WHAT A parish, a terrible parish!"

Bridie jolted awake. *Good Lord, he's singing.*

"Oh, what a parish is that of Dunkeld!" PC Harris looked over at Bridie. "You're awake! That's good. We're almost there."

Bridie glanced around the car, trying to find the cat that must have crapped in her mouth while she slept. "Good. Could use a glass of water."

"Oh, aye. Probably jet-lagged if you haven't been here long. Have you? Been here long, I mean. I find it usually hits you Yanks about the second or third day. Knocks ye right out. I knew one bird came over . . ."

Bridie leaned her head back on the window none too gently. Truth be told, she knocked into it fairly hard in the vain hope that the jarring might make her go spontaneously deaf.

"You're probably wondering what I was singing."

No such luck.

"No." She didn't think he heard her. Certainly gave no sign that he had.

"A Silly Wizard song. I thought of it 'cause we turned off the A9 just south of Dunkeld. That's how I knew we were almost there. See those mountains?" Harris pointed out the windshield toward a line of high rounded hills in the distance. "Aberfeldy's between us and them."

"Thank God."

"What?"

"Nothing."

"Oh, aye, all right. Anyway, Dunkeld had this preacher who decided . . ."

Bridie began hitting her head against the window repeatedly and begging the mountains to approach quicker. They never had a chance to, however, because PC Harris's cell began to ring. And after a few moments conversation with the person on the other line, he checked both mirrors and did a tight three-point turn. Bridie looked a question at him.

"Tayside decided to help out after all," he said. "They've taken Matheson to divisional HQ in Perth."

"Where's that?"

"Nae more than an hour back the way we came. Och, that looked like it hurt. Why'd you hit your head against the window like that? Anyway, this preacher . . ."

AT WESTERN DIVISIONAL Headquarters, Bridie bummed a pack of cigarettes from a blessedly silent constable with faded RAF tattoos on his forearms, and pushed through the door into the interrogation room that held Sandra Matheson. It looked remarkably like the room Bridie herself had been in just yesterday: low table, couple of stout wooden chairs, no windows, one door, miserable fluorescent lights.

"Who the fuck are you?" Sandra said.

Bridie took her time and eyed the girl up and down, taking in the blue eyes and the long blond hair, the thin legs under her peasant skirts. Thought about her flashing those pretty eyes at Hamilton and Fraser, maybe showing a bit more leg than strictly necessary when she shifted in her seat.

She's pretty enough to get away with that, Bridie mused, *but probably not for long.*

The eyes were sunken, the hair starting to hang lank, the legs probably covered with track marks behind the knees.

I wonder how long since her last fix.

"I said, who the . . ."

"I heard you," Bridie interrupted. Sliding a chair in front of her, she sat down, arms crossed. She stared at Sandra and didn't say anything more.

Frowning, Sandra leaned back in her chair, and fixed as defiant a look as she could muster on her face. "Listen, Yank," she began.

Amazed that the girl had pegged her as an American in three words, Bridie interrupted again. "Smoke?" She pushed the cigarette pack across the table.

Sandra paused with her mouth open. "All right." Grabbing a smoke, she said, "Light?"

Bridie made a show of checking her pockets. Patted herself down. "Sorry, no."

"Bitch."

Bridie shrugged and resumed her silence. Sandra sat with the cigarette in her mouth for a moment, then angrily tossed it back on the table between them. Folding her arms, she sat back in her chair and tried to outlast Bridie.

She didn't make it long.

"What is this?" She managed to get it all out before Bridie could interrupt her.

Bridie didn't answer. Didn't even move.

Sandra snorted. "Why give me a fag and no light? You get off on petty torture? I'll be out in an hour and have two smokes to make up."

Bridie smiled and shrugged. "Didn't have a light. Said I was sorry." Leaning forward, she said, "Sucks to want something so bad and not be able to get at it, doesn't it?"

"Like I said, I'll be out in an hour."

"No," Bridie said, shaking her head, "you won't be." She picked the cigarette off the table and put it back in the pack. "You know the rules in this country better than me. They can hold you for forty-eight hours for no reason. No fucking reason." She picked up the smokes. Tucked the loose one back into the pack, then looked at them with a wan smile. "Doesn't seem civilized. But they're your rules, not mine." She stood. "Forty-eight hours, Sandra. Shape you're in, you won't make twelve."

She knocked on the door, a constable opened it, and she walked out without another word.

IT WAS THREE hours before Sandra called for her.

"If this is about Douglas," she said, "I knew him. We were friends and all. But we weren't that close, like. I don't know anything about his grandmother's death."

Bridie turned around and walked out without speaking.

IT WAS DARK when Sandra summoned her again. She was pale. Shaking a little.

"Look, I don't know anything."

Bridie shook her head. "Twelve hours," was all she said before leaving.

"SEE," BRIDIE WAS saying to PC Harris by the water cooler, talking as much as she could as a preemptive measure, "it's like torture. I'm for sure going to get some information this way. She needs a fix bad. Another few hours she'll tell me she can fart diamonds if she thinks I'll let her go. The problem is assessing whether any of the information is even remotely truthful." The cop by the interrogation room waved to her. "Ah, the princess requires my presence."

SANDRA LOOKED BAD. Her eyes were red from crying, and her hands shook madly when Bridie handed her a cigarette. Sitting on the table, Bridie lit it for her this time.

"All right, Sandra. Tell me a story so we can all get out of here."

Sniffling, Sandra muttered, "But I don't know anything, like."

"Now, c'mon, girl, we're past all that." Bridie patted her head like an older sister. "You know plenty." Bridie took a stab in the dark. "You were there the night she died."

Sandra's head shot up, her eyes wide like a frightened colt. She looked away just as quickly. "I wasnae."

But it was too late. Bridie caught the look and leaped off the table, grabbing Sandra's head in her hands.

"What'd you see? Who killed her?"

"I didn't . . . She was . . ." Sandra's smoke flew out of her mouth as she tried to wriggle free from Bridie's grasp, but Bridie squeezed hard.

"What did you see?"

"She was dead when we got there!"

"We? Who's we?"

With a surge of inhuman strength, Sandra wrested her head from Bride's grasp and shot backward out of her chair. The chair clanged to the ground and Sandra scuttled into the corner of the small room. "No one. I just meant me. Only I was there." She hugged her knees to her chest.

Bridie crushed the smoke under her foot before following Sandra into the corner at half speed, not wanting to spook the girl more. When she reached her, she put her back against the wall, and slid down till she was seated, still moving slow. She pulled out the pack of cigarettes again, this time putting one to her lips and lighting it with a wooden match. Taking one drag to get it lit, she turned to face Sandra.

"C'mon, girl," Bridie said, "have a smoke."

Sandra didn't look up. "I can't," she muttered.

"Sure you can." Bridie reached out and lifted Sandra's chin with her left hand. Plucked the cigarette from her own mouth, then lowered Sandra's quivering bottom lip with just the tip of her thumb and placed the smoke there. "Go on."

Sandra took a deep drag. Bridie watched the cherry's glow reflected in her eyes.

She's a pretty one, she thought again. Slipping her left arm around her, Bridie pulled the girl in a little closer. Sandra sighed and took another pull off the cigarette. "There, that's better," murmured Bridie. "Now, tell me who was with you, and you can walk out of here before your smoke's done."

Sandra stiffened at the suggestion. "I can't. They'd kill me."

Bridie took Sandra's hand in hers. Stroked it gently. "I won't let them, little one."

Sandra gazed up at Bridie, her eyes unnaturally large in her gaunt face. "The Craic brothers," she said. "Donnie and Jackie."

Bridie didn't show any reaction, just patted Sandra's hand again. "Crack brothers?"

"Aye. Only spelled Irish, like. 'Craic.' For good times." She frowned. "Kind of a joke, like. 'Cause they're such bad news. It's not their real last name."

"Do you know it?"

"No. But it probably rhymes with craic. Rhyming slang, you know?"

Bridie didn't know. But she was pretty sure Hamilton would.

"That's a good girl."

Sandra sniffled. "Can I go now?"

"Just a few more minutes." Bridie stood and extended her hand to Sandra, who took it gingerly. Bridie hauled her to her feet. "Have a seat." She knocked twice on the door and when the constable looked in, aped writing on a pad with her hands. He brought a small notepad and pen momentarily and Bridie sat down across from Sandra.

"Tell me a story," she said, smiling softly at the girl and touching her lightly on the back of her hand. "Tell me a good one."

• • • oobel • • •

The snares were all sprung and empty. And the hobs were back on watch, twice as wary as before. Oobel flew into a rage when he found his ruined traps, stomping the holly bushes to the ground and pulling out handfuls of earth-brown hair from his long beard. But soon enough he was calm, and eyeing the house from the cover of a last, undamaged holly.

"Oobel must be tricky," he hissed, stroking his still plentiful beard thoughtfully. "Oobel must be sly, or he'll never have the fleshie for his own."

He wracked his brains for new ideas. It was a painfully fruitless process. Oobel was not a natural thinker. He could craft snares and cast small spells, but he preferred the smash-grab-and-swallow to anything that required more intricate plotting. He'd come up with one plan to get to the fleshie, and it had been foiled.

But he knew one who was wise and sly and evil beyond measure. Even Oobel was afraid of her.

But he needed her now.

"I will offer her the blood. I will offer her the soul. Then perhaps she'll let me eat the flesh and bone."

As he scampered off into the darkness, Oobel whispered her name to himself, perhaps as a salve to his fear.

Mercy.

seven

Scott stumbled. Yes, the sure-footed, athletic ex-soldier tripped over a patch of air and almost fell, nearly dropping the baby as well. He managed to catch hold of a sapling with his free hand and stayed upright.

"What's happening?" he asked the air. It answered.

"The *apé hana* is working toward your heart," the Voice said. "We must hurry."

That doesn't sound good.

"How can I hurry if I keep tripping?"

The Voice didn't have an answer for that one. Sighing, Scott began to pick his way forward over terrain that suddenly seemed a lot more treacherous than it had been a minute ago.

"*Hub, hub, hub,*" the Voice urged him on. Then suddenly, "Stop!"

Fletcher squeaked discontentedly as Scott pulled up short, jostling him.

"At your feet," the Voice went on. "The plant with the lightly furred leaves. Tell it your need is great and gather as much as you can."

Scott reached down for the plant.

"Stop!"

He froze. "What now?"

"Tell it your need is great."

"Tell it what?"

"That your need is great."

"Um. Okay."

Scott looked down at the furry ground cover. "Plant, my need is great. May I gather you?" He paused to give the plant time to answer. It proved as talkative as the Holly had been. "I'll take your silence as a yes."

Stooping, he yanked a bunch out of the ground aggressively. Fletcher giggled at the sudden movement. The smell as the leaves crushed in his hand reminded Scott that he hadn't eaten all morning.

Maybe the Voice wants me to make soup when we get home.

"That will do," the Voice said. "*Hub, hub!*"

"Settle down, Sarge." Through the trees, Scott could just make out his house. "We're almost home."

BACK IN HIS home, Scott felt even more like an idiot than when he was outside talking to the plants. Now he was beating himself up with them.

Following the Voice's instructions, he'd wrapped the plants he'd picked—sage, he thought it was—in a bundle before drying them in the oven. Then he lit the bundle on fire. Now he stood shirtless in his living room whacking himself in the face and chest with the flaming wad of dried plants, chanting nonsense syllables the Voice had taught him.

To make it worse, the Voice seemed quite disappointed in his performance.

"You squawk like a wounded crow. Sing! *Nigamo!*"

Scott tried to add some melody to his chant. "*Wom-pan-ni-you. So-wa-ni-you. Pah-ta-tun-ni-you.*" He spun clockwise during this part of the chant as the Voice had instructed him to, still swinging the flaming sage around in what he thought was a rather dangerous manner. *Wouldn't take long for this little house to burn to the ground.* He worried about the smoke and the baby, and forgot the next line. "*Na-nu . . . uh . . . er . . . mama-you?*"

"*Chickachava!* Now the crow has died!" The Voice sputtered incoherently for a minute, than finally said, "Stop. You are either healed or dead. We shall know in the morning."

With that reassurance, the Voice fell silent. Scott crushed the aromatic herbs into an ashtray and sat down. He really wanted a cigarette, but didn't need visions of Fletcher dying of emphysema right now.

"Dead?" he asked. "I feel fine."

The Voice didn't answer.

Sighing, Scott stood and went to the bedroom to check on Fletcher. Exhausted from the morning's adventures, the baby had gone to sleep after only three sucks on his bottle. He lay on his side, now, snoring softly.

"You must protect the child," the Voice said.

Scott nodded.

"Why are you not?"

"What?" Scott's raised voice made Fletcher wince, and he quickly retreated from the bedroom. "Of course I am!" he hissed. "I'm right here, aren't I?"

"And you think you are enough?"

"Yes. I was a soldier, you know."

"Fool! He needs more than physical protection." The Voice paused, then went on in a conciliatory tone. "I am sorry. I forget how much time has passed since the old ways were known. Even the new ways brought over by the coat-men are old now."

Scott flopped onto the couch. "Coat-men? What's a coat-man?"

"You are."

"I am?" Scott waited, but a clarification didn't come. "Never mind. How do I protect the child . . . er . . . nonphysically?"

"I will teach you."

"Um . . . good?" He was getting used to talking to thin air. *It should feel weirder than it does. But I was never good at talking to real people, anyway. This is somehow easier.* "When?"

"Do you have any scissors?"

"I think so."

"*Pautauog.* Bring them here."

Heaving himself off the couch, Scott went to the kitchen and rummaged through a drawer. *Pens, AA batteries, playing cards, Scotch tape, electrical tape, duct tape, loose screws*—he chuckled— *There we go!*

"Scissors!" he exclaimed, holding them up like a trophy. The Voice said nothing, and Scott looked a little sheepish as he walked back into the living room.

"You will need some twine."

"You couldn't have told me that while I was in the kitchen?" Not that the kitchen was far away. He didn't even have to open a door to get to it.

It's just, he thought, *the principle of the thing, dammit.*

Scott turned and went back into the kitchen, sneaking a peek at the sleeping baby as he went by the bedroom door. Searching through the same drawer, he managed to come up with some kite string, though he couldn't remember the last time he'd flown a kite or even figure out why he had any kite-flying supplies in the first place. *Maybe Bridie bought it for me. She's always trying to find me something to do outside the house.*

"Got it," Scott said, much less triumphantly than before. He went back into the living room. He looked down at the scissors in one hand, the string in the other. Said scornfully, "I feel better equipped already."

"Go to the child's room." Scott thought the Voice sounded more natural when it was giving orders. "Tie the scissors above his bed. Make sure they are open."

"First of all," Scott said, "its not Fletcher's room. It's my room. My bed, too. Well, not totally mine anymore, I suppose. Maybe it's ours." He shook his head. "Doesn't matter. How am I supposed to tie something to the ceiling?"

"*Tahaspunayi?*" The Voice sounded exasperated. "*Chick-achava, notammehick ewo!*" Scott was certain he heard a sigh this time. When the Voice went on, it sounded as if it were talking to a child. "Perhaps you could pound a nail into the ceiling?"

Scott nodded. "That *is* a good idea." He glanced toward the bedroom. "I'll wait till Fletcher wakes up though." Scott sat down on the couch and closed his eyes. But only for a second.

The Voice broke into his rest, nails on a chalkboard. "*Pasuck-quish.* Rise. The scissors now. Then there are more supplies you will need. And you will not find them here."

"But Fletcher . . ."

"You must go to town. You will know when the child wakes."

"You're not ever supposed to leave your kid alone in the house. What if town is too far away for me to be able to get his messages? What if he needs me right away?"

"You will hear him. And he will not be alone."

"Great. Got an invisible guy and an infant ordering me around." Scott heaved himself off the couch. "All right. What do I need to get?" *Maybe I can sneak a smoke while I'm out.*

SCOTT STOOD ON his bed tying the scissors to his bedroom ceiling. He'd gone with two nails instead of one so each hole in the scissors handle got its own twine attached to its own nail. Just seemed sturdier to him. Surprisingly, the hammering hadn't awoken Fletcher. In fact, the baby seemed to be sleeping more soundly than before, thumb tucked in his mouth like the stopper of a bottle. Scott tied the last of his knots and looked at them critically. He didn't know any good knots—he was a Marine, not a sailor—so he'd just tied a lot of them. They weren't pretty, but they would defeat easy untying. The sharp ends of the scissors now pointed down. At the bed. Where Fletcher lay sleeping. Scott glanced from the scissors to the bed and back again.

"And this is supposed to make him *more* safe?" he asked.

"It is a ward," the Voice said.

"And the other stuff I have to buy? Wards, too?"

"Wards, protections, prayers." The Voice sounded like a particularly bored instructor at camp. "Most are defensive in nature. To attack, you would do well with the weapons you are accustomed to. Cold steel harms everything, seen and unseen."

Scott thought that was the most the Voice had said at one time. Not a pleasant subject though.

"I'm not accustomed to weapons. Not anymore." The Voice said nothing in reply. "Listen, if you're going to watch my kid, I need to know your name. Can't let a complete stranger babysit."

"My name?"

"Yes, your name." Scott climbed off the bed. Looked again at the scissors pointing down at Fletcher and shook his head. "What are you called?"

"I have been called many things. The first peoples called me *Mundoo* and *Achak*. To the West I was called *Wakan-Tanka*, to the North, *Torngasak*. I have been called *Askuwheteau* when I watched over the sick and *Abbomocho* when I took them home." The Voice paused. "If it would make you more comfortable, you could call me by the name the Coat-men gave me when they first came across the great waters."

"What was that?"

"Satan."

Scott blinked. "Um . . . No, I don't think that would make me more comfortable."

"Very well."

"What was the first one you said?" Scott scratched his head. "Monroe?"

"Mundoo."

"Okay. Mundoo it is."

"Go then," Mundoo said. "*Anakish*. Go and I will watch over the child. And when you return, you will arm for battle."

I don't think so, Scott thought.

But he grabbed his keys off the counter and asked the empty room, "Okay, what do I need again?"

IT WAS THE Stop and Shop this time, and not just because they would have a bigger selection. Scott didn't want to risk running into Traci at Cumberland Farms, and having to explain why he didn't have his baby with him.

Oh, I left him alone with an invisible guy, Scott thought as he walked through the automatic doors into the giant grocery store. *And "those who toil for me freely."*

A middle-aged woman with salt-and-pepper hair gathered into a casual bun shot Scott an alarmed look and abruptly decided that she didn't need a cart quite yet.

Crap. Did I say that out loud? Sighing, Scott pulled a cart from out of the long line. Watched the woman teeter away on decidedly unsensible shoes. *She's just lucky I didn't come the way the Voice wanted me to: M9 tucked into my belt, commando knife gripped in my teeth.*

Then he creaked and wobbled his cart toward the herbs and spices aisle.

More sage. Then rosemary, bay, garlic, and pepper. Then . . . He fumbled his list out of his pocket. *Oatmeal, salt, red cloth, and red thread—not sure if I can find that here. Maybe there's some red napkins or potholders. What else? Bread, the herb of Midsummer— whatever the hell that is. I should get a baby carrier while I'm here so I don't have to lug Fletcher around when I'm out talking to plants. Speaking of plants, there's daisies on the list. Is there a floral section in this place?*

Sighing mightily, Scott tucked the list away without reading to the end and started searching through the many bottles of spices for what he needed.

HE WAS OUT of the herb aisle and down to bread on his list—he had, in fact, found a bright red potholder for sale, as well as a baby carrier that attached to his chest like a reverse backpack— when he got his first vision from Fletcher. It was brief, just a few seconds, and wasn't even disturbing; just a view of the baby lying in the bed glancing around disconsolately. Nothing horrible happened, or seemed about to happen, and it faded within moments. Scott froze in the dairy section of the supermarket and waited for more, but nothing came.

I better get home, he thought. *Seems Fletcher is up.*

Scott didn't know why he wasn't getting horrible reminders of why he should be home caring for his baby, but he sure wasn't going to complain.

Would've been hard driving home with that shit in my brain, anyway.

He scanned the rest of the list.

Hope the Voice isn't too attached to the rest of this stuff. Because I think I'd better get home.

He double-time marched to the checkout line then double-bagged as fast as he could. Paid cash for his items and ran for his car. Bags in the backseat and him in the front, ripping the seat cover just a little bit more in his haste. He blew a yellow light screeching out of the lot onto Route 9, earning himself a few honks and lazy birds, then he was weaving through traffic and pushing uphill into Amherst. He didn't want to risk traffic by going all the way through town so he skirted the center of town to the south. Trees whizzed by as he pushed the little Honda hard through the S-turns on North Valley Road, then he was rocketing up and down hills through Pelham and Shutesbury, heading for home. Gravel flew as he slid into the driveway, and he slammed the car into park before it was even at a full stop. Leaping out, he ran to the door.

He heard singing.

What the—?

Scott left the keys in the lock as he scooted inside to see who was singing. As soon as he was in, he recognized the singer. The Voice.

"What's going on?" Scott asked as he entered the bedroom. Fletcher lay in the middle of the bed gurgling happily as the Voice—rather, *Mundoo*—boomed out what Scott presumed was a Native American lullaby.

Mundoo held one last note for a moment or two before saying, "The child enjoys music. I thought to keep him happy till you returned."

Scott looked at the baby, chewing contentedly on the back of one pudgy hand. "Looks like you succeeded. He'll be hungry now, though."

"Feed him quickly then," Mundoo said. "*Hub, hub, hub.* Night will come soon. We must get the wards up."

Scott bent and scooped Fletcher up. "The enemy," he said. "He'll be setting more traps?"

"No. He is not a patient creature. I think he will try a more direct attack next."

"Oh." Scott thought about his pistol. His real knife. *Not yet. I still might just be crazy. Well, more crazy.*

"And I think he will bring assistance."

Scott moved into the kitchen. Grabbed a bottle and some formula out of the cupboard. Put water in a pan and cranked the dial on the stove to "Light."

All one-handed! he thought. *I'm getting good at this.*

"What kind of help? And why is he after Fletcher?"

"He is after Fletcher because that is what he does. As for what kind of help . . ." Mundoo paused. "I do not know."

There was a quiet *whoosh* as the gas caught fire. Scott leaned back against the sink and watched the blue flames lick the bottom of the pan.

"Reckon we'll find out soon enough."

"Yes," Mundoo answered. "I am certain we will."

eight

Hamilton peered at Bridie over a cup of weak tea.

"Craic brothers?" he said. "Sandra Matheson said that she, your brother, and the Craics all showed up at your grandmother's house in the morning after partying all night and found her dead already?"

They were back in his office, and though muted by the walls, the ringing phones, clacking keyboards, and rough cop voices coming from the station's main room jangled Bridie's nerves. She thought about looking out the window but decided not to bother.

I'd just see gray. Gray sky. Gray stone. Gray country.

"Aye." *Christ, I'm starting to talk like them.* "Only she wasn't telling the whole truth." Bridie shrugged. "I couldn't get her to break on the rest, though. And she said that "Craic" isn't their real name. Mentioned something about rhyming slang."

Nodding, Hamilton said, "We don't like to come right out and say things here in Scotland."

"Could have fooled me."

"Well, that may be, but when a Glasgow man says he just 'had a jam tart,' he doesn't mean he just ate."

"What *does* it mean, then?" Bridie scrunched her eyebrows up and tried to sip her tea. *Awful stuff*.

Hamilton gave her a schoolboy grin. "Means he just farted."

Bridie just stared at him. "Tart. Fart," she said slowly. "Is there anyone in this country who matured past the age of twelve?" Hamilton just cackled. "Okay, so we're looking for two brothers whose last name rhymes with 'crack.'"

"Maybe."

"Maybe? I thought—"

"It's worse than just rhyming the word. You might say something that means something else that rhymes with what you want to say."

"I'm guessing that if I knew what the hell you just said," Bridie mused, "I would think it was the stupidest thing I'd ever heard."

There was a knock on the door and a fresh-faced constable poked his head in. "I've got the Alison's Close reports."

"Desk," Hamilton said.

The constable shot Bridie a self-conscious smile as he took two steps into the room and dropped a sheaf of papers on the already report-covered desk.

Hamilton waited till the young man left, then said, "Well, you'll notice most of the famous Scots were engineers or soldiers, not orators." He took a sip of tea. "For a while there, heroin was known as 'Arthur's Seat.'" Bridie tried, but couldn't think of any word for heroin that rhymed with "seat." "Arthur's Seat is also Arthur's Crag. Crag—"

"Skag," Bridie finished for him. "Cute. So, now we're looking for two brothers whose last name might rhyme with crack, or craic, or a word that means crack, or means something that sounds like crack . . ." Bridie gave a deep sigh. "This'll be the first time I've needed a thesaurus for police work."

Hamilton swiveled in his chair and hit the spacebar on his

computer. "Well, a lot of geezers don't take it that far. Maybe it'll just rhyme with craic." The screen came to life and he pecked at the keys a few times. "Why don't you get some air. This could take a bit."

"You have my cell number."

"Aye."

Smoothing her skirt down, Bridie stood. Felt Hamilton's eyes on her briefly. "All right. Call me if you get anything."

BRIDIE TRIED TO stroll idly through the tiny park across from the station, but she couldn't relax. They were close; she could feel it. They had the name—*well, almost*—and a good description of two witnesses to the murder. Witnesses who hadn't been interviewed. The cops hadn't even known they were there.

If we find them—Bridie corrected herself—*when we find them, I'm not leaving it up to Hamilton to do the Q&A. I'll get the story out of them myself.* She gritted her teeth in a smile so full of malice that a young man who'd been ogling her put his eyes to the grass and moved away. *Get it out of them the hard way if I must.*

Leaning against the low stone wall surrounding the park, Bridie scanned the people within its confines. Several families were enjoying a picnic lunch while their respective children commingled in a rough game of tag. A businessman talked on his cell. A couple in the shade of a small tree went at it like they'd need a room soon. A man with sunken cheeks and rugged clothes furtively smoked a hand-rolled cigarette. Bridie inspected them all and moved on. She was looking for two tallish men, both with close-cropped hair and tattoos, one heavily muscled, one thin but not frail. But she knew she wouldn't find them here. This neighborhood wasn't rough enough, the locals mostly smiles and nods and "Morning!" 's. No, she would find them someplace dark, someplace quiet and mean. Under a rock, where bugs and worms dwell, or behind the fridge where the cockroaches hide. They knew something, these "Craic brothers," and they'd gone to ground because of it. And when Bridie pried them out, she wouldn't stop hurting them till they'd told her everything.

Pushing herself off the wall, she headed back to the station. She couldn't wait out here any longer. If Hamilton hadn't found anything yet, he was just going to have to deal with Bridie looking over his shoulder, leaning on him.

Bridie was good at leaning on people.

"I GOT A hit," Hamilton said as she entered his office. Fraser stood behind him in a long tan coat, arms folded.

"Off the computer?" She rushed up next to Fraser and looked at the screen, expecting mugshots of the two brothers. It was blank. Computer was off.

"No. Computer's flippin' useless." He grinned. "Only you Yanks rely on it." He nodded at Fraser. "Fraser called the pubs down around Lothian Road. Found a bartender who would talk."

Bridie turned to Fraser. "He kick them out one night?"

"He tried to," the big man said, a beatific smile on his face. "They kicked the shite out of him, instead."

"Bet they'll wish they'd killed him once we track them down." She smiled back at him.

Hamilton stood. "Bartender seems to think they already tried."

THEY DROVE OUT of the square and into the big roundabout, exiting to the right up Leith Road. Calton Hill loomed to their left. She wondered if it was her brother's finger the cops found up there.

What happened, Douglas? To you? To Grandma McClaren? And where are you?

They turned onto Princes Street, a wide thoroughfare with

upscale shops on one side and a quaint park running along the other. Even midweek midday it was packed with people ducking in and out of shops, eating bag lunches on the grass, standing in line at the lights. A lone piper dressed in a dark kilt played on a street corner, cap at his feet to catch coins.

Hamilton kept the car on Princes Street long enough for Bridie to wonder why it hadn't changed its name six times like all the other streets did, then swung left onto Lothian Road. They didn't stay on that long, taking several swift turns onto smaller streets whose names Bridie didn't catch, until they started seeing pubs with signs on them reading, "Dances for £5!" and "Most Exclusive Club in Town!" and "Best-Looking Lasses in Auld Reekie!"

Seems the pubs down around Lothian Road were mostly strip clubs.

"Lap-dancing clubs, we call 'em here," Hamilton said.

"That what the Craic brothers got kicked out of?" Bridie asked.

"No," Fraser answered from the driver's seat, "and more's the pity. Haven't seen a woman naked in nearly a year." He winked at Bridie in the rearview. "It'd be longer but my wife makes me get the leg over on her birthday."

"Mind your manners, big man," Hamilton chided him. "There it is. The *Sgian Dubdh*." He pointed at a low building of black-painted stone and Fraser pulled the car over onto the double-yellow line in front of it.

"That's us here then," Fraser said, unfolding out of the car. Hamilton and Bridie followed suit. Down two steps, and they pushed through a thick black door into darkness. They had to let their eyes adjust a moment before they could see any details. Not that there were many to see. The pub was nearly devoid of ornament, the monotony of the black walls broken only by a cloudy chalkboard that might have once held drink specials, and maybe a dozen thin, sheathed knives hanging on nails behind the bar. The only illumination in the place seemed to come from one of those machines covered in flashing lights and symbols that Bridie assumed was for gambling. She'd never seen anybody playing one however, so she couldn't be sure.

Behind the bar stood a man shaped like a Greek column. From the neck down he was the same width, alternating between muscle and fat to keep his dimensions the same. Bridie was well trained in self-defense and couldn't think where she could hit this guy that would hurt him.

Someone else hadn't shared her confusion, however: he had the yellow-green of old shiners surrounding his eyes and a number of recently healed cuts on his cheeks and forehead. When he gave a mirthless grin in greeting, Bridie saw that he was missing several teeth.

Course, who isn't in this country? she thought.

There was only one other person in the pub, man or woman, it was hard to tell, just a mop of gray hair face down on the bar, half-full pint glass of pale yellow beer next to it.

"Yer the filth then," the bartender said by way of hello.

"Aye," Fraser said, seemingly unfazed by the label. "Ye know the Craic brothers?"

Hamilton slid a spiral notebook out of his coat pocket and flipped it open. Pulled a pen from the rings.

"Know 'em? I'll fuckin' kill 'em, I see 'em agin." The bartender spit on the floor behind the bar. "Who's the bird?"

"Witness," Fraser said. "What're their names?"

The bartender cackled. "Fer fuck's sake, you coppers are usless as tits on a bull, aren't ye? Ye don't even know their names?" Fraser didn't say anything. Hamilton stared at the blank notebook.

Bridie tried to look witnessy. "They're wanted for murder, that right?"

"Aye. A brutal one."

"Likely to do a long stretch?"

Fraser nodded. "Maximum, I imagine."

Suddenly the mop of gray hair lifted its head. "Gie us another pint of Bud, ye wee fuck."

Bridie still couldn't tell for sure if it was a man or woman.

"Shut yer hole!" the bartender yelled. Then he turned back to Fraser. "Their name's Bass. Donnie and Jackie Bass."

"Any idea where they might be?"

"Nae clue." The bartender chuckled, breath whistling oddly through his missing teeth. "Why the fuck would I talk to you useless bastards if I knew where they were?"

Bridie spoke up. "Why *are* you talking to us?"

"Useless you may be when it comes to settling things. But yer damn good at finding people. And I can't settle up for these," he pointed to his eyes, his missing teeth, "if I can't find the bastards."

"And you can 'settle up' with Donnie and Jackie when they're in prison?"

The bartender showed his seven teeth again. "Even easier than I can out here."

They didn't get anything more from him. Back on the street, even the gray sky of Edinburgh was a relief after the darkness of the pub. Bridie squinted and thought about the things people were willing to do to "settle up."

Wonder what I'll have to do to settle up for Grandma McLaren, she thought. *And I wonder if I'll enjoy it?*

She shuddered as she got into the car. Hamilton noticed.

"You all right, Bridie?"

"Got a little chill," she said, a blatant lie in the seventy-degree weather.

Hamilton shrugged and sat down. "Gayfield, Fraser, and don't spare the horses."

BACK AT THE station, Hamilton said, "Computer might be a bit more use now that we've got a name to give it."

"I'll stay here this time," Bridie said. She didn't have to wait long.

"Got it." Waving her over, Hamilton pointed to the screen. The expected mug shots were there. Seemed both brothers had done some time for a variety of crimes: assault, trafficking, robbery . . . From the look of their records, they wouldn't stay outside long. "Donald Morgan and John Arthur Bass. Donnie's the big one. Health freak. Doesn't drink or smoke. Shoots up, though. Don't know how that figures into his lifestyle. Works out all the time, either on the weights or on some poor bastard's face. He's not particular. Jackie is thin and quiet. Smokes a lot."

"Last-known address?"

"Aye, got it. But they won't be there."

"Course not," Bridie huffed. "But it's a place to start."

"I got something better. Fraser!" he yelled out the door. "Our troublesome brothers have a mother in your old stomping grounds."

Fraser's bulk suddenly filled the doorway. "The garden of Eden known as Glasgow?"

"Aye." Hamilton turned and winked at Bridie. "If you didnae like Edinburgh," he said in a broad imitation of Fraser's accent, "you're gang tae luv Glasgee."

"Oh, will I?"

"Oh, aye," snickered Hamilton.

Fraser's shoulders shook in a healthy chuckle as he echoed Hamilton. "Oh, aye."

THE DRIVE TO Glasgow was long and boring, but Bridie's spirits began lifting about halfway there.

"I'll be damned," she said. "An actual highway."

Fraser turned from the passenger seat and looked back at her. "Aye, and Glasgow's a *real* city, not some jumped-up country steading built around a ruined old fort."

Tapping the steering wheel idly, Hamilton just laughed. "Oh, how you Widgies do go on."

"Widgie?" Bridie said.

"Short for Glaswegian."

"If you say so."

When they reached Glasgow, Bridie smiled. *Pollution, grime, tall buildings, crowded streets*—"It's a real city, by God!"

Hamilton peeked in the rearview mirror aghast. "Jesus. She likes it." He shook his head. "No accounting for taste."

Fraser laughed. "Get off the motorway. Traffic'll be shite this time o' day."

THEY STOPPED AT Strathclyde Police HQ to get permission to go see Donnie and Jackie's mother. The Chief Inspector told them to pick up a couple of DIs at the Govan Station.

"Just two?" Fraser asked. "Govan changed so much we don't need the whole division?"

"Govan's gone through a bit of regeneration," the chief said. "Practically posh now."

"I'll believe that when I see it," Fraser said.

Winding down streets now that changed names as much as their Edinburgh counterparts—*must be a Scottish thing*—they crossed over the M8, passing Kelvingrove Park and then the Royal Hospital for Sick Children.

"Don't suppose they have a Royal Hospital for healthy children?" Bridie said.

"No," Hamilton said. "House of Commons runs that one."

They took a tunnel under the River Clyde and Fraser asked, "Why didnae ye just take the M8 right there?"

"You said the traffic was shite this time of day!"

"It's no that time of day anymore, is it?"

"But—"

Fraser cackled. "I'll drive when we get to Govan."

The Govan Police Office achieved what Bridie thought was a neat trick: it managed to somehow look both more modern and more run-down than the Gayfield Station back in Edinburgh. There was nothing modern-looking about the two Govan detectives they met. They were a matched set of old-school bulls, both short and thick with bushy eyebrows and piggy eyes set close together. Probably had matching blackjacks and throw-down pieces tucked into their undershorts. The two DIs squeezed into a Glasgow municipal police van and took off into midday traffic. Fraser took over the driving duties in the Edinburgh car and followed the "Widgie Filth"—Hamilton's term for the two cops—on a short jaunt back across the M8 and one stop down the A8 till they reached a herd of dilapidated tenements near a sports arena.

"This the spot?" Bridie asked.

"Aye—22 Woodville Park down by Ibrox Stadium," Fraser replied.

"Doesn't look too regenerated."

The sandstone buildings were covered with graffiti up to the height of where a man could reach, and one enterprising soul must have leaned out a window to scrawl "Fenian bastards suck a dick" one floor from the roof.

Fraser laughed. "Och, trust me, this is a fair bit better than it was. Used to be, you couldnae come into Govan with less than a hundred PCs at your back. You had whole families—sons, daughters, uncles, cousins, grannies—all living in the same building. And if you tried to take one of them out, you'd have to fight the whole rabid lot of them. Had to find them first, as well. Sons living with uncles three floors up, father still pulling money from Social for him; daughters rooming with granny till she drops a brood of her own. Fuckin' animals."

Hamilton put a hand on Fraser's shoulder. "Where'd you grow up again?"

"Govan," Fraser chuckled. "And I miss it, I do."

He piloted the car past number 22 a few hundred yards and pulled over. All three got out.

"All right, she's on the main floor. We'll go right up and knock," Hamilton said. "You two," he pointed to the Glasgow DIs, who were out of their car and approaching, "cover the back. Bridie, you're with us."

"Nae chance," said one of the inspectors, ever so slightly fatter than his partner and sporting a red-veined drinker's nose. "The lass stays in the car."

"Wait a damn minute, they told me I could—"

The inspector ignored her and spoke to Hamilton. "When—and if—we turn these geezers over to ye, she can ride on their laps all the way back to Edinburgh if ye like. But till then it's our city and our show. She's no a cop in this country, so she's no going through the door." He poked a finger at Fraser. "You two take the back, and *we'll* take the front." He finally turned to Bridie and spoke right to her chest. "And you, lassie, get yer skinny arse in the car." Then he and his partner marched toward the door.

"Widgie bastards," Fraser muttered.

"Don't worry, Bridie," Hamilton said, already rushing across the street. "We'll get them."

Bridie swore and sat down in the passenger seat. "Fucking cops," she said, turning to watch as Hamilton and Fraser backtracked up the street and ducked around the back of number 22.

The two Glaswegian inspectors waited till they were out of sight, then went through a glass door into the entryway of the five-story building. They pulled open a second interior door and were gone from sight.

Bridie shifted forward in her seat. Adjusted the mirror so she could keep an eye on the door. Scanned the street professionally. There were no pedestrians visible and very few cars passing by. Quiet neighborhood, except for the roar of the highway nearby. She rolled down her window and heard some children playing. *Can't imagine where they're playing.* The front yard of the tenement was not only small, but was mostly dirt and rock, with a few patches of hardscrabble grass. Then she got it. The tenements weren't as big as she had thought. The buildings each curved around in an "L" as if a section had been carved out of each to make a center courtyard. She couldn't see the back of 22, but she could see a similar design in a building on the corner facing away from her. The courtyard there had just a touch more grass than the front, with mottled old toys lying abandoned and the occasional piece of run-down playground equipment rusting in the wet air.

She could see one of the kids now, standing at a short slide, not climbing it or sliding down it, just hitting it slowly with a two-foot piece of rod iron to a rhythm only he understood.

She checked the rearview: both doors still closed, place looked quiet. Scanned the street again. Two pedestrians now, coming from in front, silhouetted against the gray sky. Males, though, just from the way they walked. And tall. As they came closer, Bridie noted that one was broad in the shoulders and thick in the legs, but with a waist thin and tapered. Like he worked out hard. Maybe took some steroids, too. And the other was of a height with him, but thin. Scarecrow thin. And smoking.

"Oh, shit," Bridie said aloud and fumbled in her purse for her cell phone. "Shit." She dialed Hamilton's cell number and hit send. The two men were close enough now that she could see their features better. Donnie and Jackie Bass. Had to be. "Pick up, Hamilton! Pick up!"

"Bridie? We're out the back watching—"

"They're here, Hamilton! Outside!" The boy at the slide spotted the Craic brothers and ran out to greet them.

"What, Bridie? Who's here?"

"Donnie and Jackie. The fucking Craic brothers!"

The boy was talking excitedly to the two men, pointing at their mother's building and then at the car Bridie was sitting in. Jackie took one look at the Edinburgh police vehicle and took off running the way he'd come. Donnie took only an extra second to grab the metal rod from the kid's hand and sprinted after his brother.

"Oh, shit," Bridie said into the phone, then tossed it on the driver's seat, kicked open the door, and started after them.

• • • Mercy • • •

Mercy did not like Oobel. But then, Mercy did not like anyone. Mercy was over two-hundred years old, dead, yet still living on, sustained by blood and fear and her own iron will. It was not an existence suited to lasting friendships. She didn't like other creatures, but they did have their uses.

"So," she breathed, her voice rasping and popping like an old phonograph, "You say you need my help. But what do I get in return?"

Oobel looked up at Mercy in her small mausoleum, but he couldn't really see her. She was cloaked in mist and shadow, and seemed to be in the shape of a young girl in a long concealing gown. Or a shriveled, shrunken corpse. Oobel wasn't sure. "Blood, Mercy, blood. A blood so sweet—"

Mercy gave a dry cough of a laugh. "Of the man-thing you wish me to defeat? I can have his blood any time I wish." She suddenly disappeared in a swirl of gray smoke, and he feared that his interview was over and she was gone. He also feared that she wasn't. Then he jumped as her voice whispered directly in his ear. "As I can have yours." Just as suddenly she was in front of him again, flouncing down on the floor of the mausoleum. Definitely a young girl this time. "But you know I prefer the blood of my own family."

Oobel shivered. "Not the blood of your own kind. Nor the blood of the man-thing." Oobel hopped from one foot to the other to his rhyming. "But the blood of a babe not man nor fey; a babe with the power of a king."

Mercy's head swung around and sightless black holes in a desiccated skull stared at Oobel. "A babe of power?"

"More than I have ever seen. More than there has ever been."

The skull turned into a young woman's pleasant fleshy face. "That might make a fine meal." Rotting yellow teeth appeared as the girl smiled. "And who knows? Maybe the babe is related to me. That would make it even better. The best."

Oobel shuddered. He didn't know how that would make it better. He didn't want to know. He just wanted to feast.

Mercy was going to make that happen.

· · · nine · · ·

Scott jolted awake on the couch. It was 8:16 P.M. He hadn't remembered dozing off. In fact, his memories of the past few days
were kind of fuzzy. Blinking twice, he stood and looked around.
His house was transformed. No longer the lonely home of an im-
poverished disabled veteran, it now was filled with diapers and
creams and baby toys—some bright-colored and plastic, some
rough-hewn from sticks or woven out of cattails.

Baby toys?

Stumbling to the wall, he flicked a light on to see better. The
sun was just setting and it got dark quick in the hills. He wanted
to look at the toys closer. He didn't remember buying any toys.
And he certainly didn't remember making any. And . . .

There's something I need to do tonight . . .

Scott leaned against the wall, trying to think. His mind was all
foggy as if . . .

As if I hadn't taken my pills!

Scott scrambled toward the kitchen. Dizziness made him stum-
ble. Missing his pills made him dizzy. He fumbled in a cupboard
and came out with several pill bottles. Wrenching them open, he

dumped most of their contents on the counter with a muted clatter. He grabbed a red one, a white one, and two yellows, popping them in his mouth in rapid succession.

Somewhere, a baby cried.

Shaking his head at the incongruous noise, Scott grabbed a carton of milk from the fridge and washed the pills down. Strange visions started playing in his head, a child being tortured, strange creatures capering about . . .

Nightmares.

Scott leaned against the counter and waited for the visions to pass.

Takes about twenty minutes for the pills to kick in, he thought.

The visions didn't pass. If anything they seemed to grow stronger. Scott pressed his eyes shut, but that made it worse. He took another swig of milk and wished he had something stronger.

No, that'd just screw up the pills. The baby's crying subsided into gasps for breath. And now he heard a voice, deep and booming.

"Why do you not help the child?"

Scott started at the sound and dropped the milk carton. Milk splashed to the floor and spread out slowly, seeping into cracks in the linoleum like blood into sand.

"Oh, it's bad this time," he said. "Voices." A shudder started at his shoulders and worked its way down his arms. The baby screamed again and Scott started at the sound. "Real bad."

"Help the child!"

Scott glanced hurriedly around. There was no one there.

I'm really losing it this time.

The sun dropped fully below the hillside, and it was night. Suddenly, Scott saw a new vision.

I will meet a girl outside. And she will lead me to a graveyard. We will enter a tomb hand in hand.

Though he didn't see himself coming out of the tomb, the vision was comforting nonetheless. Voices and baby toys and screaming children he wasn't used to. But disturbing visions starring him? He'd lived with those since the war. And he knew what to do with those.

Just follow along, you can't stop them anyway.

Stepping over the puddle of milk, he headed for the front door.

"*Tonokete naum?*" said the disembodied Voice.

And now the voices in my head are speaking in tongues, Scott mused. His hand was on the doorknob.

"Where are you going?" the Voice asked.

Scott paused. "Since you're a figment of my imagination, you should already know." Turning around, he spoke to the empty room. "But if you must know, I am going outside to meet someone." He grinned, but there was no humor in it. "And they're going to take me to the grave."

"No! Do not go!"

Scott shrugged. "It doesn't matter. You can't stop it. These things I see always come about."

"No," the Voice said again. "Do not give up hope."

As if I have any to give up, Scott thought and turned toward the door. But before he did, a cool breeze passed across his eyes, caressing them. It smelled of pine and musk and fresh running water. For a moment, Scott's foreboding left him.

"Turn," said the Voice. "Turn and see your *matwauog.* Your soldiers."

Scott looked over his shoulder, hand still on the doorknob. The once empty room was now filled with little people. Real little people. Their skin was dark and craggy, and they wore rough clothes of brown and dark green. All were armed. Scott saw a long knife slung from one's belt, another had twin hatchets strapped crosswise on his back so that the blades peeked over his shoulders like big lethal ears. A foot-tall man wearing a green beret got Scott's attention by stomping the end of a spear twice his size on the floorboards. Scott tore his gaze away from the little man's pleading eyes and onto a small woman, almost as stout as she was tall, with a brown apron draped over her clothes and a tiny whisk broom held before her like a quarterstaff. There were more women in brown scattered among the men like the first few leaves of autumn on a field of green.

In the middle of these little people stood a tall glowing figure. The more Scott looked at the figure, the more it changed. Now a black bear, now a wolf, now an elk with moss dripping from its horns. Even a giant turtle standing on its hind legs that stared at Scott with old sad eyes. Most often, the figure was a man, lean yet well muscled, wearing only a loincloth. A single golden feather poked out of his long dark braid.

The glowing figure spoke. "Do not leave."

For no reason he could name Scott thought a single word: *Mundoo*. Then shaking his head, he said, "You don't understand. You aren't real." The vision swirled in Scott's head, like all the ones from the war and after: pain and horror—but familiar and unavoidable. "But this is."

He turned the knob and went out the door.

HE WAS BARELY down the steps when he saw the girl from his vision. She stood in the driveway, pale and slight, dressed in an old black dress, like something a Victorian lady would wear to a funeral.

"Hello, Scott," she said, her voice a cloud of old cigarette smoke.

The scene matched his vision. Scott felt like he had when they'd had him on Risperdal at the VA hospital. *Ethereal.*

She spoke again, and it was as if the wind blew through her open mouth. "Come."

She turned and began walking away; Scott followed behind. Leaving the driveway immediately, she entered the woods, moving smoothly over the rough ground while Scott stumbled in the dark. He couldn't see her feet beneath the long, dark gown.

I wonder if she has any?

Scott didn't know how long they traveled. He couldn't tell the time for once. The moon came up and moved across the sky behind the thin canopy of trees. Stars appeared and disappeared: Orion's belt forever pointing to the Dog Star, Pelaides like a tiny Dipper, the North Star, cold and bright. He was amazingly calm during the journey, feeling as if he were going where he was meant to be. Where he could finally be at peace.

However, at the edge of his mind the nightmares remained—skinned children, howling spirits, capering demons. But he knew they would soon be gone. When they reached the tomb, the girl would lead him inside, and everything would be over—the journey, the pain, the fear.

They were as far into the forest as Scott had ever wandered—farther perhaps. He recognized nothing. Familiar pines had been replaced by leafless pale birch like arboreal bones. A mist had started lifting from the ground, matching the fog in Scott's mind. He followed the girl down a gentle slope covered in luminescent fungus, its pale glow blanching her face, turning her eyes into dark hollows when she glanced back at him.

"Come," she breathed, "we are almost there,"

At last they came to a tumbled-down stone wall where a rusty iron gate hung broken and open. The girl glided through without touching it, Scott close behind. They were in an ancient family graveyard, a half dozen stones scattered on the ground, covered in moss, their inscriptions too weathered to be read, the skulls and angel wings that adorned them nearly worn away. By the far wall was a small mausoleum.

Stone and bone, Scott thought. He'd have to duck to get inside.

The girl put out her hand and Scott took it.

"You're cold," he said.

The girl smiled and pulled him toward the low structure. "Then you must warm me."

As they approached, Scott could just barely read the name over the open door, the gray stone glowing in the moonlight.

Mercy Brown — 1772–1792

Shivering, Scott ducked low and followed the girl through the door. Once inside, he stepped away from the door and moonlight shone in on a stone sarcophagus that filled the center of the small chamber.

"You look tired, Scott," the girl said. "Lie down and rest. We have come far this evening."

"Where will I lie down?" he asked.

The girl ran her hand over the pitted stone of the sarcophagus. "Here, love."

Nodding, Scott turned and sat on the edge. Then he lay slowly back. The girl held his head and guided him till he was prone. Her hands were ice cold. So was the stone.

"I am cold now, too," he said.

The girl leaned in. "Then we must warm each other."

Her face was close to Scott's. He reached out to touch her smooth pale skin, but she easily pressed his arms back to the stone, then put her lips to his. They were cold, her mouth dry. She exhaled into his open mouth, her breath tasting of dust and decay.

The cold stone he lay on seemed to rise up and envelop him, and Scott's mind drifted away to the distant sound of a tortured child's screams.

• • • TEN • • •

Bridie was out the car door and after the Craic brothers as if fired from a gun.

And I wouldn't mind having a gun right about now, she thought.

No gun, but she blessed her choice of slacks and sneakers for today's excursion.

Would hate to have to slip off my heels and run barefoot.

The Craic brothers ducked off the main road immediately and into the entryway of another tenement. Bridie wasn't far behind, the door just slamming shut as she reached it. She could see them in the courtyard through the scratched glass as she wrenched the door open and shot straight through. They sprinted to the right as Bridie burst outside, yelling, "Stop! Police!"

But why would they? she thought. *It's not like I can shoot them.*

They turned the corner out of the courtyard and out of sight. Bridie came out behind them just in time to see them duck around the edge of another tenement building.

Christ, place is like an anthill. Two turns and I already don't know which way I'm heading.

The buildings were all identical, built for savings, not style. Even the graffiti had a sameness to it, the taggers maybe bored after countless years of poverty, or the slogans and symbols too alien to Bridie to have any impact. Or maybe they were just blurred and unreadable given she was in a full sprint.

Grabbing the wall to help her, Bridie careened around the corner and knew something was wrong. The Craic brothers should have been about twenty yards ahead of her and still running flat out. There was nothing but a thin shadowed street between two tenements, and some garbage piled against a wall, some of it bagged, most of it not. The brothers were nowhere in sight.

Ambush! her brain screamed and without slowing she threw herself to the ground, scraping her palms on the concrete. Hearing more than seeing something whoosh through the air where her head would have been, she rolled and saw big Donnie stepping from a hidden doorway and stalking after her with the rod iron.

Where's Jackie? Bridie thought frantically. *They'll come at me from both sides.*

Leaping to her feet, she twisted away from where she thought the next attack would come. Jackie was where she expected, a giant knife in his right hand. He slashed at her—*good technique but not expert,* some part of her brain noted—and caught her just below the right breast. But she was twisting and spinning and it didn't feel like it dug deep and she was leaping away from Jackie as he cut and slashed and stomped forward.

Leaping away from Jackie. And right toward his brother.

Donnie smiled as Bridie jumped practically into his lap, lifting his weapon for a skull-crushing blow.

Forward, forward, she thought. Closing with Donnie, she blocked his arm at the apex of his swing before he could bring his giant strength into play. Then she fired a closed fist into his Adam's apple. Something crunched and she hit him in the same spot again, jackhammer fast. Three times, four. Then she ducked past him and let him fall. He crumpled into his brother's arms.

She got her back to a wall and panted, watching as Jackie lowered Donnie to the ground, never taking his eyes off her. A quick glance left and right told her no weapon was at hand. And Jackie's positioning cut off any escape. Bridie breathed hard, her heart about to pound right out of her chest. That was all right, she found she didn't want to escape.

Donnie's eyes were wide and panicked, and he worked his mouth open and closed like a fish out of water.

Bridie bared her teeth. Some might call it a smile. "I crushed his windpipe."

"Aye," Jackie said. With his knife still in his hand, he brushed the hair out of Donnie's face. The big man gurgled and gasped for a second or two, then became quiet.

Jackie stood. He didn't speak again. He charged.

He came at her in a low crouch, knife in front. Bridie's eyes were locked on the knife. It was a hunting knife, the back edge serrated for tearing the hide of big animals. Her blood dripped off the tip. Jackie swept the knife across his body, drawing Bridie's attention with it and he put a hard left fist into her gut. The breath went out of her in a rush, and the knife came back at her eyes. Bridie leapt back desperately, bounced off the wall, and managed to get a foot of air between them.

Idiot! she thought. *He can hit you with more than just the knife!*

She didn't have time to think more because he was back on her again, knife slashing back and forth, drawing attention away from his left hand. He got in close enough to pop her in the side with another left hook, but she was ready and took it like they'd taught her in boxing, arms up and elbows tucked in, and it didn't do much damage. Then she jabbed at Jackie's face to move him off and danced away to her right. Away from the knife.

He won't feint with the knife, forever, she thought.

But he kept hitting her in the side and stomach, content to fake with the knife, wearing her down with body blows. She had to respect the knife. He wasn't going to kill her with punching—not immediately—but one good shot from the knife and she was a goner.

And it was working. The shots to her midsection were taking her breath; the bleeding wound on her chest was taking her blood.

I can't keep this up for long, she thought desperately. *And he's keeping his chin tucked down. I won't get him like his brother.*

She did land a jab on the nose, but it was more surprise and pain that backed him off, rather than actual injury. And when she tried to close to finish him, he almost got her with the knife.

I'm going to have to try something crazy. Get that knife out of his hands. Maybe shoot the leg and take this fight to the ground.

She started backing up, faking weariness and injury. It didn't strain her acting skills much. She was hoping for Jackie to get careless, leave her an opening. But he was not a careless man. He just used the openings to continue pressing his aggressive, yet cautious attack.

Suddenly Bridie heard Hamilton calling from nearby. "Bridie!"

"Over here!" she croaked, breathing too hard to make much noise.

The prospect of company seemed to spur Jackie to action, and he pressed the attack hard, swinging the knife in earnest now. He wanted to end it fast. Bridie gave ground, looking for the opening she knew would now come.

There!

Jackie telegraphed an attack. Bridie couldn't say how, it was all moving too fast. But instead of backing up, Bridie stepped forward and a little to the right as Jackie swung the knife in. Raising her left arm, she let the attack through, and it missed her side by a hair's breadth. Then she slammed her arm to her side, and trapped his forearm there, wrapping her arm around it like a tentacle. The beginning of pressure on the elbow, and the knife clattered to the ground.

Gonna break the fucker.

Most people try to pull back when a limb gets trapped, and that just helps the trapper sink their grip in and gives them time to set up their next move. But Jackie had enough brawling experience to know that most fights were won by moving forward, and he grabbed hold of Bridie with his free hand and pulled her in. She snaked her right arm around his other forearm.

Okay, I'll break both your arms.

Jackie headbutted her.

She saw it coming. It was the only thing he could do, after all. She ducked her head so he couldn't get her nose, but the impact was still solid on the top of her head. White streaks flashed across her vision and her grip loosened. It must have stunned Jackie as well, because he just pushed her away and staggered backward three steps.

"Bridie!" Hamilton called, closer now.

Jackie looked at her, looked at the knife on the ground behind her. And ran.

Bridie watched him go, gasping for breath. "Over here!" She managed a shout this time, then sat down with her back to the wall.

Hamilton and Fraser came sprinting around the corner moments later. Fraser ran to Donnie and kicked the rod iron away from his hand. Then he knelt and took his pulse. Hamilton ran to Bridie.

"You okay, Bridie?"

Bridie's eyes flashed with anger and she thought, *Do I look okay, you idiot?* But for once she didn't say it.

"It looks worse than it is," she said. Glancing down at herself, she saw that her silk shirt was soaked in blood.

Then again, maybe it's worse than it looks.

She leaned her head back against the wall . . .

"Bridie?"

And passed out.

• • • MERCY • • •

Mercy stood over the prostate man, exhausted and annoyed. She didn't understand. It had taken most of the night just to get him out of his house and here to her home. She hadn't the time to properly enjoy him, nor even the time to return and tell Oobel to begin his attack. She would have to sleep, and soon, before the sun came up.

Scooping the man up easily, she sniffed at his mouth, his neck. *He does not seem different than any other.* The man snuffled in his sleep and cried out. *But he should be still!*

Mercy passed a withered claw over his eyes and he settled.

I cannot continue this for long. She needed to rest and rejuvenate. It had been a long night.

Laying the man on the ground, she blew a cold breath out the door of the tomb. "Come," she sighed. Then pulling the stone lid of the sarcophagus aside, she slid inside. Watching the shadows begin to slip away, she waited for them to arrive.

If I am forced to wait much longer, she thought angrily, *the punishments I devise will not be pleasant.*

But within minutes she sensed their approach. And soon after, two teenagers, a boy and a girl, entered the tomb, both dressed in baggy black clothing and thick makeup. They didn't speak or look at the prostate man, but stared blankly at Mercy until she spoke.

"Bind him. He resists me, I do not know how. I cannot reach some part of his mind. Some madness protects him." She shook her head. "Bind him and guard him till I wake. I will deal with him then."

Then with a scraping and grinding sound, she slid the lid back over herself, lay back in darkness, and slept.

· · · Eleven · · ·

Seven-fifteen A.M. *You can't tell from in here,* PFC Scott Stewart thought, *but the sun is shining.*

Here was a low-ceilinged room, with stone walls and ceiling, devoid of furnishings except for a plain table—stone—directly in front of him. His hands were tied and fastened to the wall behind him, but his feet were free and he was able to rise. Two Iraqi guards, plainclothed and smoking, glanced in his direction as he struggled to his feet.

Searching his mind, Scott couldn't recall how he'd gotten here. And he didn't know why he hadn't seen this coming. *Don't even remember being on patrol.* In fact, everything was a little hazy and unreal. He remembered a house in the woods, a baby . . .

Scott shook his head. *Must be drugged. Have to concentrate on getting out of here.*

He tried to assess the situation critically, just like he'd been taught in survival training. Tried to push the prospect of torture to the back of his mind. He eyed the room—*one exit, open*—his captors—*just the two it seems*—and tested his bonds—*Not a real professional job of knot tying, could maybe wrench free.*

But first he needed to get off this wall. And get those guards closer.

"Do you have a smoke?" Scott asked the two Iraqi. He noticed that one of them was a woman. No more than a girl really. *Odd. Coulda sworn she had a mustache a second ago.* "*Sigara?*"

They looked at him blankly. Scott used head bobs and eyebrows to try to point to their thin cigarettes. Seeming to understand finally, they glanced at each other, then strangely they both stared at the table for a moment as if it would tell them what to do. When the table said nothing, the man approached and pulled out a pack of smokes.

Seven-eighteen, Scott sensed. He didn't sense anything else. No visions of this Iraqi couple beating him or torturing him or shooting him. *Guess I'm good to go,* he thought.

The guard came close, holding out a cigarette. *He's young, too.*

"*Shoo kran,*" Scott said and took it in his mouth, then leaned in for a light. When the guard flicked his lighter, Scott twitched his head back and rammed his forehead into the man's face. Blood exploded from the Iraqi's nose. Scott could taste it, salt and copper, warm on his lips. He threw himself forward, straining at his bonds as the bloody Iraqi staggered backward.

He broke free of the wall—but not of the rope holding his wrists together. Cursing whatever rusty nail they'd driven into the stone wall—*something stronger and maybe the ropes would have given first!*—Scott charged forward, hands still behind his back. He drove his shoulder into the bleeding guard, and knocked him to the ground, then turned toward the door. The girl was there, holding a wickedly curved knife. She came at him amateurishly and Scott kicked her square in the chest, then shot for the door as she stumbled. But his feet tangled in hers and they both went down.

He couldn't break his fall with anything but his face.

Luckily the floor was dirt, not stone. Still, he hit hard and was stunned for a second—long enough for one of the guards to leap onto his back. Then pain hit him in the scapula, the ribs, the low back, and he knew he was being stabbed.

Roaring in agony, Scott tried to roll out from under his attacker. He got hit three more times before he managed to stick an elbow into someplace soft and get some room to move. Rolling once, he levered himself into a sitting position, then with another inhuman scream, tried to wrench his wrists apart. The two guards were up now and coming at him. The tendons in Soctt's neck bulged and pain shot up and down his arms. He heard a sharp crack and suddenly his left wrist went numb.

But it slipped out of the knot.

Able to use his right arm again, Scott was on his feet in a split second. One of the guards was on him. He couldn't tell which one; he had eyes only for the knife. It came at his stomach, and he inhaled and turned, just like he'd been trained, grabbing the knife hand and pulling it counterintuitively close to his body. His injured left hand couldn't hold it there for long, but it gave him enough time to punch the guard three times in his already broken nose.

Guess it was the boy.

The boy went down and the girl was there. Scott slapped away her slash at his face, grunting with the pain of it through his left hand, then grabbed her by the throat with his other hand. He drove her back against the wall till her head hit with the dull thud of a melon hitting pavement and she went slack. Her knife dropped to the ground. Scott glanced back to see if her compatriot was still down. He was and Scott squeezed hard on the girl's throat, deciding to cut down on the possibility of pursuit.

But her features shifted strangely, and where there was once an Iraqi girl, there was now an obviously American teenager, with too much makeup on and a black T-shirt with some band's logo on it. Scott dropped her and leapt away. She crumpled to the ground.

The hell?

Glancing at the boy writhing on the ground, he saw that he was no longer Iraqi either. And the room was now a tomb. Scott had no idea what was going on, but he knew he wanted no part of it. He staggered out the door, bleeding from a half-dozen places.

The bright desert sun hit him, and he shaded his eyes only to see pine trees looming over him. Blinking, he caught a metallic glint in the distance and instinctively made for cover. Gunfire crackled and he almost dove into the sand before realizing it was the snap of dry twigs on the forest floor that made the noise. He blinked again, and he was on the streets of Fallujah and army buddies marched beside him, grim-faced and hard for ones so young. *Blink* and they became gravestones and Scott knew they were long dead.

Meaning I'm back from Iraq?

"I'm deep in it," he said this time, meaning the madness. But he looked at his left wrist, already blackening and probably broken, and he felt his back turning cold where he'd been knifed and saw the blood pooling in his boots, and he knew some part of it was real, anyway.

I wonder if I just killed two innocent people? But they came at me with knives, didn't they? They tied me up!

But he couldn't be sure, and he doubled his pace, bursting through the iron gate and heading toward home. Or base. He still wavered between desert and forest.

I don't think I killed them, he thought hopefully. *Just hurt 'em real bad.*

"Whatever I did," he said, and looked around. Checkpoint. People crowded the road, refugees and families and beggars and wounded, all trying to escape; some with Semtex strapped to their chests so they could drag a few infidels to meet Allah with them. "And wherever I am, I gotta call Bridie."

Forest now, and Scott recognized some landmarks: a fragment of stone wall, a giant boulder shaped like a bearded head, an ancient fallen oak with saplings sprouting from its exposed roots. He was only a half-mile from home.

I don't think I'll make it.

He was light-headed from blood loss and felt ready to pass out at any moment.

"Come on, Scott," he said, "Just like in the war. Just 'cause you're dying, don't mean you can stop fighting."

As soon as he spoke, he was back in Iraq.

"Stewart!" his sergeant yelled. "You hit?"

"Yes, sir!"

Scott was running between buildings, head low, waiting for the bullet that would finish him.

Courtesy of Mikhail Kalashnikov.

"Can you still fire?"

"If I had a weapon."

Scott tripped over a rock and sprawled to the ground. He thought he heard the sergeant call his name again, but realized it was just a crow calling to its mate. There were two in the tree overhead, black eyes staring at him.

Carrion eaters.

"I'm not dead yet." He pushed himself to his feet. The ground beneath him was alarmingly bloody. "Close, though," he muttered.

Now, new horror hit him, as scenes of a child being tortured and eaten sprang unbidden into his head. He staggered.

"Not again."

Again?

Stumbling like a sailor on a three-day drunk, he bounced off a tree, a wall, a burned-out tank. His surroundings whirled and faded and he saw himself back in Mercy's tomb. Saw the child flayed and dying. Saw Bridie bleeding in the arms of a handsome policeman. Saw his brother, only bigger and broader than he remembered him, sitting on a throne of antler bone and staring at him with eyes as black and emotionless as the crows' had been.

Scott was practically blind with the visions and landscape shifts, but he still put one foot in front of the other, making for home every time he could see the forest. And the whole time he was thinking, *What did I mean, "Not again?"*

He ducked as an RPG whizzed overhead, and braced himself for an explosion that never came. Edged left to shadow a stone wall he knew ran toward his property, then back right when a soldier yelled, "Fire in the hole!" He found the wall again and managed to stay with it long enough to lurch out onto the road by his house. He could see his driveway a hundred yards ahead of him. Two steps, three, and he thought he could hear his blood spattering on the pavement. A dozen more, and men were yelling in badly accented Arabic at a car coming up the dirt road he was running down. No, a paved road. There was a car in each, bearing down on him. He didn't know what was real anymore, so he just kept going forward, quick-time march, *got to get home.*

Both cars began honking, and Scott howled an answer as he pressed forward. He could see inside them now. See their shocked and terrified faces. The sergeant yelled, "Fire on that vehicle, Private!" but Scott didn't, maybe because the vehicles in question were filled with women and children, or maybe just because he wasn't holding a gun. One car swerved and the other stayed straight and Scott threw himself to one side before either of them reached him.

Tumbling painfully, he felt the rocks and gravel searching and finding all the puncture wounds in his back, but at last he fetched up in his driveway. He lay on his side and stared at his front door so tantalizingly close. But his legs were numb and lifeless. He couldn't stand. He tried to drag himself forward with his hands, but his left was too mangled to grasp anything. Scrabbling at the gravel with his right proved useless. Scott let his head drop.

Survived the war to die ten feet from my front door.

He thought maybe he should compose a death poem, like the old Samurai used to, but he couldn't remember how many syllables a haiku was supposed to have.

Maybe Douglas will write something for me, he thought. *He was always better at that kind of stuff.* Chuckling, he coughed blood onto the ground. *Useless in a fight though.*

Scott's eyes began to close, but just before he lost consciousness, he saw his front door open. A horde of strangely dressed little people poured out, scanning left and right warily as they ran to him. A dozen of the stouter ones lifted him up and carried him toward his house, where a tall dark man with a long braid and a strange glow about him waited in the doorway.

Then Scott closed his eyes. And died.

Twelve

Bridie?"

"Hrmmm?"

"Stay with me, Bridie."

Bridie could hear the steady hum of a car engine and felt the movement of the road beneath her. "I'm here. Just mighty tired."

"You're not tired," Hamilton said. "You're in shock."

"That, too." She opened her eyes. She was in the backseat of the police car, her head cradled in Hamilton's lap. "Why's your shirt off?"

He smiled, inclining his head toward her chest. "Bandage." He had his shirt wadded up and pressed hard right below her right breast.

Bridie raised an eyebrow. "Enjoying yourself?"

"I believe he is, lass," Fraser said from the driver's seat. "We're going to take ye to hospital."

"Nah. I'm fine. Let's get after Jackie." Bridie sat up. Her head swam and she fell back into Hamilton's lap. "Let's get after him in a minute or two."

"Relax," Hamilton said. "We'll get him. Guys like him don't stay hidden for long."

"They'll run a few pints through ye at hospital," Fraser said, "and you'll be up and about nae problem in the morning."

Bridie sighed. "I almost had him."

Hamilton smiled down at her, something like pride in his eyes. "You got the big one all right, though. He'll no see another sunrise."

There's one for you, Grandma.

Bridie sighed. "Aye. All right." She lay back and watched the tops of gray Glasgow buildings whiz by.

Fraser pushed it hard, and the fat Glasgow detectives cleared the way; they were at Southern General Hospital in very little time. The ER—*or whatever they call it here,* Bridie thought—was crowded, but she was whisked through without a wait. In no time at all she was in an examination room, a female doctor kneeling in front of her, her blonde ponytail bobbing up and down as she stitched Bridie up.

She looks too young to be a doctor.

"I thought British health care was supposed to be terrible," Bridie said, "but you seem real good at this."

The doctor glanced up, mouth pinched and eyes narrow, but her face softened when Bridie winked at her. "Aye, but I'm no British."

"You're not?"

"No, I bloody well am not! I'm Scottish." The doctor got back to her stitching. Her ponytail bobbed in time.

Like a flesh seamstress, Bridie thought.

"But . . ." Bridie tried to read the doctor's name tag. "Doctor Ryan, aren't these the British Isles? And do you have a first name I can call you? It seems too formal calling you 'Dr. Ryan.' What with my shirt off and your hands on my breast."

Doctor Ryan looked up again. "Kate." She moved her left hand down an inch or two. Off Bridie's breast. "There's no bloody Britain." *Stich, bob.* "Scotland and England united their kingdoms. That's why there's a United Kingdom." *Stitch, bob.* "But that wasnae enough for England, so they invented Britain to justify their bloody land grab." She pulled the last stitch tight and snipped the suture off. Standing, she looked critically at her handiwork. "We sat a Scot on the English throne and still they think they own the damn place."

"But you sold them your Parliament, didn't you, Kate?"

Little crow's feet appeared around Kate's eyes, and Bridie realized she was closer to her own age than she'd first thought. "Och. You're having me on! Where'd you learn about Scottish history?"

"My Grandma was Scottish. And loved to talk about it."

"And a proud one it seems." Kate knelt again and rubbed a thin layer of ointment on the wound.

Bridie nodded. "Till the day she died."

"I'm sorry for your loss," Kate said, real sympathy in her voice. Gauze went on next, fastened with surgical tape.

"Me, too." Bridie thought of the crime scene photos and shuddered. The movement made her wound sting. "Ouch."

"Dinnae do that again." Kate stood and grabbed a shirt that was hanging on the door. "Now get dressed, love. We'll get you out of here quick-like. Back to that handsome policeman of yours."

Bridie put an arm out and Kate slid one sleeve on. "And wouldn't he like it if he *was* mine."

"Now, be kind to the poor lad. He went clothes shopping for ye. Got ye this shirt." She helped Bridie into the other sleeve. "Don't stretch. You'll ruin my good work."

"Fraser said you'd keep me overnight. Run a few pints through me."

"Och, men are such babies. You didnae lose enough blood to need any replacing it. And when the care's free, we don't like to keep ye around for more time than we have to."

Bridie pouted her lips. "Aw. I was looking forward to spending more time with you, Kate."

Bridie thought the doctor blushed a little. But she said, "Your loss, love."

"I'm sure it is."

Kate practically pushed her out the door. "Now off with ye! I have other patients to see to."

HAMILTON WAS DEEP in conversation with Fraser when Bridie entered the waiting area but sprang to his feet when he saw her. "What are you doing up?"

Some young tough in a leather jacket and bloody T-shirt stared daggers at Hamilton, either jealous of his good looks or suspecting he was a cop. Looked away quick enough when Fraser stood up and up and up, though.

"Dr. Kate says I'm okay to check out." Bridie grinned. "Let's go get Jackie."

Frowning, Hamilton said, " 'Fraid I have some bad news on that end, Bridie. Widgies say we have to leave town."

"What?"

Fraser took a sip of something hot and black from a Styrofoam cup. From the smell, Bridie hesitated to call it coffee. "Guess they don't like you killing their citizens."

"Touchy bastards." Bridie started to shrug but stopped the motion when her stitches pinched. "That's all right."

The two men stared at her silently for a moment. Hamilton was the first to speak.

"Really? It's all right?"

"Yeah." Bridie motioned for the cup from Fraser and he handed it to her as she sat down beside him. "It's like you said, guys like him don't stay hidden for long." She took a sip. Still wasn't sure whether it was coffee or not. "Besides, we can work it from the other end. I'll squeeze Sandra again for . . ." Hamilton and Fraser were looking at each other sheepishly. "What?"

Fraser's mouth pursed like he'd just sucked on a lemon. "Just got a call from . . ."

"They lost Sandra," Bridie interrupted.

Fraser nodded, managing to look embarrassed and angry at the same time.

"Now, Bridie . . ." Hamilton began.

"You guys are unbelievable! Are there any goddamn *cops* in this country?" She threw her drink hard into a wastebasket and brown liquid spattered the wall. Pain spiked across her chest where the stitches stretched but it just fueled her fire. "You can't tail a ninety-pound girl with a heroin problem? What happens if you have to arrest some actual criminals?" A baby started wailing across the room, and the mother took time from comforting it to glare at Bridie. She didn't notice. "Good thing I fought the Craic brothers myself. You two show up to help, they might have actually killed me."

The admissions nurse called to Bridie from across her desk. "Miss! I really can't have you yelling like that."

"Can it, Colleen," Bridie snapped. "I'm leaving." She stomped to the door. Turned back to Hamilton and Fraser. "You guys coming?" Then she walked out without seeing if they followed.

THE HOUR-LONG RIDE back to Edinburgh was deathly quiet. Bridie sat in the backseat lost in angry thought, wound starting to burn as the Novocain wore off, and neither Hamilton nor Fraser tried to snap her out of it. By the time they got off the motorway the silence was almost a physical presence, a fourth passenger that had stolen their voices. When Hamilton's phone rang, no one seemed to know what the sound was for a moment. When he finally answered, his voice was raspy and rough.

"Hello? Yes. No. But, sir . . . Aye, all right." He hung up. "Well, Bridie, you're off the hook."

"What?"

"For killing Donnie Bass."

"Didn't know I was on the hook."

"Well, you were. But not for too long. No one wants to raise a fuss over a bag of shite like Donnie." Hamilton spoke to Fraser. "Turn it around. Back to Glasgow."

Fraser raised an eyebrow. "What's left in Glasgow for us?"

"The airport," Hamilton said. "And not for us. For her."

"What?" Bridie said again.

As they pulled into the big roundabout by Gayfield, Hamilton turned in his seat and looked at Bridie. "It's over, Bridie. You're going home. The chief constable wants you gone. We can't have some crazy Yank girl running around killing Scots, no matter how much they deserve it."

They circled past the Leith Road exit, past the Gayfield exit.

"Wait . . ." Bridie began, but the look on Hamilton's face stopped her. He had decided his course of action—or rather his superiors had—and nothing she could say would convince him otherwise. "I'd rather take the train back. Aren't we right near the station?"

Fraser, about to exit back the way they'd come, passed it by, as well.

"Don't be ridiculous," Hamilton said. "We'll take you."

Frowning, Bridie went on. "I've been sitting in this car or lying in a hospital bed all night and day. I'd just as soon travel in something I could stand up in for a while. I'd like to get my toothbrush, hairbrush, pack my bag, too."

"It's been packed for you and shipped on ahead." Hamilton looked sheepish. "Actually, we're supposed to sit on you till you get on the plane. Keep you out of trouble."

Bridie sighed, thinking that at least the Scotch police were efficient about something. "Fine. But stop at the station anyway. I have to pee like crazy." Taking her purse in her lap, she hooked the strap over her shoulder.

"Dinnae mind me," Fraser grumbled, "I'll just circle this wee roundabout all damn day."

"Aye, all right, hit the train station," Hamilton said. "Then off to the airport, nae bother?"

"Nae bother at all," Bridie said. "Frankly, I'm sick of this country."

"About time," Fraser said and put on the lights. Winking at Bridie in the rearview he said, "It's an emergency, right?"

She nodded fast. "Gotta pee! Gotta pee!"

They roared out of the roundabout and banked onto Princes Street. A sharp left onto Waverly Bridge, then another down the hill and into the station itself. Hamilton leapt out and opened the door for Bridie.

Chanting, "Gotta pee, gotta pee," she walked fast into the station proper and was swallowed up by the hordes of travelers.

Hamilton sat back down in the car with a huff.

"Where's she going?" Fraser asked.

Hamilton peered at him. "To the bathroom. Haven't you been paying att—" He stopped speaking and looked at the spot where Bridie had disappeared into the crowd. Then twenty feet to the right where the bathrooms were. "Oh, shit."

Pouring out of the car, the two cops sprinted into the station. They didn't take two steps past where they'd seen Bridie last before they knew a search was useless. They tried anyway—they were professionals. But the station was loud and crowded and had more exits than two men could cover. And Bridie was a professional, too.

She was gone.

• • • MUNDOO • • •

Mother Earth, I offer this tobacco
Grandmother Moon, I offer this tobacco
Grandfather Sun, I offer this tobacco
Taubot neanawayean
I thank you

"Will he recover?"
Mundoo looked down at the speaker, one of the foreign *Manitou*, hobs they called themselves. "It is not for me to say."

I offer this tobacco to the four directions
To the East
To the South
To the West
To the North

The hob pushed his acorn cap way back and looked up at Mundoo. "Please tell no tales to Wee Jake. You have been chanting your native magicks over him for half the day. If it is not for you to say, then whom do I ask?"

I call on all my relations:
the winged nation
creeping and crawling nation
the four-legged nation
the green and growing nation
and all things living in the water

Mundoo frowned down at the little creature. He was unaccustomed to being addressed so impudently. The immigrant spirits usually kept their distance, but the arrival of the babe had upset the balance somehow. Made them both more brave and more frightened. A poor combination, and one certain to cause calamity.

And all the honored clans:
The Deer
The Bear
The Wolf
The Turtle

"I have healed his body," Mundoo said after a pause. "But I cannot touch his mind. It has gone somewhere even I cannot follow. He must return himself."

His feet, my feet, restore
His limbs, my limbs, restore
His body, my body, restore

Mundoo looked down at the prostate man, pale, so pale, even after his healing.

"But first he must want to return."

Taubot neanawayean
I thank you

• • • • Thirteen • • • •

Scott was gut shot. Worst thing that can happen to you. All you can do is die. If you're lucky, you have a sip of water left in your canteen and a bullet left in your gun. Quench your thirst, then blow your brains through the back of your skull. Avoid the hours of agony before the inevitable end.

Scott had neither.

"All I have," he groaned, "is sand."

Miles of it. He was on top of a dune, staring out at trackless desert, wind-blown ridges making it seem he was afloat in the middle of a great brown sea.

"Water, water everywhere . . ." Racked by bloody coughs, he stopped speaking. His world narrowed to the ragged hole in his stomach, the blood in his throat, the ravaging thirst he knew was a product of the mortal injury he'd received. When he came to, he was stretched out on the dune still, but twice as weak as before. He had no gear, no rifle, no sidearm, no canteen. Didn't even have his boots.

One ruined set of desert camos and a CD-sized exit wound in my belly, Scott thought.

He tried to convince himself to get up, or at least crawl somewhere to try to get help, but he knew it was hopeless. He was too far gone. If he were lying on a hospital table with the world's best trauma surgeon prepped and ready to go he'd still be a dead man. And he hadn't even seen a mirage of a hospital in the vast desert that surrounded him.

I wonder how I got here? Not that it matters.

Scott looked up at the cloudless sky and got ready for death.

Again.

A new wave of pain hit him, and stopped him from wondering why he would think *again*. For no reason he could imagine, an old Navajo prayer was running through his head:

May I walk with beauty before me
May I walk with beauty behind me
May I walk with beauty above me
May I walk with beauty below me
May I walk with beauty all around me

Turning his head, Scott coughed blood onto the ground. "Prayers aren't going to help," he said to the crimson sand.

"Depends on who's doing the praying," answered the sky.

Scott looked up to see a tall young man standing over him. He was maybe fifteen or sixteen, with shoulder-length black hair and startling blue eyes. He was dressed in faded jeans and a navy blue, long-sleeved T-shirt. As he knelt down next to Scott, he could see that his hands were covered in complex Celtic patterns drawn in henna ink.

"What do you mean?" Scott asked. "And who are you? And what are you doing out here?"

The young man laughed. "I mean nothing, same as I am. And I am out here to help you."

"I don't underst—" Scott began, but pain cramped his abdomen and he went fetal with it.

The young man knelt beside him, looking concerned. "Father," he said. "Let us leave this place."

Blinking up at him, Scott said, "I'm dying."

"No, you're not." The young man put his right hand over Scott's wound. "Not anymore."

Amazingly, the pain disappeared. Scott sat up. Looked down at his stomach. The wound was closed. Gone. Not even a scar. Even his shirt was healed, no longer ripped and blood-spattered.

"What's happening?" Scott said.

The young man stood and held out his hand. Helped Scott to his feet. "Nothing. None of this is real."

Scott looked out at the desert. Felt the sun hot on his face. Smelled the dry air. "Feels real enough."

"Walk with me."

The young man turned and started walking. Scott hurried to catch up. He hadn't taken more than two steps when the ground beneath him changed and his combat boots were crunching through brown pine needles and red and golden fall leaves.

"What the . . . ?"

"It's not real," the young man repeated.

"But I recognize this place." *It's a tiny house, but big enough for just you, Scotty-dog. Far enough from Amherst that you won't run into anyone, but close enough that you can drive in quick for food or smokes when you need to.* Scott frowned. *Bridie's voice saying that to him. When?* Peering through the forest before him, Scott saw a thin drive leading up to a small white house. Only room enough in the front for two windows, one door.

The young man stopped. "Of course you recognize it. It's your home."

"My home?"

The young man began walking up the drive and Scott followed. As they neared the house, Scott saw something strange: a tiny man, no more than a foot tall, standing guard at the front door. He wore a forest green tunic and leggings to match. Scanning the treeline back and forth with eyes squinted, he held a spear as thin as a matchstick in his right hand as if ready to skewer the first thing he spotted coming out of the forest. His gaze passed right over Scott and the young man.

Scott took two strides up the front steps and stopped. Waved a hand in front of the tiny man's face who never stopped scanning the distance.

"Okay," Scott said to his companion. "What the hell? What is that?" He pointed to the little man. "And why can't he see us? And who are you? And . . . and all those other questions I asked before!"

The young man smiled and stepped up beside Scott. "That is a hob. One of my mother's people. And he is here to help you." He pointed to the closed door. "Let's go inside."

Scott reached for the door handle, but his hand passed right through it. Before he could react, the young man pushed him in the back, and he stumbled forward, passing through the door with just a brief cold sensation as if he'd walked through a paper-thin waterfall and come out dry on the other side.

"I'm dreaming." It was a relief. Here he'd thought he'd finally gone *completely* bat-shit crazy, and it turned out he was just dreaming.

"In a sense," the young man said. "But not all of this will fade when you awaken." He swung his arms out and Scott surveyed the scene. An uncluttered room with a worn sofa and a nicked-up coffee table. More hobs sat on both items, or cross-legged on the floor. There were some hob women as well, thicker-set than their male counterparts, and dressed mostly in brown.

"Not hob women," said the young man, as if reading Scott's mind. "Brownies, actually."

"More of your mother's people?" Scott asked. "Also here to help?"

The young man nodded. "Come."

Scott followed as the young man wove through the room and its occupants. Literally *through*. Even though he knew he was dreaming, Scott tiptoed around the creatures, and eschewed the direct route the young man had taken through the couch. They stopped at an open door at the rear of the house and looked inside.

My bedroom, Scott thought. Isolated memories came back to him then: battles in the desert; long nights strapped to a hospital bed even though he was unwounded; his sister, Bridie, leaning over him, a concerned look on her normally fierce features; Bridie arguing with doctors, nurses, officers—anyone who dared to talk to her; Bridie taking him home, taking him here.

Scott saw a body on the bed—*my bed*—and knew it was his own.

"Am I dying?" he asked.

The young man shook his head. "No. Not anymore."

There was someone else in the room with him, an unusually big man, yet well proportioned, wearing a leather loincloth. He was chanting in a language Scott didn't recognize.

Though by the looks of the chanter, he thought, *I'd guess he's Native American.*

"Is that another of your mother's people?"

"No. My mother's people are not gods."

Scott blinked and looked again at the tall man. "He's a god? He here to help, too?"

The young man frowned. "More or less. But like all gods, he has his own agenda. And he'll demand sacrifice."

Before Scott could answer, the tall native turned around and looked right at Scott. "There you are," he said. He didn't reach out, but Scott could feel hands on his shoulders pulling him toward the bed with an irresistible strength.

"It's all right, Father," the young man said. "It is time for you to return."

A thousand questions rushed to the front of Scott's mind, but he only had time for one:

"Why do you call me Father?"

Then he was lifted over the bed and saw his own form beneath him, face drawn and haggard with pain just recently faded. Then he fell into darkness.

SIX FIFTY-THREE P.M. Even in his sleep, Scott knew what time it was. *Though I guess I'm not sleeping anymore,* he thought. *And I know who I am, too.* It had been a while since he'd remembered that. But he found that all the strange events of the past few days were in his memory now: finding Fletcher on his front step, seeing the bearded man, the Voice of Mundoo speaking to him, his dreamlike trip into the woods with the girl and the fight that followed.

I was hurt in that fight, wasn't I? I must be doped to the gills to not be feeling anything.

He also remembered seeing a whole bunch of little people— not little like midgets or dwarves, but one-to-two-feet-tall little—standing in his living room with a big Indian guy.

Brownies and hobs, he thought, thinking of the youth in his dream. *And Mundoo is the big Indian . . . god?* Scott shook his head without opening his eyes. *Maybe it really was all a dream.*

Reluctantly, he opened his eyes, expecting to see a VA hospital room. Instead, he was in his own bed. Mundoo stood over him. Fletcher lay on his chest, whuffling contentedly in his sleep. Scott heard murmurings from off to his right. "Does he yet live?"—"Is he wounded sore?"—"They will come tonight."—"What will we do?"

Turning his head, Scott saw the doorway to his bedroom crowded with brownies and hobs, just like he'd seen in what he now had to conclude *hadn't* been a dream. They seemed reluctant to enter.

Unless I'm still dreaming, he thought, but shook it off. *Thinking like that'll just drive me nuts. Well, more nuts.*

"I live," he croaked.

With that the dam at the front door burst and the little people charged in, a tide of tiny limbs clambering on and over him, sharp elbows and knobby knees poking him in painful spots.

"Ow," he protested. "Watch it!" It made no difference; they would not be denied. A brownie with a giant nose tousled his hair as another with ears to match stretched his left eyelid high to examine his pupil. Two hobs in matching tunics poked at his abdomen. Something was tickling his feet under the covers. Someone stuck a finger in his ear. And everyone was asking questions of him all at the same time.

"Shall we hold the front?"—"Shall we guard the rear?"—"Have you always been a warrior?"—"Does this hurt?"—"How about this?"—"What's your favorite color?"—"What's your name?"—"Do you fight for pay or pride?"—"Do you like apples?"

"Hold on!" Scott roared, and pulled the finger out of his ear. It turned out to be an entire arm, and the hob at the end of it smiled sheepishly as Scott put him down on the bedspread. "One at a time. You in front with the acorn cap. What's your name?"

The hob in question climbed up onto Scott's chest and proclaimed, "Wee Jake o' the Knockside Hills, I am." He was a comical-looking creature, with knock-knees and knobby arms that he held akimbo to avoid his protruding belly. But he also had a look of martial determination on his face that kept Scott from smiling at him. "And I was asking what are we to do when Mercy and Oobel come this eventide? For they are sure to come for the babe."

"Who are Mercy and Oobel?" Scott asked. "And why would they come for Fletcher?"

"Oobel is him that's been setting all the traps you freed us from," Wee Jake said. "And Mercy is her that called you from the house. Oobel comes to eat the child."

"*Eat* him?" The little hob had said it so matter-of-factly that Scott was certain he'd misheard him. But then he remembered his visions. Something reaching into the child . . . "Eat him? Like, for dinner?"

"Yes." Wee Jake scratched his chin. "I do not know why Mercy comes for the child. Perhaps she only comes for you."

"Why would she come for me?"

"I know not. But I ask again, what are we to do?"

"Well, we'll . . ." Scott began, but then stopped. Looked around at all the tiny concerned faces staring up at him. *What will we do? I don't know. Mercy will come, and I'll go with her again, and then Oobel will come and feast on the flesh of all who oppose him.* He shook himself. *No good captain would tell his troops something like that before battle.* He tried to think of something his commanders would have said, but remembered that most of the good ones didn't say much. *"Remember your training and don't get dead." That's no help, these little guys don't have any training.*

He finally said the only thing that made any sense when surrender was unacceptable and negotiation wasn't an option: "We'll fight!"

There was a faint roar of approval from the small crowd on his bed.

Wee Jake waved them quiet after a moment. "Fine words," he said, "and well spoken. But how will we fight? Words man no shield wall, they fire no bow. And though we could possibly defeat Oobel on our own, we are no match for Mercy and her magicks."

The other hobs nodded in agreement, little brown and green caps bobbing up and down. The brownie with the big nose began weeping and wailing, sending tears rolling down her giant proboscis like quarters down a chute.

Scott put a hand up and waited until the brownie was quieted some by her friend with the ears. "Mercy tricked me before. I think most of her magic is trickery and illusion. It was her servants who actually hurt me."

Mundoo spoke. "Killed you."

Scott blinked. "Killed me?"

"Yes," another hob chirped. He had a fresh youthful face and wore a tiny green skullcap pulled low over his eyes. "Killed you dead as a brick. Dead as a stone. Dead as a pigeon that's had its head stove in with one or the other, till its brains spilled out and worms came and feasted on—" He was brought up short by Wee Jake slapping him on the back of the head hard enough to scoot the skullcap over his eyes entirely.

"Jemmy Mickle-tot! Can you not see the Steward going pale in the cheeks?" Wee Jake asked. "He is not ten breaths back from the dead and you speak of worms and brains and Puck knows what else!"

"Sorry, Jake." He pushed the cap back off his eyes.

Wee Jake slapped him again. The cap went all the way over his nose this time. "*I* need not your apology!"

"Oh." Jemmy said. Pushing the cap back till only one eye was exposed, he tensed for another blow. When none came he swept it off entirely and bowed low to Scott. "My greatest apologies, Steward," he said formally.

"My name's Stewart. Scott Stewart. With a 'T' at the end."

"And a fine name it is," Wee Jake said, "and none can say it is not yours." From under the brim of his acorn, he fixed Scott with a firm stare. "But the Steward is what you are."

Steward of what? Scott almost asked, but the answer came to him immediately: *Fletcher. I've been chosen to watch over him.* Who had chosen him and why were questions he decided to get answered at another time. Right now he had more pressing problems.

"All right. It's not long till nightfall and we have to get our defenses in order." He looked at Wee Jake. "Who's in charge?"

"You are."

"No, I mean, who's in charge of you hobs. And brownies," he said, nodding to the womenfolk.

Wee Jake furrowed his brow. "I do not understand."

Scott shifted and Fletcher's little fingers dug into his chest, a leftover ape-instinct allowing him to hold on without waking. "Who leads you?"

"You do, Steward."

"But before I arrived. Who led you?"

"No one."

Jemmy and the other hobs nodded their agreement. "How did you all come to be here?"

Wee Jake looked thoughtful for a moment then said, "We were called. By the babe."

Scott looked down at Fletcher. He certainly didn't look capable of calling a horde of mythical creatures to his aid. *Course he hadn't had too hard of a time getting me to do what he wanted.*

"Okay." He supposed it didn't matter much now. *Another question for later. I get the feeling those are going to pile up.* Shifting Fletcher to his left arm, Scott pushed himself to a sitting position. He could feel the beginnings of a monstrous headache building at the base of his skull. Fletcher squawked and squinted one-eyed at Scott. "Hush you," Scott said, "We're trying to win a war here." Seemingly appeased by this, Fletcher closed his eye and was soon breathing deeply again.

"So, what is your plan, Steward?" Wee Jake asked.

Scott didn't answer immediately. *I don't have enough intel to plan an operation.*

"What do we know about Mercy and this . . . Oobel?"

It was Wee Jake who answered. "Oobel came from the land of the dark forest, where he fought the dire wolves for fat babies left alone in the wild. He is a scavenger and trickster and prefers the easy meat of the young, the sick, and the old. But he is capable of stout combat if cornered."

"And Mercy?"

"Mercy is a native creature, born of fear and sickness and mysterious death. She takes over the mind and thus the body of those she hunts, draining first their blood and then their soul. She has minions to do her bidding but rarely needs them outside of the daylight hours."

Thinking of the goth teenagers unconscious or dead in Mercy's tomb, Scott said, "I think she has two less minions than she used to."

Wee Jake shrugged. "It matters not. She can bend you to her will and we have no weapons that can harm her. It is odd, however."

"What's that?" he asked, thinking *What could be odder than the conversation I'm having right now?*

"I have never heard of her hunting outside of her family."

"Maybe we're related," Scott suggested, but Wee Jake shook his head. Scott didn't ask how the little man knew that for sure. "Well, how do I kill her if I happen not to get bent to her will?"

"Cut out her heart and burn it."

"Really?"

Wee Jake looked away. "That is what is said. You will have to discover for yourself if it is true."

"Great." The sun was orange now, and the shadows were slanting hard across Scott's windowsill. *Seven-fifteen. We don't have long.* "All right. Are there sentries out?"

Nodding, Wee Jake said, "Some of our more farsighted brethren walk the perimeter."

"Bring them in. I don't want Oobel picking them off in the dark."

"Is it wise to turn a blind eye to that same darkness?"

Scott carefully slid Fletcher off his chest and onto the bed, then stood and stretched. The promise of a headache blossomed into a stabbing pain right behind his eyelids. "I want Mercy and Oobel in close. If I can figure out how to keep my mind out of Mercy's control, I think I can finish them quick."

"How will you do that, Steward?"

"Superior firepower."

Wee Jake raised an eyebrow at him, but Scott didn't elaborate.

"Watch the windows. I have to talk to Mundoo for a minute."

When all the little people had cleared the room, Scott turned to Mundoo and took an involuntary step back. Mundoo was now a giant stag, the tips of his antlers brushing the ceiling of Scott's bedroom. *Well, that's kind of disconcerting.* "Um, got any ideas?"

The stag shifted its head to one side as if pondering the question before answering. Then Mundoo's voice echoed from the stag's mouth. "Mercy and I have never been in conflict before. I know of no way to combat her hold over you."

"It didn't feel like a hold," Scott said. "It felt like I was doing what I should. She called me and I went to her. I'm sure if I remembered Fletcher I would have stayed. But I couldn't remember him. I couldn't . . ." Scott blinked twice rapidly. Then smiled. "I have an idea."

"*Nowecontam.* And not a moment too soon."

"What do you mean?"

Mundoo's expression didn't change, but his body went from stag to bear. "Mercy comes."

• • • • Fourteen • • • •

Passing by the bathroom entrance, Bridie spotted an exit sign. It pointed away from the street, away from Hamilton, away from the direction of first pursuit. She broke into a run, purse pounding against her side. People turned and stared, but she needed distance before she started worrying about the trail she was leaving. Signs that said she'd exit onto Calton Road pointed her up a set of stairs. She took them three at a time, dodging around a girl in a denim mini-skirt before plowing through a group of young men in kilts and soccer toffs. She was on a curving, twisting walkway now, construction to her right, train tracks to the left and below her. A stone wall appeared in front of her, and she felt a brief jolt of panic before seeing stairs breaking left. Leapt down them and was once again outside.

Left or right? she thought. Then quickly, *Doesn't matter.*

Left into a short tunnel, bridge overhead, another above that a hundred yards past. It was far less crowded here, a few students walking, some people leaning on the back doors of businesses smoking. Bridie ignored them. Sprinted forward. Her stitches stung and she hoped she wouldn't split the gash open again. It'd be impossible to disappear if she were drenched in blood.

There was another set of stairs to her left, looked like it led up to street level. She jumped up them. Sure enough, she was on the sidewalk. She began walking, quick but casual, and stopped attracting quite as much attention.

Need to change my profile, she thought, stripping her coat off. Digging in her purse, she pulled out a white hair-tie. Had her locks up in a loose bun in moments.

Won't fool Hamilton and Fraser, but it might buy a minute or two from the other cops when they call it in. Now where am I?

She spotted a street sign: Leith Street.

"Shit!" She was heading right for the station. A walk light began beeping, and she crossed the street with the crowd, veering off onto the first side street she saw. She was behind the St. James shopping center, once again walking through groups of workers taking smoke breaks. The road wound back and forth for a block or two then came to a T on a sloping hillside street. She figured Edinburgh center was off left-handed. God knew what was off to the right. But straight in front of her was the bus station. It gave her an idea.

THE ENTRANCE TO the bus station was a short hall completely barren except for a screen mounted high on the wall with bus departure times. Bridie scanned till she saw Glasgow, read the other information. Seemed straightforward: *Service 900 City Link Fifteen-thirty.*

Fifteen-thirty, she thought. *Three-thirty P.M. and it's twenty after now. Perfect.*

Round the corner of the hall was a snack machine, and round another was the station itself, a study in off-white blandness with the occasional electric-blue recessed light. Lockers to the left, one-story-high glass to the right with the buses parked on the other side. Past the lockers she came on a half-dozen ticket windows, red electric signs above them flashing their service. There was a little line at the one advertising *City Link—Glasgow*. A Norman Rockwell-looking family with two freckled children waited patiently behind a dirty young couple wearing tattered backpacks, while a teenage boy in the tattooed, pierced, and leather-jacketed uniform of disaffected youth finished his transaction at the window. Bridie pushed past them, slapping her purse down on the counter just as the teenager walked away.

"Ma'am, ye can't—" Mr. Rockwell began before Bridie cut him off.

"Shut up," she said, "I'm in a hurry."

The young couple said disapproving things to each other in German. Bridie looked through the window to where the ticket vendor, a pinch-faced man in a uniform vest, looked at her disapprovingly. As she pulled her wallet out of her purse, he shook his head.

Don't push it, she thought. *You want to make an impression, not attract security.*

"Fine," she huffed, and stepped to the back of the line. The Rockwells didn't look at her the whole time they waited, though the German girl stared at her as if she were a zoo exhibit. When Bridie got to the counter, the vendor didn't speak to her. Just sold her a one-way ticket on the fifteen-thirty to Glasgow, clucking his tongue all the while. He got a good look at her, though.

Bridie took her ticket without comment and left the counter. Found a cash machine and took out as much money as it would let her. Then she retraced her steps, past the ticket counter, past the lockers that blocked the ticket vendors' view of the exit nicely, around the corners, down the hall, and out onto the street. Turned toward the center of town and started walking.

Hamilton and Fraser weren't fools. But they had to figure Bridie would try to make for Glasgow. They'd cover the bus stations, taxi stands, ask the long-haulers about hitchhikers. And if the ticket vendor didn't remember the Yankee bitch he'd sold the one-way ticket to Glasgow to, Bridie would turn in her Women's Intuition card. With any luck, they'd concentrate their search for her there.

But Bridie wasn't going to Glasgow. She was going to go to ground here, in Edinburgh, and let the heat die down. Cops always had other things they had to do. They couldn't chase her forever. Besides, Hamilton was right, guys like Jackie don't stay hidden for long. But Bridie didn't think he'd resurface in Glasgow. Just by the way he'd fought, he'd seemed smarter than most. She figured he'd know they were looking for him in Glasgow. He'd need a place to go, and he has contacts in this city. He'd come here. And when he did, Bridie'd be waiting for him.

THE WALK BACK to Edinburgh center wouldn't have taken more than a few minutes if Bridie hadn't made any stops. But she made a whole bunch of them. First, a clothing store. Paid cash for a flower-print summer dress, changed in the dressing room, then walked out wearing it. Stuffed the bag with her slacks and her hundred-and-twenty-dollar silk top from Saks in a garbage can. Tried not to cry thinking about a homeless person digging it out and wearing it.

Next stop was Hair by Bridget, a downscale salon a few blocks off Princes Street, for a spiky, dykey, buzz cut. Then another clothing store, this time for jeans and a sleeveless black T-shirt. Left wearing the new outfit again, and another homeless person got a new look. Last stop was another salon for a dye job.

"What color ye looking for, dearie?"

"Blonde," Bridie said. "Really blonde."

When she stepped out of the salon, she didn't think her own

brothers would have recognized her. Of course, one was a drug-addled criminal and the other a case study for posttraumatic stress syndrome, so she didn't know if that was a fair test.

It was getting late in the day; Bridie had to find a place to go to ground.

PRINCES STREET, THE Royal Mile, Grassmarket, Bridie cruised the touristy spots looking for a place to spend the night. But she had a problem. She couldn't stay at a place that asked for an ID. She'd need a no-questions-asked, cash-for-crash kind of establishment. Of course, she didn't know the city well enough to have any idea where to look. She knew Lothian Road wasn't great, but if Hamilton and Fraser didn't buy the bus trip, they'd go through the same thought process she had and look for her there. And they'd still send a roller out to check on the known flophouses in town just in case. She could probably stay in one safely in a couple of days, but for now she had to avoid them. Nor did she want to sleep on a park bench and get rousted by a random beat cop. She could change her appearance, but she couldn't do a damn thing about her accent. The cops would be looking for an American girl, and if they found one, Bridie imagined they'd bring her in and let Hamilton or Fraser get a look at her.

And then it's a plane ride back to the U.S. if I'm lucky, she thought, *and a decent length stay in a Scottish prison if I'm not.*

She was on High Street now, next to a short building that looked like the top of a castle tower had been chopped off and pounded into the ground. There was a long thin column stretching out of its center with a white unicorn on top. Bridie leaned against it, relaxing for just one minute. The stone was cool against her back, a pleasant feeling after walking for so long. Eyeing passers-by, she decided if she got tired enough, she'd just pick someone up at a bar and spend the night at their place.

If I can find one with teeth. She shuddered. *No, I'm not that desperate. Yet.*

A middle-aged soccer mom herding three preteen girls with Union Jack bags on their shoulders came over to where Bridie stood. Her smile at Bridie spoke more of exhaustion than emotion as she told the girls, "Stay close," and sat heavily on the ground, back to the stone wall. Bridie nodded to her absently. Two young men with enough tattoos and piercings for probable cause approached on Bridie's other side. She watched them warily as they lit up cigarettes and began loitering with intent. Then an elderly man with pants riding about eight inches too high led an age-appropriate woman up to Bridie's left, while a family of five carrying plastic bags adorned with the logos of Princes Street boutiques approached on her right. A young couple who would have been attractive if they dressed better and showered occasionally came next, along with a family of swarthy southern Europeans, a pair of cowboy-hatted American youths, a couple who were either gay or French—Bridie couldn't tell—and a middle-aged woman in a white silk shirt with a black name tag pinned to the breast pocket.

Bridie slid down next to the soccer mom who was staring hard at the two smoking hoodlums.

"What's going on here?"

Soccer mom tore her gaze away and looked at Bridie. "Sorry. Quit three weeks ago and I'm bloody dying for a fag." Her accent was pure London. "What did you say?"

"What's everyone showing up here for?"

"You're not here for the tour?"

Bridie raised one eyebrow. "What tour?"

"The tour of the vaults." The woman looked back at the smokers and sighed. "Should be starting soon. I think that's our guide." She pointed at the woman with the name tag. "She's going to take us underground."

Bridie's eyebrows shot up. "Underground?"

"Yes. Apparently there's a whole bunch of caverns and rooms under the town. Person could get lost in there without a guide."

Or a person could lose their guide and stay there overnight, Bridie thought happily and got to her feet. Sauntering up to the woman with the name tag, Bridie asked, "I'm interested in the tour of the vaults. You the guide?"

"Oh, aye," said the woman in a pleasant voice. "Last one of the day."

"Got room for one more?"

"Aye. Six pounds, please." She looked down at her watch. "It's an hour long. We'll be leaving in about five minutes time."

Bridie pulled her wad of cash out of her purse and gave the guide a ten-pound note. Got four heavy gold pound coins in return. Leaned back on the building to wait.

"O.K., gather round, folks," the guide said after a few minutes had passed, "and let me tell you the centuries-old tale of how a great bridge was built and of the community that grew in the sunless vaults beneath it. I'll tell you of the leatherworkers and publicans and whiskey runners who lived and died there and how those famous murderers, Burke and Hare, traveled its dark tunnels with fresh corpses for sale." She lowered her voice theatrically, and her small crowd had to lean in to hear her better, "I'll tell you how it became known as 'The most haunted spot in all of Britain.'" She turned and began walking up High Street. "Follow me."

Bridie and the rest of the group did as she asked. Haunted or not, she was glad to be getting off the street. If you could call this cobblestoned mess a street. Her nerves were starting to fray from keeping away from the cops. *Is this how criminals feel all the time?* she thought. *Shitty life.* With any luck, she could ditch the tour near the end of the hour and lay up till morning. Mix into an outgoing group the next day, then mingle with the holiday crowds during the day. Do the tour again tomorrow night. That might be enough time for the cops to lay off and for Jackie to come to town. Then Bridie could start hunting in earnest. She didn't know the town now. But she'd done some undercover work before; she was sure she could start making some contacts given a little bit of time.

Hell, she thought, *this'll be easy.*

They tromped down the Royal Mile and Bridie smiled for the first time all day. In a few minutes she'd be going underground. Really underground.

• • • MUNDOO • • •

Mundoo chanted no more. The Coat-man's body was healed, his mind returned—though the latter was not of his doing. Mundoo watched him dozing on the small sofa and thought of the many times his people had helped the Coat-men in the past.

Sickly creatures they were when they first came, pale and short with no skills in hunting, no knowledge of planting, no desire to honor the earth and live off its freely given bounty. He frowned. *Without my people they would have all perished that first winter. Without the game we brought them, without the* maize *we grew, their colony would have withered and died.*

Shifting into bear form, Mundoo stood on his hind legs, bristly fur on the top of his head just brushing the ceiling, eyes black as a moonless night sky staring down at the sleeping Coat-man.

Would that they had perished, he thought. *All my people had to do was stay away. Let winter claim its own.* The bear's lips parted, exposing canines as long as a man's thumb. *Or I could have sent signs to the wise men. Made warriors descend on the Coat-men's pathetic encampments, killing all who dwelt there. Burn their buildings to the ground, their ships to the waterline. Sacrifice their children to the angry gods of the vanished* Tawantin Suyu, *clubbing the pale creatures on the head or tearing their hearts from their chest.*

Mundoo sighed as he became the Turtle. *But that is not my way, nor my people's.* He turned away, showing his shell to the sleeping man, jigsaw patterns of green and gold criss-crossed with ancient scars like accusations. The Coat-man slept on, oblivious.

And I help one of them again, when I could just let him fall victim to their own monsters and Manitous.

The air shimmered around the turtle and Mundoo was human again, though his eyes were still black and pupil-less like the Bear's had been. He spoke aloud.

"But I am a foolish spirit of a foolish people, and we have always followed our way, even when it meant our destruction." Reaching out a hand, he shook the Coat-man's shoulder. "Steward."

But I am not so much a fool that I have learned nothing from my people's destroyers. The dark in his eyes shrank to pupil pinpoints rimmed in brown irises and white sclera; a human's eyes, though old beyond measure. *And if they were uninterested in learning our ways, perhaps it is time to teach them something about their own.*

He shook the Coat-man's shoulder again.

"Steward, it is time to awaken."

· · · Fifteen · · ·

Scott was on the couch. He didn't know how he'd gotten there or how long he'd been there. But there he was. On the couch. And someone was calling his name.

"Steward, it is time to awaken."

Well, almost calling his name.

"It's Stewart. With a 'T.'"

"Mercy is here."

Mercy? he thought. *What the hell?*

"What about love and kindness? They here too?"

"*Chickacava.* Your plan has not worked then."

"I don't who you are, or what plan you're talking about, or what *chickacava* means." Scott made to push himself up off the couch. "But, I—"

As he stood, he noticed some unfamiliar weight hanging off him. Looking down, he saw he had his M9 tucked into his belt, just left of center for a right-handed crossdraw. His commando knife was in its sheath on his right hip. And hanging from his chest in a flower-print harness was a baby.

A baby? "What the hell?"

The baby started to cry. The sound triggered something in Scott's head and a word popped into his mind.

Fletcher.

"Fletcher," he said cautiously. Then, "Fletcher!"

The name came to him, and with it, everything else. Mercy's spell faded in an instant. He smiled down at the baby.

"It's okay, Fletcher. Uncle Scott's here." Poking his finger at Fletcher's belly, he cooed softly at him. Fletcher stopped crying and smiled up at him.

"Mercy is here." Mundoo stood before him in human form. "And Oobel is with her."

Scott face twisted into a feral smile. "Well, I'll go greet them then."

Pulling his M9 out of his belt, he popped out the clip and checked it. Fully loaded, fifteen rounds. He slipped it back in and jacked a round into the chamber. Flicked the safety to FIRE. Looking down at Fletcher, he said, "Sorry, little guy, this might get loud." Then holding the gun behind his back, he marched out the front door.

IT WAS DARK, but not yet full dark; Scott had a good view of his front yard and the woods beyond, the pines looking like posts in a rod iron gate. The driveway was clear, though there was a little room behind the Honda where a small creature could hide. *Something the size of Oobel, maybe.* His unmowed lawn was likewise clear. There was movement in the trees to the right of the drive, but nothing solid for him to track and fire on.

I'll need them closer.

"Hello, Scott." Mercy was in the driveway again, her black dress undulating in a nonexistent wind. Scott thought he saw her eyes widen when she saw the baby strapped to his chest, but she made no mention of it.

"Come," she said and began moving toward the forest.

Scott came down off the steps without answering. Out of the corner of his eye, the movement he'd seen in the woods coalesced into a small man with a long beard.

Oobel. Scott recognized him at once.

Time for a threat assessment, he thought, trying to view the situation with a dispassionate eye. *It would have been easier with Fletcher in the house. They probably would have split their forces and I could have taken out Mercy while the hobs held off Oobel's attack. But with Fletcher strapped to me, they'll both come at me.* Scott and Mercy approached the woods where Oobel waited eagerly, wrenching at his beard with long fingers. *Mercy's hold on me is broken, but I don't know what kind of physical assault she can mount. Oobel will attack physically, but still might be the less dangerous of the two.*

Oobel was now six feet away, Mercy only three.

Mercy it is then.

Scott brought the M9 around in front of him, not bothering with a shooter's stance at this range and planted a bullet right in the back of Mercy's skull.

Or tried to.

The gun fired, but the bullet passed right through her with no visible effect. She turned, hissing at him like an angry snake, her face now a bare skull.

"Shit." *Switch targets!* Taking two steps backward, he pivoted and fired three rounds at Oobel, who was suddenly moving jackrabbit-fast away from him. The first two rounds missed—it had been a long time since Scott had tried night shooting at a fast-moving target—but the third rewarded him with a squeal of pain and a spurt of blood. It didn't bring the creature down, though.

Scott had no time to congratulate himself on his fine shooting;

Mercy was on him, hissing and screaming, long fingernails jabbing at his eyes. Half-turning to shield Fletcher from her claws, he earned himself a raking gash down his shoulder. He fired his pistol under his arm, just hoping the noise would distract her, and yanked his knife out of its sheath left-handed. Then turning back to face her, he swung the knife in a backhand slash that caught Mercy in the ribcage. The knife bit solidly and the smell of decay hit Scott like a fist.

Staggering back, he saw Mercy look down at her chest in wonder. A jagged rip in her dress ran upward from just over her right hip to her left breast. Beneath the rip, no blood seeped, but Scott could see a long cut through necrotic flesh and rotten tissue.

Steel slices where bullets fail, I guess. He held his breath and took a step forward. *Knife it is then.*

Mercy turned and disappeared into the dark woods swifter than anything living could move. Scott brought his gun up and sighted down the barrel where she'd gone, then faced toward where he'd last seen Oobel. No sign of him. He turned completely around twice, keeping his footwork clean and his sight down his firing line. There was nothing. The woods were quiet and empty.

He stepped slowly back to the house, scanning the darkness. Halfway up the steps, Fletcher let out a burp and looked up at him hopefully.

Scott said, "Oh, you're hungry, are you?" He flicked the safety on the M9 back on, then laughing, went inside.

SCOTT STOOD IN the middle of pandemonium. The hobs were jumping and cavorting in a wild martial dance, making impossible leaps as high as his chest. The brownies were well below that, hugging his ankles and weeping tiny rivers of joyful tears. Fletcher smiled happily and tittered whenever one of the leaping hobs sailed past. Only Mundoo looked somber. Scott raised an eyebrow at him in query.

"They will return," Mundoo said.

"No they won't!" shouted a hob. Scott struggled to remember his name. *Jemmy Mickle-tot. That was it.* Three other brownies had managed to find a bottle of Pabst and tip it on its side. They were filling anything they could with beer. Jemmy held a bottle cap brimming with suds in both hands and slurped noisily. "The Steward gave them a right good scare. They're probably still running!"

Scott undid the baby carrier and put Fletcher carefully down on the couch. Tickling his feet, he sat down next to him.

"No," he said, "Mundoo is right. They'll be back."

The din died down as one by one the little creatures stopped jumping around to better hear the Steward. One last hob went whooping through the air, but was quieted angrily by two others when he landed.

"I certainly scared them," Scott went on. "Hurt them, too. But mostly I stung their pride. And I don't think they'll stand for that." Looking down at Fletcher, he remembered all the visions he'd had of him being tortured and eaten. *I must protect him.* "They'll be back. And they'll bring all the help they can get."

Jemmy turned ashen. Wee Jake stepped up.

"Steward," he said somberly, "perhaps you should take the child and flee. We will hold them here as long as possible."

As he considered that suggestion, Scott saw in his mind the Honda capsized by the side of the road, dozens of grotesque creatures climbing over it, reaching clawed hands into the broken windows.

"No. We won't flee." Scott stood and walked to the window. Pushing the blind aside just a crack, he peeked out the window at the darkness past the driveway. Shapes might have been moving in the darkness; he wasn't sure. "We'll fight them here. On home ground."

Wee Jake nodded solemnly, straightening his acorn cap helmet. "Home ground."

Tossing his bottle cap of beer aside, Jemmy pulled a black stone knife out of his belt and checked the edge with his thumb. The other hobs adjusted their armor and checked that their weapons were in good shape. The brownies snapped the ends off their brooms to make quarterstaffs and several produced wicked-looking ceramic knives of their own. One brownie ran off into a cupboard, returning minutes later with a three-legged contraption that held a wheel as big as she was and one flat pedal. As Scott watched, fascinated, she sat at it and worked the pedal, setting the wheel spinning fast. Seeing a spool of what looked like wool on one end, Scott decided it was usually used for spinning thread. But one by one, the brownies and hobs stepped up to it with their knives out, grinding an edge on the stone-rimmed wheel.

It was an army preparing for battle.

"All right," Scott said at last, trying to remember what little he had read about battle strategy when he was considering officer training. "We'll need to set up a perimeter. Who has ranged weapons?" About half a dozen hobs raised small bows over their heads. "Back corner of the bedroom. There's a trapdoor that leads to an attic crawlspace. Got to be some holes in the roof you can fire through."

"Yes, Steward," they said as if he were their squad leader, then scampered off into the bedroom.

"I need sentries at the windows. Pick those with the keenest eyesight. Two to a window, in case one drowses off. The rest of you get some rest. I don't think they're coming back tonight."

"I need no rest," Mundoo said. "I will keep watch as well."

"Well, I do," Scott said. "I was dead not too long ago. It takes it out of a guy."

If he was expecting a chuckle from Mundoo, he didn't get one. "What of the child?"

Scott stepped back to the couch and picked up the baby carrier. "Fletcher stays with me. I don't know if Mercy will try to take me again knowing that I can break her hold. But if she does, I'll need Fletcher with me." Scott turned toward the kitchen. "And I need to feed him."

He felt a tap on his foot. Looking down, he saw a wrinkled little brownie holding up a baby bottle as big as she was. It was full and warm when he bent down to take it from her. He squirted some on his wrist. Perfect temperature.

"Thank you."

She bowed and waddled away. Scott plugged the bottle into Fletcher's mouth and walked into the bedroom as the baby sucked hungrily at it. The trapdoor was open.

"Hey, guys," he yelled up it. "You see a wooden crate up there?"

"Yes, Steward. Shall we bring it down?"

"Can you? It's pretty heavy."

Scott heard high tinkling laughter. "We're quite a bit stronger than we look. What's in it?"

"Extra ammunition."

And I hope I don't need it.

Within a minute the crate came sliding through the trapdoor on thin ropes. The hobs lowered it onto the bed and Scott levered it open with one hand. Small black cardboard boxes with a red-eyed-wolf logo and the words "WOLF Performance Ammunition" printed on them in red and white filled the box, as well as four empty M9 clips. Scott grabbed the clips and two of the boxes. After ensuring that both boxes were labeled "9mm Luger" he dumped them onto the bed. A hundred copper-jacketed bullets spilled out. Scott stared at them for a moment, than swung his feet up onto the bed, careful not to knock any of the bullets on the floor. Fletcher was almost done with his bottle and was looking sleepy.

When he falls asleep I'll load the clips. Then I'll get some rest myself. Once the battle starts, I might not get another chance.

Scott watched Fletcher work the bottle. Watched his eyes start to close. He thought hard about the upcoming battle, about the deployment of his little troops, about his choice of weaponry. He got no visions of imminent disaster. No horrific views of dead babies or dying hobs or brownies bawling over his mutilated body.

"I think we're going to be okay," he whispered to Fletcher.

Fletcher didn't answer. He was fast asleep.

And only a baby anyway, of course.

· · · sixteen · · ·

When the hell does this underground tour go underground? Bridie fumed silently. They'd just spent ten minutes in an alley learning all about how Edinburgh sat on a volcanic plug and about how the Flodden Wall and the loch and the castle kept everyone bottled up in the town, well into the eighteenth century. And now they stood next to a bridge that looked like a street due to all the houses built on it and were learning about how the city council, greedy as any modern-day politicians, decided that now that they were all out of real estate to sell on, over, and around South Bridge, they would try selling the land *inside* it.

I don't care about any of this! Bridie shouted in her own head. *I just want to get underground!*

They were walking again now, Bridie barely paying attention, when the matronly guide stepped off the street and unlocked an unassuming little door. She led them through the door onto a set of stairs and down.

Finally.

A few flights and they were in cool quiet darkness.

"I like to ask everyone to be silent for a moment," the guide said. "We're underneath the bridge now. There are cars driving directly over our heads, people in the houses walking about, but you can't hear a thing, can you?"

Bridie nodded along with everyone else. It *was* quiet. Quiet as the grave. She looked around. The floor was dirt and uneven, the walls old gray brick. The ceiling vaulted high overhead, its bricks made of the same stone as the bridge. A candle and a few floor lamps did a poor job of piercing the darkness. Bridie figured the effect was intentional.

Can't have the most haunted spot in Britain lit up like a dentist's office.

"Now gather round in a wee circle, and let me tell you the story of Mr. Boots—as nasty a piece of business as you'll ever see—who stalked these corridors centuries ago searching for abandoned children. Children he would murder in cold blood!"

As the guide talked, Bridie scouted the edges of the room. There were a few thin passageways but they didn't lead far enough off to hide in. A full-sized passageway led away from them, but it was well lit and looked well traveled. Not what she needed.

"And even today, Mr. Boots still stalks the Vaults. In fact, not too many years back, a young lady was attacked while on our tour. Witnesses say that a cloud of smoke appeared above her then swept into her body. She fainted, her features turning—just for a moment—into those of an old, evil man who cackled and grinned as the poor girl collapsed to the cold, cold ground."

The crowd gasped appreciatively at the end of the ghost story and eyed the numerous shadows with newfound respect.

Spooky, Bridie thought. *Wonder if she'll tell the one about the killer with the hook hand that gets stuck in the young couple's car door handle.*

Bridie had never been impressed with ghost stories.

Maybe if I hadn't been a cop and seen the terrible shit that real people do to each other. She pressed her lips into a thin smile. *Or maybe if I hadn't got kicked out of Girl Scouts . . .*

The guide waved them into the next room.

"Watch your step," she said, shining a weak flashlight on the ground as her group filed past her. The ceiling was lower here, and made the space seem even more cramped. Bridie started to feel the weight of the tons of stone and dirt above and around her, but she shook it off quickly.

Can't get claustrophobia if I'm going to spend the night here.

The guide gathered them in a half-circle in front of her, as she had in the last room and launched into another story.

"When workman complained of hearing eerie moans while excavating the Vaults, they immediately brought it to their foreman's attention. He told them to get back to work, but they were terrified by the ghostly noises and refused. Now, the foreman was a big man and afraid of nothing, so flashlight in hand, he stomped bravely into the blackness of the excavation shaft."

Bridie still wasn't seeing a spot to slip away. This room had only one exit, and they were all obviously going to be exiting through it when the guide finished this next story. Bridie tapped her foot in impatience as the guide ramped up the tension with descriptions of the "ghastly moans" and "eldritch shrieks" that echoed down the tunnel to where the foreman bravely marched.

"Let's wrap it up," Bridie muttered under her breath.

"But when the foreman saw a light in the Stygian gloom that shouldn't have been there, he realized that the workmen had driven a hole in the wrong wall and broken through to a local business that made its home on the other side: a massage parlor! That was the source of the moans and groans and painful exclamations." The crowd guffawed and the guide gave them a professional smile. "Now watch your step again."

Bridie became even more frustrated in the next room. *Six pounds wasted if I can't find a way to slip out before we get to the end of the tour.*

Once again, the guide used her flashlight to guide the group past her then gathered them in a semicircle.

"You're standing now in the most haunted place in the Vaults. Visitors have had their sleeves tugged, their ankles kicked, rocks thrown at them. They've seen old men in tophats and young women in hoop dresses and petticoats march by. Mr. Boots chases children through here and a poor lost girl asks visitors for her dolly. Take a moment and wait. Watch. Listen. You might see one of the dozens of ghosts that make the Vaults their home."

The tour continued, the guide being careful to keep track of her charges as they moved through. Many more ghost stories were told, but Bridie had stopped paying attention. She'd given up on slipping away and was trying to figure out a different way to stay out of sight for a few days. Couldn't think of one, though. She was faced with the same problems as before: the Edinburgh cops knew the city better than she did, and anyplace she could find, they could find first.

Coming finally to a flight of stairs, the guide said, "And that's us done, then."

Bridie blinked and realized that they'd traveled in a circle. The stairs before them were the ones they'd come down when they entered.

Guess being underground can really mess with your sense of direction.

"I hope you've enjoyed your tour through the most haunted spot in Britain," the guide continued. "If you'll just follow me." And she went up the stairs without looking back.

Bridie grinned. The rest of the group streamed up the stairs and Bridie just took one shuffling step behind the wall to her left and was alone. Simple as that. She waited for the footsteps to recede up the stairs and listened to the door shut. Then waited a moment. Apparently the guide didn't take a last head count, because the door didn't reopen.

She'd done it. She was tucked safe away.

"Now to find someplace to sleep," she muttered.

"Halloo! What's that?"

Bridie nearly jumped out of her skin. The voice came from down the passageway. For a second, Bridie thought she was hearing a ghost and despite her earlier bravado was seriously considering running screaming from the Vaults. But then she noticed that the candle in the first room had been blown out, and the lights turned off. She risked one more step into the room and peeked into the next. The lights were off there as well, the candles extinguished.

"Halloo?" called the voice again. Then softer, "Place fair gives me the willies. Don't know why I keep this job."

A custodian! Bridie thought happily. *Someone to come in behind the last tour to blow out the candles and shut down the lights, make sure the place is locked up tight for the night.*

The man was whistling now, and Bridie moved deeper in, retracing the tour.

Whistling past the graveyard, she thought and chuckled silently, all thought of fleeing gone. The whistling grew quieter as she got farther in, and the custodian got nearer the exit. It was near pitch black now and Bridie stopped, not wanting to risk stumbling and have him hear her.

Though he'd probably just think it was a ghost and leave even quicker.

The whistling stopped and she heard footsteps go up the staircase. Then the last tiny bit of light left with the sound of the door closing.

Bridie was alone in the dark.

"No for long," she said in her best Glaswegian accent.

Digging in her purse, she found a small plastic flashlight, a miniature imitation of the big Maglite she used to carry as a cop. She unscrewed its top till the bulb came on, then kept twisting till the top came off in her hand. The bare bulb was like a little candle, but one that gave off a surprising amount of illumination. She held it up and watched the shadows cringe to the corners of the room. Treading into the next room, she started looking for someplace to make camp. She hadn't spotted anything promising while on the tour, but she'd been concentrating on finding a way to slip away unnoticed. She thought she'd give it another look-see once she was alone.

Turned out her powers of perception were better than she gave herself credit for: there was no good place to sleep. Every bit of ground was uniformly dirty, uneven, cold, and damp. The most promising spot was right in the middle of the room the guide had called "the most haunted place in the Vaults."

"I don't believe in any of that," Bridie said, her voice sounding odd as it broke the cavernous silence. "But I think I'll stay a little farther in anyway."

She told herself it was because the most haunted place was too close to the stairs—she might not have time to get up and away if she was sleeping when the first tour came down. But truth be told, she was starting to realize just how goddamn spooky it was down here, and she didn't want to push her luck by setting up camp right smack dab in the middle of all the supposed paranormal activity.

"Pick a spot, Bridie," she chided herself. "You've got to shut the flashlight down soon and save the battery."

With the vault trail being circular, she was beginning to believe that she could stay down here for most of a few days, following tours around from a few rooms back, then laying low till the next one came down. Maybe go up top once a day for food and bathroom, then buy another ticket, and—*what do they say here? Oh that's right*—and Bob's your uncle, she'd be back underground. So if she was going to spend most of the next few days down here, she'd need to conserve her flashlight's batteries.

Conserve them for what? she thought. *Why can't I just pick up extra batteries tomorrow on my foray up into town?*

It made sense.

Just say it.

"I need the batteries for later tonight. In case I freak the hell out in this haunted little hellhole and have to run screaming up the stairs and break down the door."

Feeling immediately better having admitted her trepidation, Bridie quickly picked a spot in a place the guide had called the "wine room" and sat down. Apparently, before the bottom had dropped out of the South Bridge real estate market, fat merchants, lonely tradesmen, and probably a prostitute or three had sat in this room sucking down bottles of claret. Shards of those very bottles had been found when the place was excavated, and Bridie could see the stone shelves where the barrels had been kept. It was no posh barroom now, however; the ground was cold and damp, and Bridie's new jeans would probably never be the same. But weariness overtook her anyway as soon as she was seated.

And with good reason, she thought. *It's not every day a girl chases two guys, kills one, gets stabbed, gets stitched up, and then gets run out of town by the only people in the country she knows.*

She was exhausted. Shutting off the flashlight, she lay back on the hard-packed dirt. It wasn't in the least bit comfortable, but she didn't care. The Vaults were quiet and she was horizontal; she knew she'd be asleep in minutes.

"And if any of you ghosts wake me up," she said, "I'll have you fucking exorcised."

And with that pronouncement, she fell asleep.

··· Dearg and Darsee ···

In a dark, dank corner of a dark, dank room, two creatures—vaguely human in form—sat on their haunches and shivered uncomfortably.

"It's no fair, Darsee," said one.

"It isnae," the other agreed immediately. Then, "What exactly isnae fair, Dearg?

If there was any light in the room, Dearg's eyes would have shone angrily as he glared at his companion.

"Look at me cap!" Dearg shouted.

It was pitch black, but Darsee was a creature of caverns and caves and castle cellars—he didn't need light to see. He examined Dearg's cap as instructed. For good measure, he looked him up and down. Hairy feet, stained pants, ripped shirt, crooked teeth, warty nose, wrinkled face, the red cap on his head like a rotten cherry on a very ugly sundae.

Looked just right.

Dearg waited for Darsee to speak, but he'd been instructed only to look, and very soon was engrossed in removing an especially fascinating booger from his nose.

"Well?" Dearg finally snapped.

"Huh?" Darsee struggled to think of what they'd been talking about. "Oh! Your cap. Looks guid on you. How's mine?" He stood and doffed his own cap like a courtier. As he was almost twin to Dearg—though slightly larger in the shoulders, slightly smaller in the midsection, and a good deal wartier all over—the maneuver did not look particularly courtly.

Dearg punched him in the stomach.

"Oof. Now what'd you go and do that for?"

"My cap! Look at it!"

"I did. And—"

"It's fading." Ripping his cap off his head, Dearg shoved it under Darsee's nose. "Fading! I've had nothing to dip it in in how long? Weeks? Months?"

"I—"

Dearg put his cap back on his head. "Back in the Realm our caps never faded, our bellies never emptied." He paced a few steps away. "A fellow could be happy there."

Darsee straightened up. Rubbed his stomach. The blow hadn't really hurt that much, but if he let that on to Dearg, he'd just hit him again. "Do ye want to go back?"

"And be slaves to Lord Douglas?" Dearg snarled. He spit a giant gob onto the dirt floor. "I'd rather starve out here." Turning back to Darsee, he sighed. "Which we're like to do soon."

Darsee sat back down, found the booger again. "Too many people here during the day, and only dead people during the night. Is there nowhere else to go?"

"All the prime spots are either known to Douglas or stuffed with *Daoine Sidhe* who've escaped his rule." Dearg's already ugly face twisted into a sneer. "You think those toff nobs would have us?"

Darsee sniffled softly. "No."

"Then be quiet and let me—" Dearg's nose twitched violently for a fraction of a second, setting the warts wiggling to and fro. "Do you smell that?"

Sucking air through his big nostrils, Darsee smiled. "I do."

Dearg sniffed the air, once, twice. "It is alone, I believe." His nose twitched to the right and he stepped that way, seeming to follow it. "And even better . . ."

Darsee sprang to his feet and fell in behind Dearg. They were bent over at the waist, nostrils flared and sniffing rapidly. "It is a virgin."

Dearg's pace quickened. "We dip our caps in this one's blood and they shan't fade for years."

"And then we'll have a wee bit o' fun with it before we eats it, right, Dearg?"

Dearg slowed and looked back at his companion. "Oh aye," he said. "That we will."

The two Redcaps skipped out of the dark, dank room, following their noses toward dinner.

• • • seventeen • • •

S teward!"

Scott shot awake. It was still night and his bedroom was empty, the light on. Fletcher was strapped to his chest in his carrier, awake and staring at him curiously.

"Steward!" came the yell again, high-pitched and scared.

It came from above him. *The attic!*

Standing in bed, he leapt up, catching the rim of the trapdoor opening. But with the carrier on, he couldn't pull himself up to see over the edge without banging Fletcher's head.

"Be right there!" he shouted into the attic darkness. Dropping back to the bed, he said, "And I'll be right back, little guy."

He shrugged out of the carrier and put it gently down on the bed. Drew his gun and jumped again. Grabbing the ledge with his left hand, he slapped the gun down on the attic floor with his left and pushed till he had his elbow over. Then he levered his torso up and into the crawlspace. He heard scrabbling claws and smelled blood, but couldn't see a thing.

Should have grabbed a flashlight.

Scott fired a shot forty-five degrees up and forward and heard the bullet thunk into old rotting wood. Fletcher starting squalling below him as the muzzle flash lit the crawlspace for an instant. A horrible scene was frozen in the flash of light. Two dead hobs—one torn into two bleeding halves—lay three yards in front of him while a third struggled in the jaws of what looked like a bat the size of a black lab. Scott fired blind at the creature and spun as best he could to see if there were any hobs left alive behind him. Another shot fired high and he saw blood and innards like grotesque Rorschach tests spread on the roof and walls. Not a living thing in sight.

Then a puff of cold wind hit the back of his neck, followed by searing pain as what he guessed was a claw raked across his scalp. Blood suddenly stung his eyes, but it didn't make him any blinder in the darkness.

"Screw this," he said, and reached for the trapdoor, missing it once, twice, then finally hooking it on his third try. He let himself drop back through the trapdoor, pulling it closed behind him. But before it closed, he felt another breath of wind on his face and smelled the must of wild animal briefly overpowering the firecracker tang of the recent gunfire. Claws dug into his neck and he instinctively shrugged as he fell back to the bed. Lucky he did, as the teeth aimed for his jugular dug into his shoulder instead. Rolling away from Fletcher, he dropped his gun so he could get both hands on the beast. Tried to rip it off him, but it clung fast, claws and teeth digging in. Kept rolling and they were off the bed and falling hard to the floor.

Then through burning eyes, Scott saw brownies and hobs flood the room, leaping onto him, their eager knives jabbing swiftly into his attacker. Now the bat-thing spread its wings and released its grip to try to soar up, but Scott switched tactics and held it fast to him. Within seconds it breathed its last, bleeding from hundreds of tiny wounds.

Scott grabbed his gun and stood. Hobs and brownies crowded around his ankles and the dead bat-thing. He wiped his eyes and stared at the blood incredulously. Fletcher was screaming.

Why didn't I see this coming?

"Steward! The door!" shouted a brownie.

Scott looked up in time to see the trapdoor swinging open. Barely aiming, he made the door buck and jump as he emptied his entire clip into it. Just kept firing till the slide jacked back. The door dropped shut and there was a thump as something dead fell on top of it.

Scott stood frozen.

"There is no one left alive up there," Mundoo said. "Neither ours nor theirs."

Why didn't I see this coming? Scott thought again. *I'm wounded. I've lost six men. I should have seen this coming.*

"Something's wrong," Scott said. "I should have seen this coming." His visions warned of the bad stuff. And there couldn't be much worse than this. *Could there?*

"There is no time to consider that. They come," Mundoo said.

He's right. The attic attack will be part of a coordinated assault. Probably just a feint to draw forces from where the real attack will come.

Scott glanced around. The bedroom was crowded. Brownies clucked their tongues over the mess the dead bat-thing was making of the floor while several hobs prodded it to make sure it wasn't faking. A pair of hobs were swinging grappling hooks and climbing to the ceiling to secure the trapdoor. A brownie climbed onto Scott's shoulder and began patting at his eyes with a damp cloth. Little people weaved between his legs, crawled over the bed, jumped up onto the dresser. There couldn't be more than a couple beings left in the living room. "Shit. Back to the living room!"

Too late. Scott heard tinkling glass and screams. He ejected the clip on the M9, cursing himself for a buck private who didn't know enough to fire double-taps and conserve ammunition. His little army streamed out of the bedroom as he slammed another clip home.

Two more clips after this, he thought. *Forty-five bullets. And I think I might need them all.*

Grabbing Fletcher's carrier off the bed, he slung it over his left shoulder like a woman's purse. Fletcher stopped crying momentarily with the impromptu ride, but redoubled his efforts to deafen the entire room almost immediately.

Then Scott stepped out of the bedroom and into hell.

The living room was splattered with blood and covered with broken glass. Shattered windows let in the cool autumn air, but couldn't disperse the stench of blood, rot, and decay that permeated the air. Nightmare creatures were everywhere, tearing flesh, separating limbs from bodies, ripping torsos in two. The hobs and brownies were scrambling back and forth in a panic, unable to decide whether to flee or fight. They ended up doing neither effectively as Mercy and Oobel's evil army tore them to bits.

Raising his gun one-handed, Scott forced himself to breathe slowly as he gently squeezed the trigger.

Pop! Pop! Double-taps, just like he was supposed to, and Scott put two parabellum rounds into a three-foot-tall humanoid with the head of a stag and half a dead brownie hanging from its mouth. The creature collapsed with a yowl and Scott took a calm step forward, shifting his aim.

Pop! Pop! A naked man with skin the blue of freezing necrotic flesh and a belt that was hung with skulls looked down curiously at the two new holes in his chest. Scott put a third bullet in his forehead and he toppled backward.

Pop! Pop! The crack of the pistol was a welcome relief from

Fletcher's cries and the tortured screams of dying faeries. Something flashed toward his face from his right and Scott swung the gun up, narrowly avoiding pulling the trigger and blowing Wee Jake all the way back to the Knockside Hills. The hob's acorn cap was split in half and he was bleeding from his head and both arms, but he had managed a giant leap that landed him on Scott's shoulder.

"The Steward! The Steward!" he cried from his perch. "To the Steward!"

The yell was repeated through the tiny ranks, and what fey remained clawed and crawled their way to where Scott stood firing his pistol in a staccato rhythm. Forming a phalanx around his ankles, their defense stiffened. Scott put a bullet in the face of what appeared to be a normal human, albeit dressed strangely in animal skins. The man had just begun a charge when the bullet knocked him down. Hobs streamed over the fallen man and lifted the hair at the back of his neck then put their knives into the eyes of a dog-face that had been hidden there. Scott stepped forward once more and kept firing.

The attackers paused in their assault, watching their comrades twitch and die with every loud bang of the M9. Wings that had propelled them forward murderously a moment earlier now beat erratically. Claws that still had eyeballs, intestines, and assorted soft tissues hanging from them were retracted and then snicked out again in a nervous clicking tattoo. Weapons wavered in the air instead of hacking furiously, and for the first time Scott saw fear in their black eyes.

He yelled along with Jake, "The Steward! The Steward!"

The slide on the M9 jerked back.

Empty, Scott thought and ejected the clip right to the floor. And realized he'd made a huge mistake. With Fletcher's carrier slung over his shoulder, he needed to keep one hand on the strap to keep the baby from falling to the floor. But he needed both hands to reload. The enemy seemed to perk up at the respite in noise and slaughter, and the hobs' cries suddenly sounded tinny and weak.

"Shit, shit, shit," Scott muttered.

"Steward?" Wee Jake said tremulously.

Twisting at the hip, Scott leaned over uncomfortably so that gravity replaced his left hand in holding Fletcher's carrier in place. His perch slanting horribly now, Wee Jake clambered onto Scott's head to compensate. Fletcher, if possible now even more upset, grabbed at Scott's arms with panicked fingers. Scott reached into his pocket and grabbed a clip.

It caught on the fabric.

"Oh, for Christ's sake."

A giant bat crashed through the last unbroken window, and two more flapped silently in through another. All came straight at Scott. With a roar of anger, he ripped the pocket clean off his coat and slammed the clip home.

Too late. In his awkward position, he couldn't bring the gun to bear on the lead bat. It closed like a homing missile locked on his face, but Wee Jake, with a last shout of "The Steward!" leapt from his head directly into the maw of the flying beast. He stabbed it in the eye as its jaws closed around his torso and they tumbled to the ground.

Scott didn't wait to see them land. Straightening, he regripped the carrier with his left hand and shot the remaining two bats out of the air like clay pigeons. Turning his aim on the once-again advancing attackers, he picked out the closest one, and fired into its fanged, screaming face. But something whipped across his hand, knocking the gun free and sending it flying. His trigger finger closed on nothing but air.

"The hell?"

No time to guess what happened, he needed to be armed. He dove for the gun as it skittered across the gore-slick floor, but a hairy whip closed on his wrist and yanked him aside.

Forget the gun for now!

Scott pulled the Fairburn-Sykes from his belt and slashed at the coarse band holding him. It parted easily. It was made of hair.

Scott heard a cackle and looked up to see Oobel standing on the sill of the window the bat had broken. His hands grasped his long beard near the base of his chin, and as he jumped to the floor, he brought it back over his shoulder then flung it forward like a bullwhip. Scott yanked his knife away protectively, afraid he would be disarmed again. But Oobel wasn't going for the knife.

The beard shot forward faster than the eye could follow and Scott flinched involuntarily, expecting pain, a sting, or something. Instead, it was Fletcher who screamed as the beard closed around his ankle and yanked him forward. Scott lost his grip on the carrier's strap and it flew off his shoulder. Fletcher hit the ground hard, but luckily bottom first. He was okay, but was being dragged swiftly toward Oobel.

"No!" Scott screamed. Scrambling forward, he caught a strap and yanked back. The strap went taut, and the carrier rose in the air from the tension. Fletcher howled in more than just fear now as his limb was stretched painfully.

Oobel reeled his beard in hand over hand. The floor was slick with blood and ichor and Scott could get no purchase on it. He tumbled and slid as both he and Fletcher were dragged steadily toward Oobel. But he didn't let go. He knew if he let go, Oobel would have Fletcher in an instant and be out the window and gone. He'd seen how fast the creature could move. He'd never catch him.

I won't let go, Fletcher.

The hobs launched an attack to cut the beard and free them, but they were blocked by a wave of creatures about their size, but with horse heads and long protruding fangs. Scott saw Jemmy Mickle-tot go down under the swarm.

Oobel began a chilling chant in time to his hauling. "Little fleshie comes to Oobel. Oobel drags him with his chin. He opens up his mouthie and pops the fleshie in!"

Scott finally got his foot into a crack in the floorboards and brought his progress to a halt five feet away from the window. But Oobel kept dragging his beard in, and now Fletcher was screaming in absolute agony, stretched out till it looked like he would snap in two.

Scott looked back over his shoulder at the hobs and brownies getting slaughtered. He looked at his gun so tantalizingly close. No way he could reach it in time to shoot Oobel before he was out the window and gone with the baby. Then he looked at poor Fletcher, his face red with pain and fear, his leg about to get yanked out of its socket.

"Fuck this," he stated. And let go of the strap.

Oobel fell backward with the abrupt release of pressure, and the carrier, with Fletcher in it, flew toward him.

But not as fast as Scott. He was prepared for the release, and threw himself forward. Before Oobel could regain his feet, Scott was on him. He grabbed the beard first, thinking he could control him with a good grip on the facial hair, but it came off in his hand like a gecko's tail. Oobel almost slipped away then, but Scott managed to grab an ankle, twisting it so Oobel had to flip over on his back. He sat up and pulled.

"Not so fast, you little—"

Realizing he couldn't escape, Oobel shifted his weight and

attacked with inhuman speed. He was suddenly right in Scott's face, raining blows to his head that were surprisingly hard considering they came from a three-foot-tall man. Scott tucked his chin down so the punches landed on his forehead where they were unlikely to do much damage and concentrated on keeping his hold.

If I let go, he'll grab Fletcher and run.

Scott kept hold of the ankle and worked his other forearm up under Oobel's chin, forcing his head up and back. Oobel obviously didn't like this, because he stopped punching Scott and instead chomped down on his wrist.

The pain was tremendous, but Scott thought of a TV show he'd seen where an Australian man had said calmly, as the lizard he was holding extended its neck and bit him in the hand, "If they're biting you, you know you've got 'em."

Now!

Scott let go of the ankle and threw himself backward, and Oobel, his teeth clenched in Scott's arm, came with him. Lying on your back with your opponent on top of you is not normally an auspicious position to be in, but Scott had a plan. And when Oobel opened his mouth and made to leap off Scott's chest, Scott hooked his leg and tumbled him right back on top of him, but face up this time. Then he snaked his forearm across Oobel's neck, cinched it tight with his other arm, and prepared to choke the life out of the evil little bastard in a textbook rear-naked choke.

But suddenly the front door exploded inward and the biggest black bear Scott had ever seen stepped into the already crowded living room.

"Oh shit," Scott said stupidly.

The bear rose up on its hind legs, smashing a lamp that didn't hang very far from the ceiling with its head and giving voice to a roar that shook the floorboards. Spittle sprayed from four-inch long canines, and what little light that shone from Scott's remaining undamaged light fixtures reflected a malevolent red in the bear's beady eyes.

"Shit," said Scott again. He couldn't think of anything else to do.

· · · Eighteen · · ·

Bridie woke to a couple of voices having an argument. A very odd argument.

"Let us feed on sweet virgin flesh and then dip our caps," said one voice.

"I say we dip first, and then feed," said the other.

Bridie opened her eyes. She needn't have bothered; it was pitch black in the Vaults.

"If you say so," said the first voice, "but how shall we prepare the meat?"

"We shall eat it raw!"

"I thought we would perhaps cook this meal?" whined the first voice. "It has been so long since—"

"Raw!" The second voice sniffed haughtily. "It is the only way to prepare a virgin meal."

This is getting downright disturbing, Bridie thought, digging in her purse for the flashlight. *Good thing I conserved my batteries.* She got hold of the light and pulled it out, twisting the top to turn it on. *Let's shed some light on this subject.* The light was near blinding after so long in the pitch darkness, and Bridie squinted, following the beam around the room.

Bridie scrambled back a little, pressing her back against cool stone. "Who's there?" she asked, her voice cracking. *Fuck that!* "How about you show yourself so I can kick your ass?" *That's better.* She grinned ferally.

"Oh," said the first voice, "It wants to see us, Dearg!"

Swinging the flashlight toward the speaker, Bridie saw nothing but old tan bricks and a few empty wine bottles.

"Do you wish to see us, my little morsel?" asked the second voice.

Bridie didn't answer, swinging the flashlight again, trying to pin the speaker in its beam. She saw nothing.

Ghosts!

"Let's show her, Dearg. Won't that be good fun!"

"Aye, I think it will, Darsee."

Feeling a hand on her left wrist, Bridie jerked reflexively away. She made to wrench the top off the flashlight so she wouldn't have to aim it, but something grabbed her right forearm. She could feel the grip, and managed to twist her wrist, pointing the flashlight back at herself, illuminating the trapped limb.

There was nothing there.

For possibly the first time in her life, Bridie panicked. Alone in the dark, attacked by invisible creatures, all her self-defense training went screaming off into the darkness, and she turned to flee after it. Incoherent thoughts ran through her brain.

Haunted! Nothing there. Gotta get out. Get out! Get out!

The panic didn't last long, but it was enough. She was tripped up before she'd gone more than three steps, falling hard to the ground and getting a mouth full of dirt. A weight fell on her back, and another on her right arm. She reached back with her left arm, but couldn't grasp anything. The flashlight was wrenched from her grasp and flew off, the light flickering across the walls. Then her left arm too was pinned to the floor.

The second voice spoke right in her ear. "Careful, dearie. This may sting a bit."

She felt a cold ooze rubbed onto her eyes. She squeezed them shut, but whatever it was found the cracks, leaking past her eyelids to sting her pupils. The weight was suddenly gone from her back, and screaming, she lurched to her feet, swinging wildly. Opening her eyes again, Bridie saw nothing but a bright white light and thought she'd been blinded. But no, it was just her flashlight pointed directly at her face from across the small room.

"Now here's something you don't see every day," the first voice said from behind the light.

The light came off her eyes and swung to her right, where it illuminated a creature maybe four feet in height. It was dressed in rags, and had a vaguely human face, though covered in warts and cysts. Sweeping a red tam-o'-shanter from its head, it executed a grotesque imitation of a courtly bow.

"At yer service, m'lady."

Then the light swung back to the creature holding the flashlight, and he held it up under his chin, shadowing his face from below like a Halloween guide at a haunted house.

"Boo," he said.

If the creatures thought that showing their gruesome visages would shake Bridie, they'd missed their mark. She'd been shot at, stabbed, punched, kicked, and attacked in a variety of ways by numerous individuals and had always come out on top. Even though the things in front of her didn't look human, at least they were visible now. And being visible they could be fought. Maybe killed.

And Bridie didn't mind killing.

"C'mon then," she spat. "Enough foreplay."

The creature holding the flashlight blinked big rheumy eyes once. Then flicked off the light.

Shit, Bridie thought. She heard quick muffled footsteps and something slashed across her right thigh. Reaching down, her hand came back sticky.

Cut, but not bad. They're going to play with me a bit.

She was detached. Adrenaline always made her calm.

There was cackling all around her now and Bridie tried to time where it would be and make a grab. If she could get hold of one, maybe she could break its little spine.

And what were they? A pair of mutant, midget twins, who lived down here? Maybe they'd slipped off a tour like her years ago.

She didn't have time to give it much thought. A gash across her calf sent her to her knees and a blow to the face rocked her back against the wall. The flashlight came on again, showing a cackling face lit from below again.

"Oh, you're right, Dearg, this is good—"

The creature didn't get a chance to finish its sentence as Bridie launched herself toward it, feeling the gashes in her legs tear, the stitches over her ribs pop. She managed to get hold of a limb for a second, but the creature wriggled free immediately. Must have been holding the flashlight in that hand, however, because it flew into the air, landing six feet away, spinning wildly. It lit the room like a strobe, making everything look as if it were in slow motion.

Bridie saw one of her attackers blocking the doorway to her left, a malicious grin plastered to its already hideous face, while the other moved toward her on the right, disproportionately large hands holding the jawbone of some sort of predator before it.

Must be Dearg, she thought inanely. *The other one had the flashlight.*

Before Bridie could react, a third creature stepped into the room. It was smaller even than the other two, but with a gigantic nose and a gray cloak that flowed out behind it. It moved between Bridie and Dearg, and she saw a flash of white in its hand as it passed. Blood erupted from Dearg's throat, the strobing effect making it seem like it just appeared in midair before disappearing. There was a thud as the body hit the ground and then the other of Bridie's attackers uttered the single word, "Martes?" before it, too, collapsed to the ground and gurgled its last.

The flashlight slowed and stopped, illuminating a small patch of wall from just a foot away. It was eerily silent. The flashlight rolled toward her, as if someone or something had pushed it with its foot, and Bridie snatched it up like she was starving and it was made of meat. Twisted the cap off and held it over her head. Weak light filled the room.

"Bridie?" the creature before her said in a wheezing nasal voice.

Bridie was having a hard time convincing herself that this was a mutant midget. Aside from standing on two feet, it didn't look remotely human. More like a three-foot-tall rat. It's huge twitching nose even had rat whiskers on it.

"Bridie," it said again, "are hyou hurt?"

She found her voice. "What . . . er . . . who are you? And how do you know my name?"

The creature smiled. It might have been the least reassuring expression Bridie had ever seen.

"I am Martes." He toed one of the corpses. It didn't respond. "And I was sent to save you from these Redcaps."

Bridie just stood and blinked. Finally, she asked the obvious. "Sent by who?"

"By Lord Douglas. Your brother."

"Douglas? Where is he? Is he all right?" Bridie asked all in a rush. Then she stopped and realized what the strange creature had just said. "Wait a minute. Lord Douglas?"

"Come," Martes said, turning and walking out the door. Bridie followed behind, her mind struggling to make sense of what had just happened.

Those things weren't human, were they? And this . . . Martes. What the hell is he? And where are we going?

Martes stopped in the middle of the most haunted room in the Vaults and pulled a small wooden flute from the folds of his cloak. Putting it to his misshapen lips, he began to play a strange melody, at times sinister, at times airy, seemingly running through every note possible on the little instrument. He capered about as he played, skipping and hopping around the room, kicking up dirt. Bridie watched silently, unsure for once of what to say or do. She'd seen a lot of crazy stuff in her time as a cop—and no shortness of weirdness slinging drinks—but this took the freaking cake.

As Martes played, something began to shimmer in the air between her and the far wall. At first she thought that light was reflecting off the dust he was kicking up. Then she thought her eyes were playing tricks on her after so long in the dark. Then she didn't know what to think, and she just began to accept what her eyes were showing her and damn the consequences to sanity, calm, and reality itself.

The lights flared magnesium bright for a split second and Bridie shut her eyes against the glare. When she opened them again, there was a door in the far wall.

Or rather, she thought as she looked closer, *there's a door right in front of the far wall.*

The door was a single piece of old wood, carved into a circle three feet in diameter. The handle was a deer antler, the hinges bone. And it floated two feet off the ground. Bridie peeked behind it and could clearly see space between it and the wall.

"What the hell is going on?"

In answer, Martes opened the door. Impossibly, there was a dark tunnel stretching off into darkness.

"You'll have to crawl, lass," he said, scrambling up into the doorway.

"Crawl? What?"

"You'll have to crawl." He pointed down the tunnel. "To Lord Douglas. He wants a word."

Bridie stared down the tunnel. The tunnel that shouldn't be there. *Couldn't* be there.

"A word?"

Martes's eyebrows shot up and he blew air through his lips like a horse. "By my bogie's bollucks! Are ye deaf as well as stupid, woman? Get in the bloody tunnel!"

That broke Bridie out of her stupor.

"Screw you, you little monster," she said. "Tell Doug to come out here himself and talk to his sister." She straightened her shoulders. "His big sister."

Chuckling softly, he said, "Just like him, you are. Always have to do things the hard way." He slipped something out of his cloak and tucked it into the end of his flute. "At least you're not as heavy."

"Not as heavy? Why the hell does that matter?"

Martes put the flute to his mouth and placed his fingers over every hole. The note he blew was high and shrill, and Bridie felt a sting in her neck.

"Why you little . . ." she managed to get out before her knees buckled and she collapsed to the ground.

Martes sighed and tucked his flute away. "Because now I'm going to have to carry you all the way there, you big bitch."

Hopping to the ground, he hooked Bridie under her arms and with a grunt and a heave, hauled her up into the tunnel and away.

· · · Aine · · ·

Stillness.

It is a torture. Aine could think of no pain, no privation, no punishment that could match this endless stillness for pure torment.

And she had a surplus of time to think.

Still, she thought. *I am not completely without power.*

In the endless hours afforded her for thought and reflection, she tested the boundaries of her imposed stillness and found they were not as complete as she had first assumed.

For instance I can still think.

Whether this was an oversight on Douglas's part or intentionally planned to make the torture more exquisite, she did not know. Whichever it was, she was not going to waste the opportunity it gave her.

If I can think, I can send.

Douglas thought magic was all in the performance. A song or a sound, perhaps a wave of a hand to send your will into the world and make it real. But sometimes all it took was a notion. A thought drifting into the dream space. An idea that was more than an idea. More than a dream. A single sending, small but strong, that worked on the weavings of the worlds, deep in the underpinnings, where even Douglas's far sight could not see. A place where providence and prophecy were more important than logic, and a queen of Faerie held more sway than all the laws of physics.

Aine made a summons, and the fates would ensure its delivery.

NiNeteeN

The bear roared again and everyone in the house, attackers and defenders alike, froze momentarily. Oobel was the first to recover, and used the distraction to wriggle free of Scott's grip and leap for the windowsill. Scott ignored him and pulled Fletcher close to his chest. The baby seemed none the worse for wear, though he was still screaming his head off. Oobel hopped outside and was gone, leaving his army behind.

"Steward!"

Mundoo.

"Where have you been?" Scott looked at where his gun was, but decided he couldn't get to it before the bear, and it probably wasn't powerful enough to do more than annoy it anyway. Besides, some of Oobel's soldiers—a blue man, a stag-head, and a couple of smallish humanoids—were between him and the gun as well.

"Getting more help," Mundoo answered.

"Well, where is it?" *Do I leap outside with Oobel,* Scott thought, *or stay inside with the bear? Not an easy decision.* But one he'd have to make soon. The bear dropped back onto four paws and took another step inside. "Could use it quick. Real quick."

Oobel's army was closest to the door, and nearest the bear. They backed away cautiously, trying vainly to keep an eye on both the bear and what was left of Scott's army. Scott would have loved to order a counterattack, but he didn't think the half dozen hobs and seven or eight brownies still alive could manage any more than what they were doing right now: dragging themselves battered and bleeding toward him and the baby.

"Mundoo!" he cried. "Where's that help?"

"I do not understand," Mundoo said, and now Scott saw him, stepping through the doorway calmly behind the bear. "It is here." He patted the bear companionably on the flank. "*Netuspus, netap,*" he said in the bear's ear, and shifted into bear form himself. They roared together till Scott thought the roof would cave in, then the giant black bear waded into Oobel's army. With one swipe of his paw he sent three creatures flying to land in bloody, misshapen lumps in the kitchen. The claws of his other paw flashed, and a horse-head went out the window Oobel had escaped through. A ten-foot-long snake with the head of a red fox couldn't get out of the way fast enough, probably due to the knot of dead hobs it had swallowed whole. The grisly meal was revealed when the bear bit the snake in half. A backhanded blow scattered a group of horned humanoids, and the bear roared again, sending a panic through the enemy ranks.

The creatures in Oobel's army were now clawing at each other, trying to escape the bear. They made for the door, the windows; they tried to tear through the walls. But not all of them. A few of the cleverer ones launched themselves over the bear, landing on its back, gripping its fur. Knives clenched in their teeth, they pulled themselves hand over hand toward the bear's head. A hob-like creature, except for the long canines jutting out of his mouth, had made it to the window. But instead of escaping outside, he turned and gripped his knife by the point, preparing to throw.

They'll all be going for its eyes, Scott thought. *It's what I'd do in their position.*

Scott saw now that the battle balanced on a razor's edge. The bear had turned the tide in their favor, but they'd committed their reinforcements, and whatever happened in the next few seconds would decide whether they all lived or died.

And he was sitting on the floor watching.

Still clutching the crying Fletcher to him, Scott struggled to his feet, yelling, "The Steward!" and was gratified to hear an answering cry from the few remaining fey on his side.

"The Steward!" they shouted back, pulling themselves onto bleeding and broken legs and launching themselves toward the bear and his attackers. They had little hope of doing much damage, but they added to the confusion and more of Oobel's army died under the claws of Mundoo's bear.

Leaping bodily between the bear and the knife thrower in the window, Scott spun to protect Fletcher and earned a knife to his spine. But it hadn't completed its rotation and the hilt only bruised him. Before the creature could escape, Scott turned back, reaching out and grabbing the diminutive creature in his right hand. It struggled hard, but Scott was in an adrenaline-fueled rage now, and he threw it at the creatures on the bear's back.

"Boo-yah!" he shouted as he scored a direct hit. Two creatures fell to the ground and were swarmed by brownies. But there were still three creatures left on top of the bear, and a number more on the ground. They were currently just trying to escape, but if the bear went down they could turn and attack in a hurry. Scott went for his gun, kicking his way through friend and foe alike. It was still where it had fallen, none of the creatures on either side daring to touch it. Scott scooped it off the ground and came up firing. No double-taps this time, this was suppression fire, a steady stream of bullets aimed just over the bear's back as Scott strode forward. He would try to pick the attackers off the bear, but they were tucked down low. Miss an inch low, and he'd hit the bear.

And bears tend not to react well when they get shot, he thought.

Paint and plaster flew as bullets buried themselves in the wall behind the bear. Scott's ears ached from the noise; his nostrils burned from the acrid gunpowder. But he kept firing. Two of the creatures, panicked by the noise and the flash and the steady stream of bullets overhead, slid off the far side of the bear and joined their fellows in trying to escape. The third continued to climb grimly forward. Lifting itself slightly to get a good downward thrust at the bear's right eye, it finally gave Scott a clear shot. He fired the last bullet in the magazine and caught the little bastard right in the throat. But before the bullet plucked the creature out of the bear's fur, it plunged a curved bone dagger deep into the bear's eye.

"Oh, shit," Scott said, ejecting the spent clip.

The bear went mad with pain, and Scott saw now that its earlier attack had been positively restrained. Now everything in its path was a target as it struck out indiscriminately in shock and rage. Hobs and brownies went down under its claws as well as Oobel's creatures. Scott began to realize how small his house was and how close he was to a gigantic wounded animal.

"Mundoo!" he yelled. "Do something!"

But Mundoo was back in human form by the front door, watching impassively as the creature he'd brought into the house ran amok.

Scott grabbed his last clip from his pocket, hooked Fletcher's carrier awkwardly over his left elbow, and jammed the clip into the stock. The remains of Oobel's army, three horse-heads and an unidentifiable hairy thing with a moss cap somehow still perched on what Scott guessed was its head, made a halfhearted attempt to rally, but the bear swung around and broke two of the horse-head's spines with a backhanded blow and disemboweled the hairy thing with a swipe from his other paw. The last horse-head, after a quick glance at the pale intestines spilling from his comrades, decided it was time to call it a night and jumped for the window.

Scott shot it twice in the back, then turned his attention to the bear. Half-blind, it raked its head from side to side, looking for a target for its anger. Its gaze stopped on Scott and it raised up on its hind legs, huffing and growling. Scott tried to aim at the bear's other eye but it was an impossible shot from the angle. Switching his aim to center mass, he wondered if a 9mm bullet could even pierce the bear's skin.

After all the smoke and noise of battle, it was suddenly eerily quiet. Fletcher was whimpering softly, as if he didn't have the energy left to cry. A last shard of glass from a broken window tinkled to the ground. The bear's breathing was a deep rumble as it took a shuffling step forward.

Scott took a step backward. He didn't fire, hoping the bear would drop back to all fours before it attacked and give him an opportunity to empty his clip into its other eye. At least that was a vulnerable spot. Maybe he could slip by if it was fully blind.

As if reading his mind, the bear snorted derisively and stepped forward again. Scott moved back in response and spared a glance at Fletcher's beet-red face peeking out of the carrier.

"It's okay, little guy," Scott lied.

He didn't have any visions of anything bad happening, but that was no longer comforting. He was convinced his experience with Mercy had done something to his vision; he might be about to die. He'd only know it when it happened, just like anybody else.

Any other time, he thought, *and I'd be ecstatic about that.*

A step to the rear, and another, the bear forcing him back slowly, seemingly content to draw out the death of this last antagonist. Scott kept waiting for a shot that looked promising. None did. When he finally came up against the wall, he realized he had to take whatever shot was available, because in another second the bear was going to be on top of him. He pointed the pistol at where he thought the bear's heart might be, exhaled slowly, squeezed the trigger . . .

"*Moingaminge!*" Mundoo barked. "*Mattath!*"

The bear froze. So did Scott, the trigger a quarter depressed, the hammer a hair's breadth away from falling on the firing pin and starting the explosive chain reaction that would send a bullet hurtling toward the bear.

"*Mattath,*" Mundoo said again and the bear sat down suddenly and began pawing at the dagger stuck in its eye. Scott trained his pistol on the other eye, finger still holding the trigger a hair's breadth from firing.

"Mundoo?" he said.

The spirit finally answered. "It is over, Steward."

His pistol still pointing at the bear, Scott looked around the house. Bodies were everywhere, none of them moving.

"Jake? Jemmy? Anyone alive?" Glancing at Mundoo, he saw that the spirit was now flanked by two large wolves, their yellow eyes staring at him unblinking. "More help?"

Mundoo said nothing. Scott looked at the bear. It had worked the dagger loose somehow and was knocking it back and forth between its paws, whimpering occasionally as blood and fluid leaked from its ruined eye. Exhaustion washed over him, and Scott wanted more than ever to sit down, lay down, pass out. But there was more to do. He needed to check the casualties, see if anyone was still living. He also needed to secure the house. Oobel could still be hanging around, and Scott needed to be ready if another attack was launched. Flicking the safety on, he tucked the gun in his pants and pushed forward.

"What are you doing?" Mundoo asked.

Scott knelt down by the nearest body—a hob. He didn't need to check it for signs of life; its head was gone. Scott moved on.

"Checking the butcher's bill," he said.

"You must go."

Two more bodies, a brownie and a horned creature obscenely entwined in death. "Not yet. It's not safe. Besides, there might be someone left alive here."

"There are none. And if there were, they would not stay that way for long. Take the child and go."

Something in the spirit's tone made Scott look up from his grim task. Mundoo still stood in the doorway, the wolves now joined by a pair of crows that perched on his shoulders. Scott stood, and his hand crept toward the pistol tucked in his belt.

"Why?"

Mundoo frowned, making his long face look like an Easter Island head. "Because I am not a murderer of children. But he is an invader like the rest. And he must go."

Scott had a chilling realization then and drew his gun; but he didn't know where to point it. He didn't think it would hurt Mundoo or the bear. Shooting the crow might make him feel a little better, but probably wouldn't accomplish anything more.

"You wanted this, didn't you?" he asked, waving the gun to encompass the carnage of his living room. "You didn't care who won as long there was plenty of death on both sides."

"Not true," Mundoo replied. "I preferred that you won, as it would pain me to see an infant slaughtered, no matter its provenance." He smiled. "Why else would I bring assistance?"

Scott snorted. "You could have brought it at any time. But you waited till the thing was almost decided."

Mundoo's lips straightened into an expression of long-simmering anger.

"There was a balance once, Steward," he said coldly. "I was one god and many. Animal spirits roamed the woodlands unfettered, and if my people had to take one, they spoke the right prayers. But then you came, grasping and grating, with your guns and your steel." He paused to point at the dead bodies of the hobs and brownies. "With your weak *manitou* that comforted you and conspired against you in equal measure." Reaching the pointing finger now up to his shoulder, Mundoo allowed one of the crows to step onto it. Held it before his face, talking to it as much as to Scott. "My people took pity on you. You were small and weak and ill-prepared for this land. They were tall and strong and lithe. If it came to battle, they would not be defeated. But you brought with you something more, something even I could not help with." He looked past the crow and fully at Scott. "Plague. Disease. Sickness without end. My people were wiped out without even a chance at defending themselves, my woods invaded by 'settlers' and their spirits, my time as god of this land at an end."

"And this will make it right?" Scott asked.

"No. But for a time the woods will be mine once more." Mundoo paused a moment, considering something. "I think you are correct, Steward."

Scott raised his eyebrows. "About what?"

"It is not safe. You cannot go."

"Um . . . okay. I'm going to secure the perimeter then."

"You misunderstand me." Mundoo face was stone. "You cannot ever go. And I will have no Coat-man stay."

"What about Fletcher?"

"The child will be safe. I will have the animals raise him. I may be able to turn him into a weapon against his own. That would be fitting."

Scott nodded and raised his gun. *A crow first, I guess. Take out his air capability.* "Better teach me some of those prayers then, because I'm about kill a bunch of your precious animals."

Mundoo gave him a nod. Not in agreement, Scott thought, but the nod of one warrior to another on the eve of battle. The battle long denied his people. Then Mundoo raised his arms and the crows took flight. The wolves bared their teeth and the half-blind bear lumbered back to his feet.

Scott steadied his gun arm and prepared to face down a god.

But before he could, his cell phone rang.

• • • TWENTY • • •

"Bridie?"

Bridie couldn't believe what she was hearing.

"Douglas?" she whispered.

"Yes. It's me, sis."

Bridie opened her eyes. She was on her back in a canopied bed in a stone room decked out like a medieval castle. There was stout wooden furniture scattered about and lit torches in wall sconces.

What is this, she thought, *a themed motel room?*

Her purse was on a bedside table next to a candelabrum with candles guttering and emitting a scent that suggested they weren't bought at Bed, Bath, and Beyond. A tapestry on the far wall depicted a hunting scene in three panels. The first panel showed oddly proportioned beaters pounding through thick forest with drums, bells, and horns; the second, lords and ladies aboard tall horses at full gallop. In the third, the quarry of the hunt was finally shown: a unicorn, its sides pierced with dozens of arrows. Whoever had woven the tapestry had caught the scene in exquisite detail; Bridie could almost hear the dying beast's screams.

Tearing her eyes away from the tapestry, Bridie looked at her brother Douglas, who leaned over her. He was bigger than she remembered, and dressed in an outlandish costume of black cape, tunic, and breeches, all trimmed in white fur and silver stitching.

Like a punk Prince Charming.

There was also something wrong with his eyes. But it was definitely him.

Reaching out, she gently touched his face. She'd felt like she'd been chasing a ghost these last few days and now here he was, unexpectedly hale and healthy. She traded the gentle touch for a sharp slap on the cheek.

"Hey!" Douglas said.

Bridie sat up and threw the covers back. She was still wearing the muddy, bloody clothes she'd had on in the Vaults. But she felt no pain from her recent stitches and there was no sign of the injuries the two creatures in the vault had inflicted on her.

"Where have you been?" she said rather more loudly than she'd intended. "And what the fuck happened to Grandma McLaren?"

"I can explain everything," Douglas said. "No need to hit me."

"And why not?" Bridie swung her legs over the side of the bed and stood up. Douglas towered over her, but still cringed away as she waved a finger in his face. "You goddamn fuckup! You finally did it, didn't you? You finally screwed up bad enough that someone ended up dead." She remembered the dead priest and the missing finger up on Calton Hill. "Two people, maybe."

Damn it, she thought. *This isn't how I wanted this to go.*

"Listen, Bridie—" Douglas began.

"No, you listen!" *But I'm just so damned pissed!* But her voice softened. "Douglas—"

But Douglas wasn't listening to her. He was *singing*. Something wordless but tuneful. Bridie couldn't place it, but it sure sounded familiar.

What the hell? She opened her mouth to castigate Douglas

some more, but found she couldn't speak. She worked her jaw like a fresh-caught walleye. Nothing came out.

What's happening?

Looking at Douglas, she saw he had stopped singing and was staring at her curiously.

"Maybe now you'll listen." He tilted his head to one side. "You know you never listened to me, Bridie. Not even when we were kids. Once I was old enough to not be your toy anymore, you pretended I didn't exist."

That's not true!

"Oh yes, it is. You can lie to yourself, Bridie, but you can't lie to me." Douglas smiled, a cold grin that left his eyes alone. "Not anymore."

It took Bridie a second to realize that she hadn't spoken. Douglas had responded to her thoughts only.

Is he reading my thoughts?

"Not exactly," Douglas said. "But I know your true name now; I can make a pretty good guess at what you're thinking."

Well, how about this then, she thought and launched herself at him. It should have been an easy takedown. Douglas was standing way too straight, his weight distributed all wrong. Bridie came in low to hook his leg and send him to the ground.

Except he wasn't there when she arrived.

Since when does Douglas move that fast?

"Come on, Bridie." He was behind her now, with the bed between them. "Even if I didn't know your true name, anyone who knew you even a little could guess you'd do *that!*"

I didn't even see him move.

Bridie thought about charging him again, but the bed was in the way now and she didn't want to give him the satisfaction of evading her again. Instead, she just stood her ground and stared at him.

Let me speak, she thought. At him.

Douglas paused for a moment. "You promise not to yell at me again?" he said, sounding a bit petulant.

Fuck you.

Douglas laughed. "I guess that'll do." Then he whistled a short, sharp note, and Bridie could speak again.

"What the hell was that?"

"That," Douglas said, "is a bit difficult to explain."

"Try me."

Douglas tilted his head to one side. "I'll show you. Come."

Douglas came around the bed—a bit cautiously, Bridie thought—and pushed open a thickly carved wooden door to reveal a dim stone hallway. He marched out the door, not bothering to see if Bridie followed.

"Of course you'll follow, Bridie," he called. "You always have to know what's going on. Why things happen the way they do." His voice was growing weaker as he moved away down the hall. "I suppose that's why you became a cop. You're a born investigator."

Bridie grabbed up her purse and stepped into the hall. *He's right. I've come this far; I'm certainly not going to stop now.*

The hall stretched off to the right as far as Bridie could see, dotted with more torches every twenty feet or so. Douglas walked briskly away. To her left was a leaded glass window. It was night out. She could tell nothing else through the old glass.

"Hold up, brother!" she yelled to Douglas's receding back. He turned and smiled, tapping his foot impatiently as she hurried to catch up. "Okay," she said as she got close, "I'll let you show me what you have to show me. But it better be real convincing, or I'm going to haul your ass to the local cops quicker than you can say, 'Bruno, can't you just hold me tonight?' to your new cellmate.' "

Chuckling, he said, "I think you would have some trouble hauling me anywhere, Bridie. Especially to the police."

"Why's that? Whatever your midget friend shot me with can't last forever, Douglas. I'll stop hallucinating eventually. And when I do, you can be certain of an almighty ass-whooping if you don't do what I say."

Douglas looked down at her and raised an eyebrow. "You could see Martes? As soon as he arrived?"

Odd question. "Yeah, I could see the little bastard. And the escapees from the freak show that attacked me, too."

But they were invisible at the beginning, she thought. *Weren't they?*

She shook that thought off. It was impossible. *But so is mind control, and Douglas beating me in a fight and . . .*

She shook those thoughts off, too.

Has to be whatever Martes shot me with. Has to be.

They passed three more sets of torches before Douglas spoke again. "Interesting," was all he said.

"Anyway," Bridie said, trying to make her tone light. *Like we're back home, sitting around the kitchen table with Mom and Dad and Scott.* But tones had never been light then. Douglas had always been a strange and troubled child, and Bridie hadn't been very sympathetic. She didn't understand him or how his world worked. He always made choices that confused her, as if he just couldn't tell the difference between the rights and wrongs that she saw so clearly. "Anyway, why can't I take you in? Where are we?"

Douglas smiled at that and threw his arms wide. "Why, we're in Castle Douglas! Isn't it grand?"

"Actually it's pretty damn gloomy." She thought back to the family trip they'd taken to Scotland so many years ago, and the history lessons her folks had insisted on giving at every opportunity. "And isn't Castle Douglas a town? Not an actual castle? Certainly not one that's still standing."

Douglas shrugged. "If I say it's Castle Douglas, then it's Castle Douglas. That's the way things work around here. Now, no more questions. We're almost there."

They walked on in silence. Bridie wasn't ensorcelled this time; there was just no reason to ask questions that wouldn't get answered.

After two more minutes of interminable hallway, they finally reached an ornately carved and brightly painted double doorway. A family crest of some kind, featuring a white stag that was impaled with . . .

"Is that a guitar sticking out of its chest?" Bridie asked.

"Not just any guitar, but a Lowden F35 cutaway. I was very particular when I had it made." Douglas held a finger to his lips. "Now, shush." Then he knocked on the door and opened one a crack. Peeking his head inside, he called, "Honey, you decent? We've got company."

When he pushed open the doors, Bridie found herself looking into a fairy-tale throne room. A high, vaulted ceiling soared over a meticulously polished marble floor, with windows edged in molded plaster that stretched the full length of the wall. Bright glowing orbs floated high overhead, almost blinding Bridie after having been so long in torchlight or darkness. A single throne sat on a dais far across the shiny floor. It was high-backed and thin, and intricately carved out of what looked like silver.

It was empty.

Beside it was a simple wooden chair that held the most beautiful woman Bridie had ever seen. She sat straight and regal. Black, almost iridescent hair curled down around her shoulders and ice-blue eyes were visible even from across the large room, and even though she didn't move or shift position, Bridie felt as though she was staring directly into her.

Now that, she thought, *is my type.*

If Bridie didn't know any better, she'd think she was in love.

"Who . . . who is that?" she breathed.

The woman in the chair didn't move, but Bridie could feel her looking at her, through her, into her. She knew that this woman—whom she hadn't even spoken a word to—already knew her better than any of the ones who had come before. Better than the few boys she'd failed with in junior high, better than the teenage girls she'd exchanged clumsy grope sessions with in secret in high school, better even than the women she'd been with after the academy. Even better than her ex, Diane, who'd shared an apartment and a bed with her for nearly two years.

The woman in the chair knew her better than all of them already. And loved her. Bridie was certain.

"That," Douglas replied, "is Aine. Formerly queen of the Daoine Sidhe and now consort to the current Lord of the Realm." He winked at Bridie. "Me." He strode into the room like he actually *was* the Lord of the Realm, white-edged cloak flowing behind him, big black boots sending footsteps echoing off the arched ceiling. With long strides, he covered the distance to the dais quickly and stepped up. Swung his cloak to one side, sat on the silver throne. "And she is also the creature that ordered the murder of our grandmother."

Bridie gasped. *No,* she thought.

"I'm afraid so, Bridie." Douglas sighed heavily and looked down at Aine. "She's as treacherous as she is beautiful. A real black widow."

"No," Bridie said aloud this time. Her voice didn't sound right to her.

"Bridie, come here." Bridie didn't move. "Come here," Douglas said again.

Tearing her gaze away from Aine, Bridie shuffled up to the dais.

"Look at her, sis. She isn't human." He reached down and pulled the hair back from Aine's face, revealing long and pointed ears.

Bridie stared at the ears for a second then looked Aine full in the face. She hadn't moved or changed expression the entire time. She still looked angry; she still stared at the doorway.

"Why doesn't she move?" Bridie asked.

"You were right," Douglas said, ignoring her question. "I screwed up and got into trouble, and people ended up dead. But I don't know if I could have avoided it. Look around, Bridie," he said, waving his hand at the room, the floating orbs. "You think anything we used to know applies here?" He pointed down at Aine. "She called me to her. Made me her pawn. All to save her own miserable skin. And when she was done with me, she tried to kill me and everyone near me." He leaned over and grinned in Bridie's face. "But you failed with me, didn't you, dear?"

Even without moving, Aine seemed to suddenly glow with hate. Her hatred was nearly a physical thing, and Bridie took an involuntary step backward before it. The lights dimmed and the air grew cold, making Bridie shiver.

Then Douglas hummed a few notes of a jaunty tune and the temperature and light were instantly back to normal. "Stop acting catty in front of our guest," he quipped. "She's family." He turned to Bridie. "She's still sore over this whole 'keep her captive for all eternity thing' I have going." He shrugged. "Touchy bitch."

Bridie looked back and forth between the two: Aine, motionless as stone, yet still lovely enough to make Bridie's heart stop; and Douglas, her brother—though somehow more than him. *Or maybe less. Manic as all get out, at any rate.* She wondered if he was still using, and whether that was good or bad in this place.

Shaking her head, she said, "Tell me what the fuck is going on, Douglas."

Douglas stood and indicated that Bridie should take the throne. She stepped up on the dais and sat. The silver seat was cold but not uncomfortable, somehow conforming to her body despite its hardness.

"Comfy?" Douglas asked.

"Does it matter?"

"I suppose not. Let's have a drink," he said and clapped his hands. A door that had been cleverly hidden in the patterned walls opened, and a girl entered. She was raven-haired and blue-eyed like Aine, but lacked whatever it was that Aine had that made Bridie yearn to be with her. She was carrying a tray laden with a decanter of dark red wine and two long-stemmed glasses. Kneeling low before Douglas, she presented him the drinks.

"Pour," he said coldly.

As the girl obeyed, Bridie looked at Douglas and raised an eyebrow.

He shrugged. "Lord of the Realm," he said. Taking the now full glasses off the tray, Douglas said, "Leave us," and handed one to Bridie.

She sniffed at it. Eyed it critically. "I'm more of a beer drinker, Douglas."

"Live a little, sis. I'm sure you'll like it."

Bridie shrugged and tipped the glass back. She did like it. More than like it. It tasted of all the fruit she had eaten as a child. Of the juices dripping from her tiny chin, of the summer sun shining down on her as she chewed, of the love her mother and father beamed at her, their only daughter.

"Jesus," she gasped, pulling the wineglass away from her lips and staring at it. "What is that?"

"That," Douglas said, "is one of the few perks of this hellish existence I've set myself."

"Serving girls, a castle, fancy wine." Bridie sneered. "Real hellish."

Douglas smiled. Shrugged. "It's not all that it seems."

"Tell me then. Start at the beginning."

Sipping his wine, Douglas was silent for a moment. He sat down on the edge of the dais, his back to Bridie, long legs stretched out in front of him. Despite his "Lord of the Realm" getup, Bridie noticed that he was still wearing the big black combat boots he'd always favored.

"I was clean," he said and looked back over his shoulder at Bridie, waiting for her snort of disbelief. She'd heard the same thing a thousand times before—not just from him, but from all the junkies she'd busted back to rehab for the sixth or seventh time. When she said nothing, he faced away and went on. "That's why I went to Scotland. Everyone back home knew me as a junkie. Grandma McClaren just knew me as—" His voice choked up when he said her name. Bridie watched as he clenched and unclenched his fists before continuing. "Anyway, I was clean. But Aine here—" Douglas suddenly jumped to his feet and began pacing back and forth on the dais.

"Aine?" Bridie prompted.

"Let me tell you about Aine," Douglas said. "She once told me, 'My kind have always known the manner of our passing.'" He stopped, facing Bridie. "You know what that means?"

Bridie thought for a second. "She could see her own death?"

"Yep. And was powerless to stop it." He began pacing again. "Something about how prophecies work. Any steps you take to avoid your fate merely bring it about in the end. That's where I came in. I'm a Namer."

"What's a Namer?"

"I know things' true names. Or I can discover them. And

knowing them, I can change them. Change their true name, and you change their true nature." Bridie looked about to say something, but Douglas waved her off. "It's not important. What really matters is Aine. She couldn't stop her death, so she brought me over, and tricked me into bringing her back to life. Then she killed Grandma McClaren, and tried to kill me."

"Why?"

"I knew her true name. I had ultimate power over her. She needed to kill me before I learned how to use it."

Bridie looked down at Aine seated below her. "Looks like you learned."

Douglas didn't sound triumphant when he said, "Yes, I learned. And I keep her here instead of killing her, so that she will never be able to plan another resurrection. She doesn't see her own passing because I will never let her die." He stopped his pacing in front of Aine's chair. "And I will never let her go."

Bridie stared at Douglas, then jumped off the throne. "This is crazy, Douglas. None of it makes any sense."

"Of course not!" Douglas barked a laugh. "Don't you know where you are, Bridie?" Moving faster than she could follow, Douglas was suddenly at her side. He grabbed her arm and dragged her to one of the giant windows. "Look!"

She did. It was dark outside. Nothing to see.

Letting go of her arm, Douglas stepped back. Bridie turned to see him lift his arms, open his mouth wide, and let forth a note so low and loud, that she felt her organs rumble. She had no idea how he was making it. It was inhuman, the sound of a freight train or a dinosaur's footsteps or maybe the earth's plates shifting, a note huge and round that shook the walls and blew Bridie's hair away from her face. Then impossibly, Douglas added a high shrieking note, like a violin wailing on its highest string. Bridie leapt back around when she heard the window behind her shattering with a ringing tone of its own.

Out the broken window, the sun came up, creaking over the horizon unnaturally fast, as if pulled up by something.

Or someone.

Bridie looked once more at Douglas. There were beads of sweat on his forehead, and the veins in his neck were bulging with effort. The unholy noise finally stopped as he shut his mouth, bending over with his hands on his knees like an exhausted athlete. He waved Bridie's curious look away.

"Outside," he gasped. "Look outside."

Bridie did, stepping up to the window to get a better view. The sun was rising over a pastoral scene. Low green hills rolled into the distance, dotted with farmsteads and dirt tracks. A gray stone tower house poked over the horizon. Off to the left, a forest of dark twisted trees pressed in against a great stone wall that surrounded Castle Douglas. Far below in a wide courtyard, grooms tended horses, gardeners weeded a vegetable patch, and a group of ragged children played a rough game of tag.

"What do you see?" Douglas was right behind her now, whispering hoarsely into her ear.

"You're living in some sort of a medieval fair?"

"Look again."

Bridie did, and began to notice some strange things. None of the people in the courtyard looked quite right. Their proportions were off somehow. The horses seemed strange, too.

Is that one missing its skin? Bridie shuddered.

And unless her sense of distance was really screwy, the tower house in the distance was nearly a mile tall.

Then one of the children playing tag sprouted wings and took to the air, and Bridie jumped backward.

"Jesus!" she yelped as she bumped into Douglas.

He steadied her with hands on her shoulders. "You're in Faerie, Sis. Nothing you know or think you know has any bearing here."

Bridie said nothing, just watched as the child circled the others, flapping and laughing. *Things had been strange enough,* she thought, *but this takes the fucking cake.* "All right, Douglas. What the—"

"Go home, Bridie," Douglas said. "There's nothing for you to do here. I'm safe and Grandma McLaren's killer has been brought to justice."

Bridie finally looked away from the flying child and turned to Douglas. "But how—"

Douglas interrupted again. "Go home." He clapped his hands. "Take her back," he said. "And get someone up here to fix the window. I must rest."

And with that he turned and marched out of the throne room.

Bridie made to follow but found her way blocked by three feet of ugly. Martes.

Nose twitching, he said, "Sorry, luv. Boss says it's time for ye to go."

"But—"

"I'd hate to have to carry you again. You're fat as a house."

Bridie opened her mouth to spout something indignant, but closed it immediately. Decided it was beneath her to argue with this *thing.*

Do I need to stay, anyway? she thought. *I've been given answers to Grandma McLaren's death.* But she couldn't believe them. *Aine couldn't have killed Grandma McLaren.* It didn't fit with her feelings about the still woman.

Bridie nodded to Martes, then followed him out yet another hidden door.

But how can I trust those feelings? In a place like this, where magic seems to be more than possible, it seems the norm. And how can I believe Douglas's explanation? It fits the facts—what little of them I know—but something's wrong with him. Aside from the whole magic Lord of the Realm stuff. He just doesn't seem right.

The door led to a stone spiral staircase, worn with centuries of use. They went down, Martes hopping to each new step like a demented slinky. Bridie thought about pushing him down, but decided it wouldn't serve any purpose. Questioning him might be better.

"So," she said conversationally, "What exactly are you?"

"I was once a bogie," Martes replied. "But Lord Douglas 'improved' me."

"Improved you? You don't sound like you believe that."

Martes glanced once over his shoulder. "Ah, but I must. I have no other choice. I am Lord Douglas's sworn man. I am to protect him and his. At all costs."

Keep him talking. "That challenging work?"

The stairway ended and they pushed through another of the castle's large wooden doors and into the courtyard Bridie had seen from the window. The children paused in their game to stare at Bridie as she passed. She returned their looks and noted that up close they didn't look human at all. Besides the wings, their ears were pointed, their skin was an odd hue, and their eyes sparkled tourmaline hues of purple and green.

"Reasonably, yes." It took Bridie a moment to realize Martes was answering her question. "Your brother likes to put himself in rare and dangerous situations."

"That doesn't sound like the Douglas I knew." And it didn't. "He was always one to run from trouble rather than face up to it."

"Oh," Martes said, chortling, "he's nothing like the Douglas you knew. He is Lord Douglas now. All-powerful in this land, and not to be trifled with in yours. You would call him mean-spirited or perhaps even evil. And he cares only for his self-set geas to punish Aine from now till the end of time for his kinswoman's murder."

They crossed the courtyard, making for an arched gate with a thick wooden portcullis that stood open. *It smelled like a castle should, anyway,* Bridie thought. *Horse shit and hay.*

"If he is so evil, why do you stay with him?"

Martes stopped and turned to stare up at Bridie. "What do I care what your kind calls evil?" Shrugging, he began walking again. "Besides, I am his sworn man. I must protect him and his."

"And that includes me," Bridie stated.

"And all his other relatives."

Bridie thought of the beautiful Aine, motionless in her small chair. "But not his wife."

They passed through the portcullis and onto a wide track that wended its way through waist-high flowering grasses. What looked like hummingbirds whizzed from stalk to stalk, or hovered indecisively. When one flew close, Bridie saw that it was actually a tiny winged humanoid with an angry expression and a hangnail-sized knife in its hand. Buzzing briefly at Bridie's face, it backed off quickly when Martes growled at it.

How come I'm not surprised that they're not hummingbirds?

"Aine isn't his wife," Martes said. "Or really his consort. Though they have had a son together."

"A son? What?" Bridie barked. "I'm an aunt?"

Martes shook his head, though not, it seemed, in denial. "I have said too much. It is not my place to speak of what Lord Douglas deemed unfit to pass on." He stopped abruptly. "And this will take too damn long walking. Up horse and hattock!"

"Up horse and wha—?" Much to her dismay, Bridie let out a

girlish squeal of terror as invisible hands gripped her and lifted her into the air. She was six feet off the ground. And moving forward fast. *Fast.* "Martes? What the hell?"

Martes was off the ground as well, leaning back slightly and chuckling. "Relax and enjoy the ride, luv. You'll be back home soon."

"I won't relax *or* enjoy, you little shit," she huffed. But she couldn't do anything else, either, so she just frowned at Martes's back and watched the ground stream by below her.

BRIDIE HAD NO idea how long they flew or how much distance they covered. *Flying always does mess with my sense of time,* she thought and giggled nervously.

They passed over wide rivers and rolling hills and fields of wheats and grasses that were every color but green. They floated around a dark forest of giant trees that Bridie swore moved every time she looked away, and skirted white-capped mountains with peaks hidden by dragon-shaped clouds that were frighteningly realistic. They aimed for the mile-high tower house she had seen from the throne room window but never seemed to get any closer to it, then turned toward a distant hilltop fort and passed by it an instant later. The sun was beginning to set when they finally came to the sandy banks of a wide red river. The invisible hands released them: Martes gently, Bridie abruptly.

"Oof," she said and tried to lessen the impact by shoulder rolling. She came to a stop on her knees by the water's edge. Or . . .

"What is that?" she said, looking at the thick, red, viscous flow. "It looks like—"

"Blood," Martes said. "Or at least it is to you. And don't ask me to fly you over it. Your kind need something to delineate our two worlds, as if they were somehow different, not just reflections of the same truth."

"And what truth is that?"

Martes nose twitched as he scratched it idly. "If I knew that, I'd be a god, not a bogie. Now in you go."

Bridie reached out a finger tentatively and touched the river. It was warm and sticky. *Definitely blood.*

"Disgusting." She shuddered and made a face. "I have to wade through that?"

Martes grinned. "Only if you want to leave, luv."

"Oh, I think I've had enough of this place." Standing, she thought, *Come on, Bridie. You're Springfield PD. Policewoman in the fifteenth most crime-ridden town in America with only 100,000 citizens to its name. You saw this much blood on an average Saturday night back when you walked a beat.* She took a step forward, immersing her sneaker in ninety-eight-degree fluid.

"Ick."

Another step, then another, and she was ankle-deep in the Big Bloody. Knees, thighs, waist, and she began to worry that she would have to swim for it. But after a minute of walking it didn't appear to be getting any deeper and she strode forward more confidently, holding her purse over her head to keep it dry. Martes "up horse and hattocked" and floated next to her.

"Never understood why you people needed this. Of course, I don't understand a lot of your needs."

"Like what?" Bridie didn't really care if Martes understood a damn thing about humans, but making conversation was the only thing she could think of to get her mind off the task at hand.

"For instance," Martes began, but before he could finish, Bridie's cell phone gave a muffled beep from inside her purse, indicating she had a message. "Well, cell phones for one. There's no one I want to talk so much that I would carry around the means for them to reach me anytime anywhere."

Bridie ignored him and dug in her purse, pulling out her

phone and flipping it open. The message icon was lit, and a pair of coverage bars shone proudly.

"I get coverage? Here?"

"Nice plan," Martes commented. "You're halfway across the river and mostly in your world now."

Bridie checked who the message was from. Hamilton. *Probably trying to triangulate my signal and get my location.* Giving a short laugh, she thought, *Good luck with that.* Then she stared at the phone blankly for another few seconds, before saying, "I'm going to call my brother. Tell him Douglas is all right. Well, alive anyway."

Martes shrugged in midair. Bridie dialed Scott, while still wading toward the far shore.

"Hello?" Scott sounded strange. *Well, that's nothing new.* What *was* new was the sound in the background.

"Is that a baby crying?" Bridie asked by way of hello.

"Yeah," Scott said. "Got left on my doorstep."

"What?"

"Can't talk now, Bridie." There was a sharp crack—*a gunshot?*—and the connection ended.

Bridie stood waist-deep in blood and stared at the phone.

"That was odd."

"If I cared," Martes drawled, "I suppose I would ask what you meant by that. But Douglas calls me back already. Cross quickly and follow the center path. You will be back in your world before you know it."

Bridie went on as if he hadn't spoken. "He said he had a baby dropped on his doorstep." Then she blinked as Martes gasped and dropped from the air. "What are you doing?"

He came up sputtering and spitting out blood. "That idiot troll. You must go to your brother quickly."

"What?"

"I don't have time to explain. I know what that baby is. And if I know it, Douglas will know it soon. He calls me back to him, and I cannot resist."

"I don't understand," Bridie said.

Martes got himself airborne again. "No, I suppose you wouldn't. Your brother is in danger. Get to him as swiftly as possible."

"Douglas?" Bridie frowned. "Isn't he 'Lord of the Realm'?"

"Not that brother. The one you just talked to. The one who is caring for Douglas's son."

"What?"

"The son Douglas wants to kill."

"Why would Douglas—"

"No time," Martes said. "You must go. Now. Take your brother and the child far away."

Bridie thought for just a second. "This path. It takes me back to where you found me?" Martes nodded. His nose was twitching furiously now, and he kept looking over his shoulder. "My brother's house is a long way from there. Could take me days to get to him."

Martes hesitated, then wrestled a ring off his finger. Tossed it to Bridie, who caught it easily. It was thick and heavy, despite being designed for such small fingers and made of light polished bone instead of metal. Bridie recognized the dying stag motif from the throne-room door intricately carved into the face, a tiny red gem serving as the bloody wound.

"That is my signet," Martes said. "It should get you safe passage."

"Safe passage where?"

"Follow the river west. Skirt the dark forest. No, wait. Go through it." Martes was still facing Bridie but was beginning to drift away. "Time flows differently in Faerie," he said. "But you will still need to hurry if you are to get to your brother before Lord Douglas. Take days in your land and you will surely be too late."

Bridie slipped the ring into her shirt pocket. It was too small for even her pinkie. "How about if I just follow you back to Douglas and kick his skinny ass?"

Martes cackled. "Then you would just add your body to the growing pile. He cannot be defeated here." He was yards away now and picking up speed. "On the far side of the forest, on the banks of the river of blood, you will find a small hut. The creature there can get you to the proper gate."

"I show them your ring and they'll take me?" Bridie called.

"Perhaps," Martes yelled back. "Accept no gifts and trade only for fair value. You will not be lied to. Neither will you be told the truth. And do not step back into the river! There's no telling where or when you'll emerge if you do." Martes looked over his shoulder, back the way they'd come. Back to Castle Douglas. "Farewell, Lady Stewart. Lord Douglas calls me and I can do naught but obey." He put on a burst of speed and was soon out of sight.

Bridie whipped out her cell phone and dialed Scott again. She got voice mail.

"Scotty-dog. If you get this message, take the baby and run." *He needs more than that.* "Get in the car and head for the turnpike. Keep driving west. Stop only for gas. I'll call you when I get home and explain everything. I love you."

She hung up the phone. Put it back in her purse. Thought about calling someone else. But there wasn't anyone else to call. She'd only ever had poor, messed-up Scotty and perennial fuckup Douglas. Her family. She was too dangerous for anyone else. She'd known that since the night she'd been shot. Since she'd killed. She'd made herself a loner. And she'd never been more alone than now.

Bridie shook herself. "No time for fucking whining," she muttered. Fingering Martes's ring in her pocket, she stared ahead toward the path that would take her to Scotland. Then she turned and waded back toward the shores of Faerie.

· · · Aine · · ·

Douglas paced around the throne room, passing in and out of Aine's vision. He stomped and spewed, spittle spraying from his lips as he railed over his missing son, the treacherous Martes, the difficult visit from his sister.

He does go on, she thought. *Could I but speak, I would tell him how unattractive whining is in a grown man.*

Unattractive or not, Aine listened carefully to his tirade, alert for any hint that Douglas suspected her of orchestrating any of the events that troubled him. There was nothing.

Why should there be? I am completely at his mercy.

He was so sure of his hold on her that he barely concentrated when he periodically resang her. He did not try to read her thoughts anymore, he just strengthened the inevitably loosened bonds and went on his way. Why subject himself to the wave of anger and hatred that she spewed at him anytime he entered her mind? Nothing changed between singings. She was his prisoner.

Inwardly, Aine smiled. She might be motionless, but events were going forward at speed. She couldn't say that they were going according to plan—there was no plan, after all—but it was obvious that her sending had been received. The Fates had laid a hand to the weave and the threads thrummed with anticipation.

Douglas passed by her again and she didn't even try to follow him with her eyes. It would have just frustrated her. And if she became frustrated, she would become angry. And then she would spend a lot of energy uselessly straining at her unbreakable bonds. And she wanted to conserve her energies.

Events were in motion, and Aine would be ready for whatever came to be.

TWENTY-ONE

Scott shot a crow from the air and the phone fell from his ear, cracking open on the floor. Fletcher managed a breathless scream. The M9 barked and another crow went down. The bigger animals closed in snarling.

Too crowded in here, Scott thought, and jumped headfirst out the window. He scraped his cheek and jarred his spine hard but avoided breaking his neck with a clumsy shoulder roll designed more to keep Fletcher safe than avoid harm to himself. He was just sitting up when a wolf leapt much more gracefully out the same window. Scott fed it his left ankle and then the M9's barrel, blowing the wolf's brains out a fist-sized hole in the back of its head.

On his feet now, and another wolf came out the same window. Two shots center mass and it was down as well.

Just the bear left, he thought. *And the god.* He wasn't reassured. But smiling quickly at Fletcher anyway, he said, "It's all good, little guy. Uncle Scott's here."

He dodged around to the front of the house in time to see the bear lumber out the front door on its hind legs, Mundoo close behind in human form. Douglas squeezed off four shots, starting at the crotch and letting the light pull of the M9 drag his aim upward. He knew the shots hit home, but the bear showed no visible effect. Switching to head shots, he clanged four more bullets off the bear's skull. He didn't know how many rounds he had left, but it couldn't be many. Switching his aim to Mundoo, he fired till the slide of the pistol racked back empty. No effect.

"Shit," he said and tossed the gun aside, pulling his knife instead.

Mundoo's smile seemed a grim estimation of his chances versus the bear.

But something dark and large rushed out of the woods and suddenly the bear was staring down at a giant gash across its midsection. It whined like a kicked dog and looked at Mundoo with wide surprised eyes.

"Am I interrupting something?" a voice said from the darkness. There was a whistling noise and a dagger was sticking out of the bear's previously undamaged eye. It dropped screaming to all fours and pawed meekly at its eyes and stomach.

"*Chickacava,*" Mundoo muttered. Then called out, "Yes, you are interrupting. And you will flee if you do not want to face my anger."

A tall man dressed all in black stepped from the shadows and peered critically at Mundoo. He held a six-foot-long great sword in one hand as if it were a toothpick. "I don't fear your wrath, Mundoo," he said calmly. "But perhaps you should fear mine." Then he turned and winked at Scott. "Hello, Scott."

Scott squinted at the newcomer. "Douglas?"

"Aye, Scott. It's me."

"You look weird."

Douglas laughed. "I imagine I do."

"Enough," Mundoo roared. "I have heard of you, Douglas. It is said by the many new *manitou* here that you are powerful in your lands." He seemed to grow in stature, and the inner light he glowed with shone brighter till Scott could barely look at him. "But you are in my lands now. And whatever you may be, you are no god."

Douglas shrugged nonchalantly. "God or not," he said, "I know your true names. All of them. Do you want to test me in an affair that you have no real interest in?"

"It is you who interfere." Mundoo snorted. "These two are of no interest to you. Go on your way or be destroyed."

Scott had seen a lot of barfights in his time as a Marine. And one thing he'd learned, when two guys talked this much instead of throwing down, neither one really wanted a piece of the other. He wondered which one of these two was going to blink first. And if he could use this knowledge to help make it be Mundoo.

Gotta give him an out. Let him leave without losing face.

"No interest?" Douglas said. "Scott is my brother. And the child he is holding is my son."

Douglas's son? Scott thought. He looked down at Fletcher, panting and red after so long crying. *I'm an uncle, for real, I guess. Wonder why Douglas's son ended up on my doorstep?* He looked up at Mundoo, shining like the sun, then over at Douglas who twirled his six-foot sword over his head easily. *Wonder if I'll live long enough to ask him.*

"Mundoo," Scott said. "Let us go. You've got what you wanted. The woods will be yours again. Let Douglas have his son."

Mundoo turned slowly toward Scott, still keeping one eye on Douglas.

"You've won," Scott said. *There's your out.* "Let Douglas have his son."

Mundoo stood silent for a moment or two, then nodded. "*Nummauchemin.* You are a brave warrior so I shall let you go. But perhaps you would like to know what else I have heard from the new *manitou* that flee your brother's realm."

"His realm?" Scott asked, brows furrowing.

"Your brother does not come to rescue the child. He comes to kill it."

Scott looked sharply at Douglas who now held the big sword tip down and was leaning casually on it with one elbow. "Is that true?" Scott asked.

"Of course not! What possible reason—"

"It is prophesied," interrupted Mundoo, "that his son will destroy him."

Scott stared hard at Douglas. "Is that true?" he repeated.

The old Douglas, the one that Scott knew from childhood, would have wriggled uncomfortably under his scrutiny. But this new, weird-looking Douglas just shrugged. "Which bit? The prophecy? Or the part about me wanting to murder my own son?"

"All of it."

Douglas didn't answer. Instead he looked at Mundoo. "Weren't you leaving?" he snapped.

Mundoo grinned, then shifted into a wolf. "*Chickacava,* witch-man. A curse on you and yours." Then lifting his head, he let loose a howl that set the night birds chattering and padded off into the darkness.

Douglas watched him go. "Little fucking late to curse me and mine, I think. Now," he said, turning back to Scott, "what did you want to know?"

"Is it true?"

Douglas shrugged again and drew aimless circles in the dirt with the tip of his sword. "Sure. Yeah, it's true. Except for the part about killing the boy."

Scott let out a breath he hadn't realized he was holding. "I didn't think so. How could you be capable of that?"

"Oh, I'm capable. Don't mistake that." Douglas's eyes narrowed. "I am completely without restraint or remorse, I assure you. It's just . . ."

"Just what?"

"Well, I haven't decided yet."

"What?" Scott yelled. "You haven't decided yet?"

Douglas looked petulant. "It's complicated. I—"

"Well, let me simplify it for you, brother," Scott said, his voice hard. "You can't have him. If you're even *contemplating* hurting him, you can't have him. I'll raise him as my own."

Douglas sighed and lifted the sword. Rested it on his shoulder. "I'm afraid that's not an option, Scott. Give me my son or I will take him from you." His eyes softened momentarily. "Don't make me hurt you, Scott," he said, his voice just above a whisper. "If I could feel anything, I'd feel bad for what you're going to make me do. But—"

"But you're completely without restraint or remorse."

Douglas nodded. Scott clutched Fletcher tightly in his arm. Readied his knife.

"Do your worst, Douglas," he said. "Nothing bad's going to happen today. I would have seen it coming."

Tilting his head to one side, Douglas said, "Oh, you wouldn't have seen this coming." Then he whistled a discordant melody and Scott's vision went black.

"What the hell?" Scott heard a shuffling in the leaves and something slapped him in the back of the head.

"Oh, Scott. You can't see anything now." Douglas's voice came from behind him and Scott spun around. But there were more shuffling footsteps and he was slapped again. "How will you care for your nephew if you're blind?"

"Fuck you, Douglas." Taking a few random swipes with the knife, he hit nothing but air.

"Give me my son."

Scott got smacked again. The blows didn't hurt, but they were disorienting him badly. He began a simple knife *kata* from long ago training, adjusting it to exclude his left arm that still held Fletcher tightly. *Step, slash, slash, block, turn, slash.*

His wrist jarred against a tree almost causing him to drop the knife.

"Give me my son, Scott."

He slashed at the voice, hitting nothing. Something slapped him hard on the back of the hand. *Flat of that giant sword,* he guessed. His hand went numb for an instant and this time the knife did drop to the ground. Scott crouched and swept his hand over the dirt and grass searching for it, but he didn't find it before a foot pushed him in the back, sending him sprawling. He ducked and rolled, protecting Fletcher, but as he rolled onto his back, there was suddenly a foot on his wrist and something cold and sharp at his throat.

Fletcher was plucked from his grasp.

"No!"

The foot and the blade disappeared and Scott lunged toward where he thought Douglas was. He grasped nothing but air. He spun, lurched, grabbed again. Nothing. Running into another tree, he dropped to one knee but was up again in an instant. Spinning, grabbing, screaming, gained him nothing. Eventually he stood panting in the woods beside his house, hands on his knees.

"I wish I was sorry," he heard Douglas say quietly, then nothing.

"Douglas!" Scott yelled. "Fletcher!"

There was no answer.

Scott screamed until he was hoarse, then sobbing through blind eyes, collapsed to the ground. He was still there when the sun came up, though he had no way of knowing that it rose.

Fletcher.

TWENTY-TWO

Bridie reached the riverbank and clambered out. Looking down, she was startled to see that her clothes weren't stained with blood. They were sparkling like they'd come right from the dry cleaners.

"Of course, that's pretty far down the weirdness scale as far as this place goes," she mused aloud.

Scanning the horizon, she saw rolling hills covered in evening mist in every direction, their smooth curvature marred only by the occasional tree. The sun was a big orange orb, hanging on the horizon to her right. Hoping that it really was evening, and also that the sun in Faerie set in the west, she began walking toward it.

The grass felt like normal grass, springy and soft; the occasional shrubs she stepped around looked like normal earth plants, dim though her knowledge of horticulture was. The ground rose steadily, and before long she was high above the red river, a thin sheen of sweat coating her brow.

Cresting the hill, she hoped for a sight of the forest Martes had mentioned, but saw only more hills in the distance, and at her feet, a circle of dark, spotted mushrooms, maybe six feet in diameter. She stepped around it instinctively, remembering Grandma McLaren talking once about 'fairy rings.'

Grandma McLaren. With all the strangeness, she'd almost forgotten why she'd come here—*well, come to Scotland, anyway.* She thought, *I have no idea why I came here.* Grandma McLaren was dead. Brutally killed. And for a moment, no matter how strange the explanation, she'd thought she'd known what had happened. But now, with Martes's revelations about Douglas, could she trust what her brother had told her? Or should she trust the feelings that struck her when she'd looked at Aine.

Or am I tied to a hospital gurney in an asylum somewhere?

Shaking her head, Bridie headed down the far side of the first hill. "Got to get Scotty-dog safe. Then I'll sort out what the hell is going on."

The hillside was covered in mist and dew, and Bridie's feet were cold and wet when she reached the bottom. Cursing the discomfort, she forced herself to jog up the next hill.

Martes said I had to hurry, she thought. *Not that he gave me much else for useful info.*

"They won't lie to you," she said in a high squeaky voice that she had to admit didn't sound anything like Martes. "Neither will they tell you the truth." Her voice dropped back into its normal register. "What the hell is that supposed to mean?"

The next hill was relatively low and it only took a few minutes for Bridie to reach the top. Peering through the gathering mist and darkness, she still couldn't see any forest. She sighed and scampered down the other side to repeat the process. She jogged up and down till she was breathless, then settled into a more reasonable fast walk. Up a slope, search for a forest, down the other side, keeping the river on her left and the sun in her face. The process repeated itself endlessly. Bridie began to worry she was going in the wrong direction. *Maybe it was actually morning?*

Shouldn't the sun be down already? I've been walking for hours.
But the sun hung heavy in the sky, refusing to dip below the horizon. Not that she wanted to travel in darkness, but at least it would reassure her that she was traveling west.

If the sun sets in the west here, she thought again.

She was on her tenth hill, her twelfth, her thousandth—she'd lost count—when she finally saw a change in the scenery: a Dark Forest looming on the horizon, its trees as big as skyscrapers.

"Finally," she muttered angrily. But she was pleased that Martes's directions had worked and that she was headed the right way. The good feeling lasted only about another minute, because the sun chose that moment to finally go down, and Faerie went dark.

BRIDIE STOOD STILL and let her eyes try to adjust to the sudden darkness, hoping a moon would come up soon and light the area. A full moon.

Hell, maybe two moons.

But unlike other rural areas, where night brought near total blackness, Bridie discovered that when night fell in Faerie, all kinds of lights suddenly came on. A startling variety of mushrooms, moss, and vegetation that had gone unnoticed in the daylight began to glow in blue, green, and orange pastels on the ground. By the banks of the river, balls of pale yellow light rose out of the rushes and swirled around hypnotically in groups of a dozen or so. Bridie watched as a pair broke away from their group and zoomed up the hill to her.

Beautiful, she thought as they hovered before her eyes.

They drew patterns in the air, hieroglyphic trails of light that disappeared before any meaning could be deciphered from the pictures they drew. Bridie took a step toward them, and they moved away the same distance. She reached out to touch them, but they flitted just out of reach. They seemed to want to play and Bridie obliged, following them down the hill, almost skipping, as they played just out of reach of her grasping fingertips. She giggled girlishly, thinking that this was the first fun she'd had since coming to this country. The first true happiness she'd felt since Grandma McLaren died.

Grandma McLaren.

The thought of her grandmother's death was a cold splash of water in the face. And it coincided with a warm splash of something on her foot.

Bridie looked down and saw that she had unknowingly taken a step into the river. She hadn't even realized she'd come down the hill.

"What the hell?"

The lights zipped down in front of her and drew her gaze back upward. Their dance began anew, but Bridie looked at them now. Really looked, ignoring their weaving dance and their patterned tails. She looked at them, and deep inside each light she thought she could make out a squat little creature with long teeth and cat's eyes and a very hungry cast to its features. When they came in close again, Bridie swatted angrily at them, but they were too quick and floated out of reach easily.

Bridie sensed the game change then. The patterns they drew in the air went from enchanting to confusing, and she could no longer follow their movements. A low humming drone accompanied their movements.

"Screw you guys anyway," she said, and turned her back on them to march back up the hill. "I've got work to do."

She'd no sooner turned her back then there was a sharp shock of pain in her calf, as if she'd been nipped by a small dog.

"Ow!" she yelped and spun around. The lights were out of reach again, spinning crazily. One shot toward her face and she tried to block it, but it veered off and hit her in the shoulder. Two spots of blood accompanied the pain this time. Another light came in under Bridie's arms and took a good chomp of a rib. Bridie swung crazily and the lights veered off again. But only momentarily. They were back in moments, hitting her in the thigh, the head, the other shoulder.

Get a hold of yourself, Bridie, she thought. *What are you swinging at so wildly? Elbows in! Arms up! Guard your face! Timing, timing. Look for a pattern and break it.*

She got in a good guard position and balanced on the balls of her feet like a boxer, bobbing her head a few times and shifting her hands in front of her face. It was no use. One came in high, the other low, both inhumanly fast. And before they reached her, two different ones bit her in the back. Bridie spun around and saw that a whole pack of lights was on her now, a dozen darting, nipping, attackers whizzing at her and around her, each opening up little wounds that were eventually going to turn into very big wounds if this kept up.

Bridie ran.

She ran as fast and as far she could. Which was about fifteen feet up the hill, where three of the lights scooted between her feet and tripped her up. She went down hard, and an unseen rock knocked the breath out of her. The lights were on her like piranhas in the dry season, opening holes in her clothes and her skin, and sending her rolling and scrabbling trying to get away.

The ring! she thought suddenly.

Ignoring the pain of a dozen injuries already endured and a dozen more being inflicted at that moment, Bridie dug into her pocket and pulled out Martes's ring. When she held it in front of her face, the attacks stopped immediately.

"You assholes recognize this?" she asked. The lights were now hovering in the air, quivering slightly. She took a big gasping breath. "Well, when Martes finds out about this, he's going to boil you little bastards alive!"

Bridie struggled to her feet. She took a step up the hill and was gratified to see the lights giving way before her.

But not all of them. A few stood their ground.

Well, hovered, anyway.

Bridie shook the ring at them. "When Martes finds out . . ." she began, then thought, *You idiot. 'When he finds out?' Now they have to kill you so he doesn't ever find out.* She added, "And I've called him. He's on his way." She put the ring back in her pocket and walked nonchalantly up the hill. "Up horse and hattock, baby. I suggest you fly as fast and far away as you possibly can."

That seemed to settle it. The lights broke out of their group and whizzed into the distance like lightning bugs on speed. Bridie watched till they were out of sight, then collapsed to the ground.

"Ouch," she said looking at the many punctures, scratches, and cuts that covered her. Nothing looked fatal. "And I still have to hurry to get to Scott."

Grunting and sighing like a crippled old dog, she got to her feet again and headed for the Dark Forest.

• • • • caılleach • • • •

Cailleach popped the still-beating mole's heart into her mouth and swallowed it whole.

A wee snack it is, she thought, *but the gift it gies is lairge enough.*

Closing her eyes, she rocked in her chair and waited for the visions to come. She caught a few tantalizing glimpses that made no sense: a mortal woman in the Daurklins Wood, a pile of fey bodies in a room she didn't recognize, a blind man sprinting across a high bridge.

She opened one eye, then the other.

"Pliny, ye wee git," she said. "Yer nae use to me today."

The mole's tiny body was still in her lap, and she dug through its entrails with long fingernails, removing the tiny liver. She tried to read the *processus pyramidalis* but got nothing.

"Too small," she muttered. "And I've never been guid at haruspication, anyway."

Of course she knew that wasn't the problem, but she had to try to get a reading, regardless.

"Perhaps the cards."

She pulled a worn deck from her cloak and shuffled it six

times. Opening her legs so that her black skirts made an impromptu table, she cut the cards and put out a circle and staff spread. The circle was all major arcana: the Magician and the High Priestess locked in a pair, with the Tower in their past and Death in their future, Justice and the Devil at opposite poles. The staff was more varied: the Deuce of Wands, the Trey of Swords, the Hermit, the Queen of Swords.

Power and betrayal, Cailleach thought. *Unsurprising cards considering the major players. But who are the Hermit and the Queen of Swords?*

"An interesting reading," she said, scooping the cards up with a sigh. "But not mine."

It was the Usurper's, as all readings had been of late.

"Well, there's still others who can see. Perhaps I'll call on them."

She cleared her throat noisily and spit a giant green gob into the dust before her. Thrice she slashed the tip of her walking stick in the dust, forming a triangle around the remarkably round circle of spittle. She did not write the three sacred names of God around the outside, nor the Archangel's name split into three sections in the center. The Triangle of Salmon needed none of that on this side of the river.

She drew five horizontal lines of descending length next to the triangle, tipping the top one with small circles, the rest with short vertical cornices. Then she drew a circle balanced on the center of the second largest line, and made a bold stroke straight down from it, ending at the bottom line. Last she made mirror-image "B"s on the top line with long curlicues extending from their spines.

"Ipsos, he who knoweth things past and to come, I conjure and command yew to appear and shew yerselfe visibly to me, in fair and comely shape . . ."

A cloud of black smoke began to form in the area above the triangle Cailleach had drawn in the dust. It swelled and swirled until it was vaguely humanoid in shape, but with an abnormally large head.

"Without any deformity or tortuosity . . ."

The body of the darkness stayed unclear, but the head was now visibly that of a lion. It spoke, its voice a low roar.

"Cailleach, I cannot help thee. Summon me not whilst Douglas still sits the throne."

Cailleach frowned at the smoky figure. "But I'm as blind as my breakfast was, Ipsos."

"I cannot help thee," Ipsos said again. "Release me."

"Ach," she said and wiped out the seal of Ipsos with her foot, watching the figure dissipate and the air clear. Then she swirled the gob of spit through the triangle until it was a shapeless mud puddle drying in the sun.

Something was coming. Something big. Caillech could tell. Not all the portents had been blocked by the Usurper. But she couldn't see what it was. Or more importantly, she couldn't see how she could take advantage of it.

"Ach," she said again and tapped out her pipe. Refilled it from a pouch tucked deep in her cloak. Lit it with a wooden match and leaned back in her chair. "I'll just have a wee feuch and see what the day brings."

She looked out toward the red river and puffed till her head was wreathed in smoke, with just the tip of her great crooked nose poking through.

· · · τwentγ-three · · ·

Scott was still blind. He couldn't see the hand in front of his face. He'd tried. He'd held it there, pretty sure it was right there an inch from his nose, and tried to force his open eyes to see. But there was nothing. Just blackness.

Except it wasn't just blackness. It was something else. He just wasn't sure what.

When he'd finished screaming and crying, when the ground had grown too cold and uncomfortable to ignore any longer, when pain and fear and rage had finally given way to a need to do something—*anything*—he'd sat up and dragged himself to where he thought his front steps were. He wasn't surprised to miss them entirely, but he did find a tree to put his back up against.

Sitting up, he tried to see his hand. Failed. He tried to listen, hoping maybe his hearing had grown supernaturally strong to compensate, but that was either a myth or took a lot longer than a few hours to develop. Ditto with his sense of smell—though he figured he'd be thankful that his sense of smell was deadened by years of smoking when all the corpses in and around his house started to rot.

He was blind. But still, when he moved his hand away from his face something shimmered.

No, not shimmered, he thought. He didn't have a word for what he saw. *Saw isn't even the right word.*

Scott moved his hand again and tried to figure out what he was seeing. *A shimmer. A sparkle.*

Using the tree for support, he pushed himself to his feet. The *shimmer/sparkle* was back, stronger than before, accompanied by a sense of things dying, other things being born. Scott shook his head. Took a blind step forward. His blind eyes flashed and he knew . . .

If I go that way, I will never reach my house.

He turned to the right. Took a step.

Yes.

Still blind but now strangely confident, Scott walked step by slow step toward his home.

• • • twenty-four • • •

Bridie wasn't walking nearly as confidently. Though a pale crescent moon had risen, the visibility in Faerie was still poor. And as she neared the dark forest, she began to capitalize it in her mind. *The Dark Forest.* The trees were gnarled behemoths whose withered canopies still looked thick enough to blot out what little light the moon provided. Great cobwebs or moss—Bridie couldn't tell which—filled any cracks the leaves missed. Undergrowth looked to be spare—choked out by the lack of light if forest ecology worked the same here—but it would still be tough going as thick vines crisscrossed every possible path. And to top it off, the whole place emanated a menace that made Bridie feel as if she were pushing through a stiff wind to get near it.

Martes's casual 'go through the dark forest' was starting to look like a daunting task. Just getting to it was proving difficult. The soft springy grass of the hills she'd been traveling over had turned to scattered rocks that shifted and moved underfoot whenever she stepped on one. They were sharp, too, and Bridie had to pick her way across carefully, feeling every step in the many nips, bites, cuts, and gashes the faerie lights had inflicted on her. Still, she made steady progress and was almost to the forest when a briar patch sprang up in her way.

Literally.

One minute there was nothing but a hundred yards of barren, stony ground between her and the Dark Forest, then with a great creaking roar, thornbushes that looked a thousand years old burst from the ground and rose to the height of three men in front of her.

Suddenly showered with loose stones and clumps of dirt, Bridie jumped back in surprise. She managed to get her hands in front of her face in time, but earned more cuts and bruises on her already battered body. Spinning around, she tried to guess if something else was going to spring up at her. When nothing else appeared, she dusted herself off, then turned her attention to the new growth cutting her off from the forest.

A forest I wasn't exactly thrilled to enter, anyway.

The branches were wrist-thick, the thorns as big as her thumbs, and the whole patch stretched from the river to the horizon with no discernible break.

"Crap sandwich," she said.

Pacing a few steps to either side, she eyed the briars even closer. The branches were woven together as tight as a wool blanket, and unless she was a snake, she wasn't crawling through any of the spaces left over. She'd be sliced into lean Bridie cutlets in about three minutes if she tried. She grabbed a branch, avoiding the thorns. Tried to snap it in half. She might have been wrenching on a baseball bat for how much it moved.

"Crap sandwich with dill pickle and mayo,"

Bridie stepped back and looked hopelessly at the impassable barrier. Put her hands in her pockets. Felt the ring. A smile brushed her face as she pulled out Martes's ring and showed it to the bush. For a second she thought it hadn't worked, but then, rasping and grinding, the branches directly in front of her began to unweave and pull to either side. It looked like time-lapse photography in reverse, though with big creaking sound effects. As the path opened wider, Bridie stepped in, ring held boldly in front of her.

"Little fucker sure has some pull here," she muttered.

The briar patch that had seemed so daunting a minute ago, turned out to be only a few yards thick, and Bridie was through in short order. The branches closed behind her, and she marched up to the Dark Forest, still holding the ring out. She wasn't surprised when one of the trees opened two burls in its trunk to reveal wide brown eyes. A slash of a scar beneath them opened and the tree spoke.

"Put the ring away, meat-girl. We will not harm you and incur the wrath of the Usurper." The tree's voice was high and screeching, the sound of branches scraping together and wind whistling through bare branches—but stripped of any pleasant qualities. "But be quick. Your presence here disturbs us."

My presence here disturbs me, Bridie thought, but said nothing. Pocketing the ring as requested, she stepped into the forest. Like the briars, vines slithered and shot up the trees that supported them until a way was clear. Bridie stepped forward, then stopped.

"If you want me to be quick, you'd better give me some light."

The tree didn't answer, but the thick moss at the base of its trunk began to glow. The glow was answered in turn by more trees in a line that stretched to the west, not just providing enough light to travel by, but also a path for Bridie to follow.

"Thanks," she said, and began walking.

It was cool and quiet as any earthly forest, but for the sense of menace and dread. Bridie found herself starting nervously at the sound of her own feet scuffling on the forest floor, or the wind pushing a stray branch up against its neighbor.

Jesus, she thought. *I'm disturbing them?*

Hugging herself and shuddering slightly, Bridie rushed through the woods. With the vines gone and the moss providing weak light, it was fairly clear sailing, the only obstacles the occasional roots she stumbled over. The few times she tripped and fell she didn't stay down long; the foreboding she felt kept her moving fast despite the poor visibility and uneven ground. When the dread finally began to fade, she knew she was almost through.

She broke out of the forest just as dawn broke behind her.

Either I spent a lot longer in there than I thought, or time really does move strangely in this place. Bridie decided it didn't matter. Either way, she had to press on.

The red river was wide here on the far side of the forest, so that Bridie could barely make out the other bank through the pink haze that rose in the distance. Between her and the river was a long stretch of rocky beach, and beyond that a thin strip of sand that formed the river's banks. Farther down the beach, the inland terrain rose slightly while the coastal ground fell away, till the riverbank was a ten-foot cliff. The rocks that might have made a beach, instead piled up to form a natural bulwark. Perched precariously on the edge of this formation was a thatch-roofed hut built out of the same stone that surrounded it. Smoke trickled out of the center of the conical roof, and something—Bridie hesitated to use the word "someone" in this place—sat in a chair before the hut, a pipe in its mouth, staring at Bridie as she approached.

This time, Bridie pulled the ring out of her pocket immediately. Crossing the rocky beach, she held it in front of her. And she kept it held high when she reached the bulwark, despite the added difficulty of clambering over the rocks one-handed. Over the barrier now, she got a closer look at the seated creature.

It was, Bridie realized, female, and decidedly cronelike, with a long nose and leathery skin, coarse black hair sprouting from the many warts, moles, and cysts that dotted her visage. She sat comfortably in a high-backed rocking chair despite a noticeable hump in her spine. Her garments were long and black, and appeared fastidiously clean. On her scalp was a tight black skull cap rimmed with strange runic writings.

The crone peered at Bridie, then at the ring she held out. "Favored of Martes, are ye?" Her accent was broad, raw, Scots.

Bridie nodded. "One of his most favored. I need passage to the real world. To a specific spot. And I need it fast. So, I suggest you get to it."

The crone smiled at Bridie and blew out a big cloud of smoke. It hung in the air while she looked critically at the bowl of her pipe, eventually dumping its contents on the ground. The ash formed quickly into a tiny gray mouse that began to scamper away. The crone crushed it casually beneath a large bare foot. "Oh, ye suggest, do ye?"

This one doesn't seem as scared as the rest, Bridie thought. *But I better keep bluffing anyway.*

"Yes, I do," she said as confidently as she could.

"No," the crone said.

"What?" Bridie leaned in close, putting her face near the crone's. "Listen, old woman—"

"No," the crone interrupted. "Ye mistake Martes's importance to me. His protection merely means I'll nae skin ye alive and eat yer organs in front of ye." Reaching out, she ran a gnarled finger down the side of Bridie's head. "Before smoking that pretty blonde hair in ma pipe." Bridie jerked back and the crone smiled. "So, no," she repeated.

Bridie took a half-step back. *Martes isn't a big enough threat? How about little brother? See how she likes that.* "What about Lord Douglas? He'll kill you if you don't help me."

"Oh, aye. He can kill me sure as blood flows past my front door. But he cannae make me do what I dinnae want to. No creature of Faerie or Earth can. So, again, no." She paused, then raised her brows and looked up at Bridie, her eyes gleaming, "Unless, of course, you'd care to make a wee trade?"

Bridie raised an eyebrow in return. "What are you looking for? My firstborn?"

"That'd probably do." The crone cackled. "But yer no likely to have one are ye?"

That's true. "What, then?" she said impatiently.

"A service perhaps."

"What kind of service?"

"Something yer good at, luv." The crone looked slyly at Bridie. "What are ye good at?"

Bridie thought she knew the answer to that, but didn't want to come right out and say it. "How about you tell me?"

The crone smiled. She had three teeth. "Yer a warrior, luv. Yer good at killing."

Bridie hesitated, then nodded. "I am."

"A year of service, then, for a trip back hame," the crone stated. "I can always find use for a virgin warrior around here. A year—"

"No."

"What? You refuse a perfectly fair—"

"A year?" Bridie said. "Not a chance. For a simple trip stateside? No. I might give you an hour's worth of service. *Might.*"

"Half a year then."

"An evening."

"A month."

"One night."

"A fortnight."

"A what?"

"Two weeks, ye ninny."

"Why not say that then? One day."

"Three."

"One."

"Twa."

"Wha?"

The crone sighed. "Two days."

"One."

"Two."

"Okay. But two days passed either here or in the real world. Whichever comes first."

"Done."

The crone spit in her hand and stuck it out. Bridie did the same. When they shook, Bridie felt as if something clicked in her mind, like a lock's tumblers sliding into their last position. She knew she couldn't break her word on this. Seemed deals struck in Faerie were binding in a way promises weren't in the real world. She could *feel* how impossible it would be not to comply. She found she didn't mind this. It meant the crone would keep her half of the bargain.

They stood like that, hand in hand for a long moment and then, suddenly the crone pulled Bridie beside her. Bridie almost panicked, thinking the whole bargain had been a trick, a way for the old witch to get a hold of her.

But the crone just used Bridie to heave herself to her feet, then let go of her hand and said, "Well, if yer in a hurry, let's get to it." She reached into her black cloak and pulled out a gnarled walking stick. Bent over so that her torso was nearly perpendicular to the ground and leaning heavily on the stick, she set off at a surprisingly brisk pace away from Bridie and down the other side of the hill.

Bridie couldn't conceive of how the old woman was going to climb over the jumbled rocks that blocked their way when they got down the hill, but as they approached the wall, the crone knocked on the ground twice with her stick. The rocks shifted aside to reveal a rickety wooden gate. The crone pulled it open.

"After you, dearie," she said.

Bridie walked through the gate and onto a stone path. She stopped, but felt the stick poke her in the kidney.

"Keep going."

Bridie obeyed, following the path as it angled away from the riverbank and toward a distant mountain that Bridie would have sworn wasn't there a second ago.

"Now think about where ye want to gae," the crone said. "And keep walking."

"All right." Bridie thought about Scott's little house in Leverett. The peeling paint, the roof badly in need of patching, the rough drive that had been paved maybe once in the last thirty years. When she thought she had a good picture of it in her mind, she said, "Okay. Got it."

"That's it?" the crone scoffed behind her. "I hope yer better at killing than ye are at thinking, or I got the short end of this bargain. So ye know what it looks like. What do ye hear when you're there? What's it smell like? Who's there to meet ye? What do ye feel when yer there?" The stick poked her in the back again. "Now, think again about where ye want to gae. Close yer eyes if ye need to."

Bridie closed her eyes and thought again. She saw the house, and tried to remember every detail of the last time she was there.

There were birds singing, she thought. *There always were out there in the boonies.* She couldn't have named them, but she could remember the sounds: chirring and chipping, an occasional whistled yip like a kid's toy with the battery running down. *What about smells? Who the hell remembers what a place smells like?* But it came to her: *pine and grass and the soft rot of decaying leaves, sometimes the ozone zing of a storm sweeping in over the Quabbin Reservoir.*

She thought some more. *Who's there to meet me?*

Scott. Poor crazy Scott. Scott, who always looked confused when I arrived no matter how often I told him I was coming. As if he never knew if I was really there or not, but was ready to be happy to see me if it turned out I wasn't a hallucination. Her little loving brother, Scott, who was so chubby and sweet as a baby, and so tortured and hard when he came back from the war. Scott, who needed her now maybe more than he ever had before.

"Got it," said the crone. "Open yer eyes."

Bridie did. The river was gone. The path was gone. The distant mountain was nowhere to be seen. Bridie was in a green forest, facing a thick tree with a door carved directly out of its trunk.

"This gate will get ye as close as possible. Return to the gate within a year and a day to begin yer service."

Bridie turned and looked at the crone. "Thank you."

She peered at Bridie, her brows furrowed. "Why?"

Bridie had no answer to that, so she grasped the antler bone that served as a door handle, pulled it open, and stepped inside. The crone shut the door behind her, and Bridie stood in pitch blackness that smelled of wet wood.

Stretching her hands out in front of her, she shuffled forward a step. Then another. Her hands met no resistance. Five more steps, six, and she was well past where the tree should have ended. Still her hands met nothing. Another five steps and she finally felt something, though she couldn't identify the material. It was cool and smooth, like a snake's skin, and her hands tingled lightly where they touched it. Hoping it was not, in fact, a giant snake, she pressed against it firmly.

Her hands pushed right through.

She jerked them back immediately. Rubbed them together.

They seemed to be undamaged. Reaching out, she felt for holes or tears where her hands and gone through. There was nothing.

"Hrmph."

With a tingle and an audible pop, Bridie pushed her hands through to the forearm. Felt a cool breeze. Stepped forward till her body was flush against the barrier.

"Here goes," she said, then squeezed her eyes shut and pushed her face through.

The barrier was cool on her cheeks. There was a sucking sound as her ears passed through. Then suddenly she was falling forward, and she stepped clean through to catch her balance.

And opened her eyes to a scene straight out of the Far East.

A seventy-five-foot-high white dome stood in a forest clearing, a giant bronze Buddha sitting in an arched alcove carved into its side. The sunlight reflecting off the building and the tall golden ornamentation that stretched skyward from the roof made the whole structure glow as if filled with divine light. Bridie herself was on a small island in a koi-filled pond, a fallen slab of stone just a few feet away forming a simple bridge to the clearing. Several yards beyond that, a bald monk in robes of orange and red raked the stones of a Zen garden. If he was surprised by the sight of a disheveled woman materializing in the middle of the koi pond, he didn't show it. With an almost imperceptible nod in her direction, he went back to walking backward with his wooden rake.

For a moment, Bridie thought the crone had missed the mark by thousands of miles and dropped her off in China or India or God-knows-where-ik-stan. Then she recognized the place: the Peace Pagoda. For some unknown reason, when the Nipponzan Myohoji monks had finally decided to build one of their monuments to peace in America, they had settled on the unlikely location of good old nuclear-free Leverett, Massachusetts.

Bridie was maybe a mile and a half from Scott's house.

Fifteen minutes if I walk there. Bridie's feet barely touched the stone slab as she leapt to shore. *Ten if I run.*

She ran.

WESTERN MASS IS all hills and valleys. Bridie started down, down, down, flying past the unfinished new temple, past the monks' residence, through the empty dirt parking lot where Peace Pagoda visitors left their Volvos and VWs before tromping up the hill for enlightenment. The main road was paved but unlined and Bridie turned right onto it. She would have been racing against traffic if there was any, but the road was devoid of cars. She was traveling uphill now, breathing hard. Crossed another small road and she was sprinting through a long sweeping curve, chest on fire, legs aching. And still going uphill.

C'mon, Bridie, she encouraged herself. *You run harder than this at the gym three times a week.* This was a lie. She hadn't been to the gym since leaving the police. And she was still hurting from any number of small slashes, gashes, cuts, and bruises. *Okay, so maybe I'm a little out of shape. But this is for my Scotty-dog, goddamnit!*

She pushed herself harder.

The hills seemed endless—and the short run down from the Peace Pagoda looked as if it was going to be the only downhill section of the trip. Leverett Road certainly ran the wrong way. So did Chestnut Hill Road. Bridie turned up it.

Up, she thought, *up.* She was so out of breath now that she couldn't *think* in more than one syllable. But Scott's house was just ahead. She forced herself to sprint the last hundred yards.

Stumbling into the driveway, she almost tripped over a gigantic black bear. She shrieked like she hadn't since she'd been eight years old and leapt backward.

The bear didn't move. Panting, Bridie bent over and put her hands on her knees. Took a closer look at the bear. A gigantic puddle of blood spread out from underneath it. If it wasn't dead, it was only seconds away. She expanded her view, taking in the whole exterior of Scott's house. There were dead crows on the drive, a couple of dead dogs—no, wolves!—by the side window. And a few dead bodies of creatures Bridie couldn't recognize scattered among the animals. They all looked gunshot, although the bear appeared to have been killed by a gash through its mid-section

Despite her exhaustion, Bridie wanted to run. Into the house. She wanted to scream out Scott's name and charge into the house, find out if he was safe or not. But she'd been a cop too long. Whoever had done this killing might still be around. Bridie had no gun, no knife, no weapon of any kind—nothing but her hands to fight with. And if they could kill a bear they could probably kill her. It wouldn't do her or Scott any good if she got herself killed. So she picked her way carefully and quietly through the bodies, hoping to reach a side window undetected so she could assess the situation inside before making her next move.

Which is going in, she thought. *No matter what's in there I'm going to get to Scott.*

She was almost to the house when the front door swung open. Flattening herself against the wall and preparing to dart around the corner, she looked up to see who emerged.

It was Scott. He was dressed in his old desert fatigues, the browns and tans barely showing through the fresh blood that was splattered all over him. He didn't move as if he was injured, however, and Bridie hoped that none of the blood was his own.

"Scott," she said, in a short directed whisper. She was still hedging her bets in case anything else was getting ready to come out the door.

Scott cocked his head at the sound of her voice, but didn't turn toward her. "Oh. Bridie. Of course. You're here now." He took one tentative step down the stairs. "I guess I knew that," he said softly, as if confirming something to himself.

Bridie pushed herself away from the wall and ran to him, bounding up the short steps of the stoop, and stopping one below him. "Scott! I'm so glad you're okay. Listen, it's not safe." She looked around at the bodies. "But I guess you know that. We have to—" She stopped when she looked up and saw his face. "Scott. Your eyes . . ."

Scott nodded, not really looking in her direction. It didn't appear that it would matter if he did. His eyes were a pupil-less murky white.

He's blind, Bridie thought. Then said it out loud. "You're blind."

"Yes," Scott agreed.

"What happened? Who did this to you? What are these creatures? Who killed that bear?" Bridie knew she was babbling and mentally slapped herself. *You know Scott can't handle that kind of verbal pressure. Calm down before you put him in a state.*

But it was Scott who reached out his hand and put it over one of hers. "Bridie?" he said quietly. "Let's go."

· · · · **cailleach** · · · ·

Once the gate in the rowan tree clicked shut and the virgin warrior was well on her way home, Cailleach cackled with glee.

The Queen of Swords. It has to be.

It was the most minor of the new cards that had appeared in the tarot spread but still . . .

It is mine. For two whole days.

She capered around the tree, still cackling wildly. The Queen of Swords was hers. And she was connected to the Hermit somehow. One of the Major Arcana. If she held the Queen of Swords perhaps she could get the Hermit as well. And while the Magician and the High Priestess went to Death and the Devil, who would be holding the only cards left?

"Cailleach, that's who!"

Power hates a vacuum, and if a seat on the throne came open, someone would have to fill it.

"And why not me?" she asked the nearest tree.

The tree had an opinion on this matter—several in fact—but wisely chose to stay quiet. A skill trees are renowned for.

"Did not Douglas steal the throne from Aine?" she asked a young sparrow as it flew by.

"Actually, she kept the throne, he just married her for a semblance of legitimacy."

Sparrows are not known for their ability to keep silent.

Landing on a twig by Cailleach's head, the sparrow went on. "I don't know why he needed to. Powerful as he is. I mean, he could crush any one of us with just a note. You, for instance, you're feared round most of Faerie, but to him you're no more than an insect. Something to be swatted if it annoys him, but otherwise ignored."

Sparrows aren't noted for their great intellect, either.

Cailleach's hand flashed out, quick as a striking snake, and caught the sparrow before it could so much as ruffle a feather. It had time for one frightened tweet before she snapped its neck. Then she cupped the small body in her hands and blew into them as if warming them. Feathers began drifting out of the cracks between her fingers, and she took another breath. Blew again. This time blood seeped through her knobby fingers. On the third breath into her palms nothing came through and she opened her hands to reveal a pile of pale thin bones.

"Hrmph," she said and tucked the bones into a hidden pocket in her cloak. Licking her fingers clean of blood, she addressed the forest as a whole and asked again, "Why not me?"

There was no answer this time.

· · · · twenty-five · · · ·

Scott?"

When Scott heard Bridie's voice, it brought him back to himself. He'd been adrift in . . . possibilities.

"Oh. Bridie," he said. And watched as waves of possibilities shattered on the shore to become history. What *had* happened. "Of course. You're here now." *How could it be otherwise?* He took one step downstairs and saw more futures die. Others sprang to life, shimmering in his non-sight, spreading before him. "I guess I knew that."

Bridie spoke again, but too fast for Scott to follow. It wasn't important yet anyway; no possibilities changed with her words. Scott waited till she wore down and said something that made the future-ocean shift a little.

"Scott. Your eyes . . ."

He nodded, knowing what she would say next.

"You're blind."

"Yes."

Bridie spoke rapidly now, but again Scott didn't listen. He was trying to pick out individual currents in the roiling possibility-ocean.

There:

Bridie leads Scott to his car—they tear down the hill to the hospital—a kindly staff locks him away where he can't hurt himself or others—

And there:

Bridie takes Scott inside the house—the delay is too long and a door closes that should have remained open—

Scott looked out to sea, trying to see the ends of those waves. It was foggy with distance, but he could tell that Fletcher wasn't there. The future Scott never sees him again. Never learns his fate.

But the now-Scott knows it.

No. That is all. No. Look again.

There:

They argue—disagreement means delay—a door closes that should have—

No.

Perhaps there:

Scott attacks Bridie—he wins the fight—he never sees Fletcher again—he loses the fight—he never sees Fletcher again—he kills his sister—he never sees Fletcher again—his sister kills him—

Well, that one was obvious.

And I must see Fletcher again. If I don't . . .

Scott didn't want to think of what would happen if he failed to reach his nephew. What his brother would do. His brother, seemingly all-powerful, but caught now in a place where prophecy wrote history and future alike, and one's fate was inescapable whether emperor, peasant, or priest.

There must be a way. A wave.

Scott watched the breakers, the possibility-waves just about to strike the now and fuse to the present shore. Delay itself began to limit the tide, calming the ocean, all futures leading into one.

There must be another way. Another—there!

Scott saw it then: a clear path, if an unlikely one. He timed his leap and . . .

Reaching out to where Bridie's hand must be, Scott felt her warm skin, the flutter of a pulse elevated with confusion and excitement.

"Bridie?" he said. "Let's go."

THEY TOOK TWO steps down the stairs and another two up the driveway before Bridie thought to ask where they were going. She was not entirely pleased with the answer.

"You tell me," Scott said.

"This isn't the time for a guessing game, Scott."

He smiled vaguely in her direction. "I know the future," he said, "but I don't know the way."

"What the hell does that mean?" Bridie spat. But then it hit her. "The Peace Pagoda. Has to be." *Return to the gate within a year*, the crone had said.

"Yes."

"Let's take the car. I'm a bit gassed after running all the way here."

Scott nodded. They walked to the car and awkwardly shuffled around each other so Bridie could get in the driver's side.

"Oh, and we should hurry," Scott said when he was seated.

That was all Bridie needed to hear, and she slammed the car into gear. Screeching out onto the road, she wished she had a cherry to put on the roof. Not that there was any traffic to clear, but she'd always liked the noise and lights. As if to compensate, the autumn foliage whizzing by soon filled the windows with a smear of red, and orange.

"What do we do when we get there?" Bridie asked.

"You lead us to Douglas."

"I do?" Bridie downshifted and the car whined into the S-turns. "How am I supposed to do that?" But she thought she knew already. *I've been there before. I guess I'll have to find my way back.*

Scott just nodded silently.

The turnoff to the Peace Pagoda came up suddenly and Bridie cranked the wheel, sending gravel spewing behind the Honda as it hit the drive. They slewed sideways into the parking area. She thought about trying to break through the chain blocking the road, but feared a crash that might cause delay. She slammed on the brakes instead. Bridie was out before the car skidded to a stop and was quickly around to the passenger side to help Scott exit.

He was a soldier; even blind he could march. They double-timed it up the hill.

The Pagoda looked like a giant golf ball in a particularly bad lie. Bridie bypassed it and headed for the koi pond. The monk was gone. When they were across the makeshift bridge, Bridie realized she had no idea what to do now. The thought lasted only a second before she heard the crone's voice.

"Are ye ready to begin yer service?" Bridie wasn't sure whether the voice was on the wind or only in her mind.

"I have one more thing yet to do," Bridie answered. "And I need to come to your land to do it."

"Come ye then."

The air shifted before her and a door appeared, rough wood with a bone handle, twin to the one that had been carved out of the tree in Faerie. But this one was attached to only air. Bridie wondered for just a second why Scott didn't seem surprised by this, before remembering he was blind.

Well, maybe not blind exactly, she thought.

Taking his hand in hers, she pushed open the door, stepping through, and into the long dark hallway. There was no barrier this time.

"Careful, it's dark in here," she warned Scott before realizing how idiotic that was.

"Okay."

Scott shuffled forward more confidently than Bridie in the pitch black, and she let him lead her the half dozen steps to the other side.

"Door," he said, then waited patiently while Bridie searched for a handle. She didn't find one, but the door opened easily when she pushed on it, and bright sunlight streamed in. Squinting, Bridie got her bearings. They were standing in the tree she'd come through, looking out at a lush green forest. The crone was there, leaning on her stick.

"So," she said, "what is this that needs doing in my lands?" She cackled a touch. "And would ye be needing to bargain for my services?"

"No need," Bridie replied. "We just need to . . ." She stopped. *I came here with my eyes closed. I have no idea how to even get back to the crone's house, let alone get to Castle Douglas.* She looked at Scott, who was standing on one foot kind of awkwardly, his head nodding rhythmically to some music only he could hear. "Well, we are in a bit of a hurry. So I could give you one more day of service if you can get us to Castle Douglas quickly."

The crone smiled at Bridie. It was not a comforting sight. "One year."

"What? Not a chance. You'll get—"

"One year, dearie," the crone said. "Yer desperate. Ye stink of it. It's writ in every twitch of yer eyeballs, in every drop of sweet sweat on yer brow." She tapped her stick on the ground once, twice. "One year. Or ye can find yer own way."

Well, doesn't she just have me over a fucking barrel? Bridie wished she was a better poker player, but apparently her bluff had just been called. But as she opened her mouth to agree, Scott spoke up.

"No," he said. Firmly but without anger. Then he sat cross-legged on the ground.

"No?" the crone sounded strangely pleased with the idea. "Well, perhaps we can work a different wee deal. How about your companion joins you in yer two days of service."

"No," Scott said.

"No?" the crone screeched. Now she sounded angry. "Ye have no other way!"

Leaning down, Bridie whispered to Scott, "We are in a hurry, right?"

"Yep," he said happily. "But we can rest for a minute or two." He patted the ground next to him. "Take a load off, sis."

Bridie looked from Scott to the seething crone then back to Scott. Then shrugging, she sat down. "How will we get to Douglas then?"

"I think I . . . see . . . another way," he said. "Besides, I can't serve her for even a minute and you wouldn't survive a year's service with her."

"Oh, I think I'd—"

"You wouldn't survive," Scott said, his voice hard.

His words chilled her. "What are you, Scottie?"

Scott went on as if she hadn't spoken. "A few days you can do. A few days you can live through."

Bridie just stared at him.

He turned to face her, blind eyes pointed firmly at a spot just off her right shoulder. "I'm your brother, Bridie."

Bridie tore her gaze away and peered up at the crone. She had both hands crossed on the nub of her walking stick and was resting her head on them. Her eyes never left Bridie's. Nor did the flame of anger go out of them. The rest of her looked relaxed, however.

She looks ready to wait us out, Bridie thought.

"How about a couple of weeks?" she hissed to Scott.

"Hush," he said. "Just a minute more."

Bridie tried to keep her foot from tapping impatiently as they waited. "Are we in a hurry or what?" she blurted out after only a few seconds. "I mean, this bitch seems to have all the chips. What are we supposed to do? You say I can't survive, but I'm pretty goddamn tough. If we're in such a damned hurry, let's just do the deal and go. We'll sort it out later."

The crone's smile got bigger and bigger during this little speech, but Scott didn't react at all. His head was cocked and bobbing again as if the music had come back on.

"Now," he said.

Bridie looked around, but didn't see anything different. But the crone's nostrils flared and she suddenly stood straight up. Sniffing the air twice, she glared down at Bridie. "A pox on yer seer of a brother," she said. "I may not hold the Hermit but I still have you. And I'll see you soon." Then she spun in a whirl of black rags and shuffled into the dense trees and out of sight.

Scott stood. "Let's go, Bridie."

"How?" Bridie asked, getting to her feet herself. But her answer flew into the clearing, his giant nose twitching furiously.

Martes.

"Up horse and hattock," he said without preamble, and Bridie felt herself lifted off the ground. Scott was airborne as well, a slight wind ruffling his short hair. "We're late for a family reunion."

• • • TWENTY-SIX • • •

Scott decided he liked flying.

Not only am I weightless and floating free, he thought, *but for now anyway, the sea of possibilities has calmed.*

No choice he made in the next few minutes affected the future in any way. He was completely under Martes's power, and could do nothing but relax and float toward Castle Douglas. It allowed him some time to examine this new sight of his.

This side of the door, it's a lot more powerful.

Since entering Faerie, the fog in the distance had cleared. The waves were crisp, and if he concentrated, Scott could follow the current to the horizon and beyond, watch in fascination as a single event branched out into a million different futures. And not just for himself, either. He saw others' futures as well. Not as clearly as his own, but he could see. He'd seen Bridie's dead-end if she'd said yes to the crone. That was easy to spot: a big tidal wave of a future, that would have drowned her in blood—most of it her own. But now she was back on track. To what he wasn't sure. So drifting over the landscape, he let his inner eyes roam, trying to see what lay ahead for them at Castle Douglas. What he saw wasn't good.

"Scott? Scottie-dog!"

"Yeah?" he answered. Something in her tone made him think she might have been calling to him for quite some time. "What's up, sis?"

"What do you see?" she asked.

Should I tell her the truth? Scott examined the near future. The seas looked calm for at least a little ways. *I don't think anything changes if I tell her the truth.*

"I see us," Scott said. "And Douglas." His voice caught a little. "And Fletcher."

"Where? And is Fletcher Douglas's son?"

"Yes. At Castle Douglas. We're in a big, bright room. And there's a beautiful woman there." He shook his head. "Only she's not. Not really. It doesn't matter."

"Why doesn't it matter?"

Nothing changes if I tell her the truth.

Scott spread his fingers and felt the wind whistle through them.

"Because we die there, Bridie." She didn't reply. "At least, in all the futures I see so far," he added feebly. "I'll be able to see clearer when we get closer." *I hope.*

"That's real encouraging, Scott."

"Shhh, let me concentrate."

And he looked out over the sea once more to where a creature that was once his brother cut him and his sister down again. And again. And again . . .

BRIDIE STAYED QUIET. *What was there to say, anyway?* She tried to go inside herself, find a calm center, like they'd tried to teach her to do in every martial arts class she'd trained in. But she'd only ever been good at the fighting. Inner peace eluded her then; it eluded her now. So she stretched. It was a strange feeling, stretching in midair.

There was no resistance. Not even the slight tug of the water when swimming. Bridie wondered if this was how astronauts felt in space.

Of course, they get up there by the much more reasonable means of sitting on a shit-ton of explosives.

"What are you doing?" Martes asked, turning to look back at her. He was in a half-reclining position, though leaning against nothing but air. His cloak fluttered around his sides.

"Limbering up." She cocked her head from side to side, heard her neck give a satisfying crack. "Scott says were going to die. I, for one, don't plan to go down without a fight."

Martes reached into his cloak, pulled something out and tossed it to her. Snatching it out of midair, Bridie saw that it was a small knife, its blade porcelain, its hilt scrimshawed bone.

"It was a gift from Lord Douglas," he said.

A feral grin lit Bridie's face. "Well, maybe I'll give it back to him."

"Make sure it's hilt-first then." Martes frowned. "I am pledged to protect him and his. I cannot allow you to harm him."

"Then why are you bringing us to him?" She examined the knife, blinking away a few tears the wind was tugging from her eyes. It was too small for her to wield it conventionally. But she could tuck it between her middle and ring fingers, round pummel tucked into her first. *A knuckle-knife. That'll work.* It would turn a punch to the face into a deadly strike.

"You are his family. I know how much he valued his grandmother. I hope some of that extends to you and your brother."

"If you think we can talk him out of killing—"

"I have no other ideas." Martes turned away and his cloak streamed out behind him. "I must follow my pledge, even though I fight against prophecy. No choice is my own. Yet I must act. I am not allowed to stand idly by."

"If I can't use the knife," Bridie said, "then why give it to me?"

Martes winked over his misshapen shoulder. "I made no pledge to protect his guards." On the horizon, a tower house and courtyard loomed, silhouetted by the evening sun. "Are you done 'limbering?' Castle Douglas is nigh."

Bridie glanced at Scott, his blind eyes closed tight as he concentrated on something she didn't understand. Then she looked down at the sharp white blade protruding from her clenched fist. "Yeah. I'm ready."

Martes made an almost imperceptible hand motion, and they began to descend. "We'll approach on foot," he said.

"Should we wait for night?" Bridie asked.

"Do you see in the dark?"

"Um, no."

"Well, the guards do." They landed lightly, even Scott, who never opened his eyes. "Besides," Martes went on, "I would think the straightforward approach would be more your style anyway."

Bridie shrugged. "Subtlety has never exactly been my strong suit."

Martes began marching on stumpy legs toward the castle. "Well, it's always been mine. But I have no time."

Scott fell in behind the bogie, and Bridie followed. They traveled in silence through the high flowering grasses till they reached the muddy track that led to the gate. A hundred yards from the gate Martes hissed to Bridie, "The ones on the walls are mine. You take the two on the ground."

Bridie looked at Scott. He nodded at her. "Okay," she said, sounding confident.

As they approached, Bridie looked over the guards Martes had named as "hers." They were big. Six-ten, seven foot maybe. And muscular. *Probably go two-sixty, two-seventy,* she thought.

And that's without the armor. Or the big swords hanging from their hips.

"Okay," she said again, not sounding quite as confident this time.

When the three were ten feet away, the guards' swords hissed out of their scabbards in unison. A stomp and a twirl—also in perfect unison—and the tips were pointing directly at Bridie's heart. "Halt," they said as one.

"Okay," Bridie said. There wasn't a trace of confidence left in the word.

The guard on the left—distinguishable from his partner only from the faint ghost of a scar running through his upper lip— peered at Martes and said, "Martes?"

Martes didn't answer. He had a wooden flute to his lips, and began blowing a jaunty tune.

"I am sorry, Martes," the guard said, "but Lord Douglas has closed the gates for now." He nodded firmly. "Closed them to everybody."

Martes kept playing. Bridie watched as heads began appearing over the wall, guards investigating the music.

"Martes," the guard continued, his tone indicating that though he was uncomfortable telling his Liege's right-hand man to bugger off, he was going to do his duty. "We cannot let you pass."

Martes ended his tune on a loud shrill note. Bridie saw one of the guards on the wall topple forward soundlessly. She balanced on the balls of her feet, left hand open and slightly forward, right hand with the knife held down by her leg.

"We cannot let you—"

Interrupted by the sound of a dead body hitting the ground from a fairly decent height, the guards turned their heads to see.

It was only a slight movement, a mere moment's break in their well-trained attentiveness, but it was all Bridie needed.

Knife hand whipping up and forward, she leapt at the guards.

SCOTT WATCHED IN horror as Bridie's foot slipped and two feet of bone sword suddenly sprouted from between her shoulder blades.

No, wait, that could *have happened. Just one of a multitude of possibilities.*

The futures were flashing so fast it was tough to follow the real action. Bridie's foot could have slipped. The guard could have shifted his weight and let her fly past. The second guard could have looked back earlier and caught Bridie off-guard. Each of these possibilities led to quick death for Bridie and Scott. He couldn't see past that. But as Bridie's footing stayed firm, and her target kept his weight forward, as the other guard kept watching his fellow's body fall, the possibilities narrowed down to one certain action, and Scott saw:

Bridie takes a quick shuffle step forward, and reaching up, buries Martes's knife in the guard's right eye.

With one guard down, there were less futures where Bridie was killed. Scott could almost read them quick enough to comment.

If she hesitates, he thought, *she dies.*

She didn't hesitate. Instead, she stepped past the dying guard, leaving the knife in his eye.

The blade would have snapped off if she yanked on it anyway.

Arrows from archers peeking out from behind crenellations on the wall were now filling the air and Scott suddenly saw that he should stand two feet to his left. He stepped aside as a half dozen arrows burrowed into the ground beside him. Several sharp high blasts from Martes's whistle and more bodies dropped from the walls. The arrow fire began concentrating on the bogie and he took to the air, dodging arrows with remarkable agility.

Turning back to Bridie, Scott saw that if she went left she would die on the second guard's blade. No time to warn her, and he gasped in horror as she stepped that way and into the reach of the right-handed guard's weapon.

It was only a feint however, and when the guard stepped forward and swung, she was already back to her right and out of reach, before skipping forward fast around his shield side. He was too big and bulky to stay with her and she was behind him.

That's the end, Scott thought. All the guards' futures splashed into one grim certainty once Bridie was behind him. Scott saw it before it happened. The leap onto his back. The thin arm snaking under the helm, but above the chestplate. A knee in the back, and he was choked out while his powerful arms swung his weapon impotently at a target he couldn't reach.

There's a very slight possibility that she'll stop before he . . .

The guard went down on his knees, arms limp. Bridie kept her arms locked hard, looking around for other enemies.

Nope. She'll kill him.

It was quiet. Martes floated to the ground and tucked his flute away. Bodies littered the grass. Bridie let the newest one drop to the ground.

Scott looked into the future.

"We must hurry," he said.

BRIDIE WAS THROUGH the portcullis first, Martes close behind. Scott, despite urging them to hurry, brought up the rear, walking slowly but purposefully.

Well, he's blind, Bridie thought. *Can't expect him to sprint.*

The entryway was wide and high-ceilinged—probably to give the archers positioned on the walkways lining the hall a clear line of fire. There were a dozen, maybe more, bowstrings taut, arms steady.

"Hold your fire," Martes commanded.

"Keep moving," Scott hissed.

The archers tracked them with their bows as they crossed the cobblestones making for a stout wooden door across from them. They were almost to it when it flew open and a guard burst in, shouting, "Traitors! Kill them!"

Bridie was on him immediately. Wrist lock and throw, and he was between them and the archers. A split-second later he was a pin cushion. Grabbing Scott by the arm, she propelled him through the door. Martes was close behind.

"On," he said, slamming the door. "Left at the end of the hall and straight on to the throne room." Pulling his flute from his cloak, he added, "I'll hold them here."

Bridie nodded, dragging Scott forward. He stumbled.

"Are you hit?" she said.

He shook his head no. "I just . . . I'm having trouble seeing."

Pulling him to his feet, Bridie said, "That's 'cause you're blind, you idiot."

"That doesn't help." Scott steadied himself and got moving again, leaning on Bridie's arm. "I'm having trouble seeing a future where we don't die."

Hearing the sound of splintering wood and Martes's flute screaming behind her, Bridie turned to look, but Scott said, "Keep going! Stop to help him and we die."

She obeyed, but said, "But we're going to die anyway, right?"

He smiled without joy. "Let's put it off for as long as possible."

"Okay." And they jogged down the long hall to the discordant sounds of Martes's flute and screaming fey.

· · · TWENTY-SEVEN · · ·

Scott's legs were pumping, but his mind was far away, searching through future after future where he and Bridie were blown up, stabbed, pierced by arrows, turned to stone, or killed in a number of creative and mostly painful ways.

Hopeless, hopeless, hopeless.

Back in the now he spotted something close by and deadly.

"Right!" he shouted. "Go right!"

"But Martes said to go left," his sister replied.

"Too many guards left." *Both the direction and the number,* he thought. "Go right. Down through the dungeons and up through the tower. Across the bridge to the throne room."

Then he was away again before he could tell if Bridie followed his directions.

If she doesn't, all our futures will meld into one bleak one quick enough.

He backtracked, caught another wave, and followed it over the horizon.

I didn't know a body could bend that way. He saw his spine snap. *Oh. It doesn't.*

Back to the now and out again. Violence, disaster, and death. *Try again. There must be an answer.*

BRIDIE WENT RIGHT. Scott was blind and crazy, but in this place, she decided, that might be an advantage. So she followed his directions, dragging him as quick as she could down the stone hall until they reached an intersection.

"Which way?" she asked. They all looked the same: rough gray stone, alternating windows and ensconced torches, each turning off in a different direction after twenty or thirty yards. When Scott didn't answer, she charged forward.

He didn't say to turn.

The hall turned and Bridie almost fell down the stone spiral staircase that appeared in front of her.

Scott did. Lost his grip on Bridie's hand, when she stopped abruptly, and tumbled past her, down the stairs and out of sight.

"Shit," Bridie said and jumped down the worn stairs three at a time, heedless of her own safety. Reaching the bottom moments later, she saw Scott crumpled in a heap. She ran to him. "You okay, Scotty-dog?"

Scott got up quickly and grinned. "I am wounded in dignity only." He ran his hands down his chest, then held one out to Bridie. "Let's go."

Bridie gave him a quick once-over, saw he wasn't lying, and resumed pulling him on.

"Why didn't you see that coming, Scott?"

"I did," he said. "But I'm not hurt. I wouldn't have gotten hurt. So I kept concentrating on the future a little farther out."

There were no more windows in the wall, and the hall was getting darker. Bridie starting noticing a bad smell coming from up ahead. Bad enough to overpower the normal castle smell of must, dust, and burning straw.

"See anything promising?"

The hallway ended in a thick door, with a lock so big as to be cartoonish hanging from its latch. The lock looked to be made mainly of obsidian or some other dark rock, with wood bindings that had been soaked and polished till they were hard as iron. Whatever the smell was, it was coming from behind the door.

"Nope. We die." Scott sounded neither surprised nor distressed. Like a newsman reciting the same bad news every night till it lost all meaning.

"Well, keep looking," Bridie said. Examining the door momentarily, she yanked once on the lock. It stayed firm. She yanked on the latch. The lock held it closed. "Or do we die right here?" She kicked the lock. Hit it. It didn't budge or break. "Because unless you suddenly learned how to pick a lock, this is the end of the line."

"It's a magic lock," Scott said, as if explaining things to a young child. "Use your magic ring."

"My what? Oh." Bridie grabbed Martes's ring from her pocket and held it before her. "Any magic words?"

"Please never hurts."

"Please open," she said, pointing the ring at the lock. Nothing happened. "What next?"

"Touch it."

Bridie reached out and rapped the lock with the face of the ring. The ring's red gem glowed briefly as it hit and Bridie heard a click from deep within the lock. With a sharp tug, she pulled the lock open, then off, then tossed it aside, and whipped open the door.

The smell almost knocked her off her feet.

"What's that?" she choked.

"The dungeon," Scott replied. If he was affected by the smell, he wasn't showing it. "We must go through."

"Great," Bridie said blandly. But holding Scott's hand—though whether to lead him, or to comfort herself, she was no longer sure—they went in.

FOR THE FIRST time, Scott was glad he was blind. He recognized the odor; you never forget the smell of mass death. And he'd seen enough torture chambers going door-to-door in Iraq to know what he would see here if he had eyes: shackles, chains, blood-stained tables, and chairs bolted to the floor. And tools. Some perverted from their normal purpose, some made specifically for the job of ripping flesh, popping eyeballs, tearing out fingernails. There'd be piles of ears and toes and other parts; there'd be a body or three still strapped into the chairs, maybe living maybe not—it didn't matter, they wouldn't be alive for long. And there'd be a big drain in the middle of the floor so the blood wouldn't pool up hip-deep.

Scott shuddered and kept walking. Bridie's hand tugged at his and he realized she had stopped.

"Let's move, Bridie."

She didn't. "I thought . . ." she began.

"Thought what?"

"I thought I'd seen it all."

Scott sighed and squeezed her hand. "You were a cop, Bridie. Not a soldier. You've never been in a war. You don't know real madness. Real evil." He turned milky eyes on her. "You think I'm crazy? You'd have to be after what I saw in war. What we all saw." He tugged at her hand and started walking. This time she followed. "You like killing, Bridie."

"No, I—"

"It wasn't a question." Scott stepped around a body. Tripping over it wouldn't have affected his future, but he figured he'd avoid it anyway. "I can see it in your future, in your past. You think it makes you a bad person?" He smiled when she didn't say anything. "That was a question."

"Yes." A simple statement.

"It doesn't. I've seen bad people. I probably was one for a while there. A lot of us were." Waving his free hand at their surroundings, he said, "But you're not capable of this."

"But I do like killing. Just like you said."

Scott was silent for a few more paces. The smell was growing more tolerable. *Either I'm getting used to it, or we're nearing the dungeon's exit.*

"Do you know what the difference is between a hunter and a madman, Bridie?" He didn't wait for her answer. "A madman hunts to kill. A hunter kills to have hunted." Bridie pulled on his hand and stopped him. He reached out. Felt a door. "You're a hunter, Bridie. Just make sure you're after deserving prey."

He pulled the door open and dragged them onto another musty castle stairway. It smelled like a fresh spring breeze.

AFTER THE HORROR of the dungeon, Bridie took the lead again, leading up the stairway as fast as she could make her brother go. The stairs kept winding upward and upward and the irregularly spaced thin windows were dirty and fogged; they let in the light, but gave no clue as to what was outside. Still, when the stairs finally ended on an open-air platform, Bridie was not surprised to be well above the ground.

However, well above the ground was a bit of an understatement. Bridie's legs felt weak as she peeked over the side at the thousand-foot drop to the ground below. Straight ahead was a thin span of stone between where they were and the top floor of a stout tower maybe twenty yards away. It was wider than a balance beam. But not by a nearly big enough margin to make Bridie comfortable.

"We have to cross that?" she asked Scott.

"Yes."

"Do we die?"

"Yes. But not usually from crossing this bridge."

Bridie frowned. " 'Not usually?' "

"If we hurry," Scott said, "we'll make it."

Bridie eyed the bridge, one hand on her hip. "I am *not* hurrying across that."

"Suit yourself. But the air force is on its way." He pointed toward the sun. Following his finger, Bridie spotted winged creatures—but not birds, certainly with those feline features and long clawed feet—circling in the near distance. One spotted her and, giving a roar, wheeled toward the ledge they stood on. The others followed suit. "And it's a long enough drop for them to catch us before we hit." He grinned. "The futures where we die from impact are preferable to that."

"Oh, shit," Bridie drawled, making the word last for her first jogging steps onto the thin bridge. She began listing to port almost immediately, but more speed and a slight tug on her hand from Scott righted her. Pouring it on then, she was in full sprint by the middle. She didn't dare take her eyes off the beam to see how close the flying tigers were, but they'd looked capable of alarming speed. She didn't know how Scott was keeping his balance. There was no chance of falling off when she was just a few steps from the end, and she looked up to see what kind of door they were facing.

Glass. The door was a giant pane of glass.

With a lovely crystal handle, she noted inanely.

There was no going back. There was no slowing down.

"Scott!"

"Go through, Bridie."

Bridie gathered herself and leapt, hitting the center of the glass in a nearly perfect flying side kick. The door exploded inward, and Bridie went with it, shards of glass slicing her in the legs, the hands, the face. The floor was farther down than she expected and she landed awkwardly, twisting her left knee and knocking the wind out of her.

By the time she caught her breath, Scott was by her side, helping her up. Taking stock as she rose, she sensed that the knee was painful but could support her and though a disturbingly large hunk of glass stuck out of her right thigh, it was like an inverted iceberg: most of its mass was out of her leg. The rest of it was neither deep nor sticking into anything vital. She was injured, but not badly. And she was alive.

For now.

"Quite an entrance," Douglas said from his opulent throne. He was dressed all in medieval black again, one foot in its incongruent combat boot tapping idly on the dais. In his right hand he held a long dagger, in the left he cradled a sleeping infant. "I wonder if the exit will match."

WELL, SCOTT THOUGHT, *here we are. The end of the line.*

He'd been holding out hope that when they got to the throne room, new possibilities would open up. But he saw no new way to attack Douglas that didn't end in their death. No matter how fast he moved, no matter how Bridie bobbed and weaved, Douglas was always three steps ahead of them.

How does he do that? Does he see the future even better than I do?

Scott scanned Douglas's futures, most of them impossibly long. He saw Douglas perform seeming miracles, grand acts of destruction, massive transformations of himself and others. He suddenly remembered something Douglas had said to Mundoo: *I know your true names. All of them.*

He doesn't know the future, Scott thought. *But he knows us so well he can easily predict what we're going to do.* Reaching up,

Scott touched his eyelids. *He can even change us into something different if he wants to.*

Scott scanned Douglas's futures again.

There's so many. We have so few at this point. Then it hit him: *Why am I examining our futures? Douglas has a lot more options left to him. Maybe in one of them we all live.*

He dove into the wide sea of Douglas's possibilities, searching for some thin thread that would lead them all ashore.

"DOUGLAS," BRIDIE SAID. "Don't."

Douglas raised an eyebrow. "Why not? This child is half *her*." He sneered at Aine, who sat frozen in her little chair below him.

"It's half you, too." Bridie inched closer as she spoke, gauging the distance between them, trying to guess if she could reach him before he stabbed the baby. Or her. She glanced around the room, looking for some kind of weapon. Silently cursed herself for leaving Martes's knife in the guard's eye. Then she looked down at the piece of glass sticking out of her leg. *Maybe . . .*

"It's half me, as well," Douglas said, eyes fierce. "And I've never liked me much, either."

Bridie shuffled forward another half-step. "Douglas. You can't kill a child." *Two more steps and I can reach him. Maybe he's distracted enough to not read my mind.*

"I've killed so many," he said, eyes drifting away from Bridie momentarily, "I never bothered to count."

Now! Bridie's instincts screamed at her. *While he's looking away.* Pain gave her extra impetus as she tore the glass shard from her leg. One step, two, and she was almost on him, spraying blood, a red splash appearing on Aine's sharp cheeks as she passed her. Douglas's head whipped around to see her, and his grip on the infant tightened. He was on his feet impossibly fast, knife in guard, mouth opening to sing.

Scott was right, Bridie thought. *I'm not going to make it.*

But a voice so authoritative she almost didn't recognize it froze them both in place.

"Stop!"

SCOTT COULD SEE Bridie's possibilities narrowing, but he couldn't do anything about it. No action he took right now could stop her death. He saw that. If there was another way, it would have to come from Douglas's future. His was still wide open, branching far and wide—but most of the branches were—*or will be, I suppose*—drenched in blood.

He's a bloody-minded tyrant, isn't he? Scott thought.

Bridie's futures were dismal now, only seconds remaining. Desperately, Scott cast his net far afield, ignoring the bloodiest of Douglas's prospects.

If we avoid bloodshed now, maybe he avoids it in the future. I don't have time to look through all of them.

Futures shuddered and shook as Bridie ripped the glass from her leg. His gaze far away, Scott was still filled with despair as Bridie's fate was being sealed.

I've wasted the few moments we had left, he thought. *I should have done something. Anything. Instead of standing here like a blind fool.* But he'd seen the future. There was nothing he could have done.

A tear rolled down his cheek as his sister's death dance entered its final few steps.

Nothing I could have done.

But then, far in the future of one of Douglas's least possible possibilities, he saw a face he recognized. It was so unlikely, so improbable, that the twists and turns that caused Douglas to meet this person were impossible to follow.

But Scott could see where it started. Right here, in this throne room.

With the force of a drill sergeant, he shouted, "Stop!"

And the sea of possibilities exploded.

twenty-eight

Bridie was the first to break the silence. "Scott? You got something to say?" She kept her eyes on Douglas, watching for the slightest twitch of his blade in her or the baby's direction.

"Make it quick," Douglas snarled. "I believe your sister is moments away from forcing me to kill her."

Scott cocked his head to one side. "But if you kill her," he said, "you'll never see Grandma McLaren again."

Douglas flinched like he'd been struck. His knuckles whitened on his knife, and he looked so furious that Bridie thought for a second that he was going to throw the baby to the ground in anger. But a split second later he was as calm as ever. "Grandma McLaren is dead," he said in a flat voice.

"I know," Scott said. "But strange things happen here." He shrugged. "I can't explain it."

Douglas peered at him. "And what do I have to do—besides not killing you, of course—to have this unlikely reunion with our grandmother?"

"I can't see the whole way there. It's too far away and too complicated. But I can tell a few things."

Douglas settled back down onto his throne. "And they are?"

"You never see your son again."

Douglas looked down at the baby. Bridie didn't sense any love in his gaze.

"What else?" he asked.

"You don't harm us."

"Yes, we covered that."

"You don't kill her." Scott pointed at Aine.

"Hadn't planned to. What else?"

"Well, you . . . um . . ."

Turning her head, Bridie looked at Scott in surprise. *He'd sounded so confident till now.*

"Yes?" Douglas asked, arching an eyebrow.

Recovering himself, Scott stated, "You strip yourself of your powers. Here. In this room."

Douglas threw his head back and howled with laughter. Bridie almost jumped him then, but Scott was suddenly beside her, his hand on her arm. He shook his head at her.

"C'mon, Scott," Douglas said in one of the small gaps between guffaws and gasping for breath. "You'll have to do better than that." Finally getting control of himself, he let loose with a perfect imitation of Scott's stentorian pronouncement. " 'Strip yourself of your powers,' " he intoned. " 'Here. In this room.' " Then he was off again, sending peals of maniacal laughter echoing off the tall windows.

Scott pulled Bridie back a step. "Let's bind that wound, Bridie."

Looking down at her leg, she saw that it was bleeding freely now after removing the shard of glass. "Am I going to bleed to death?"

Smiling, Scott said, "Not if we bind it." Tearing a long strip of cloth from his shirt, he knelt and reached out blindly for her leg. Then he looked up in Douglas's direction. "Look at me, Douglas. *See* me."

Laughter finally subsiding, Douglas stared at Scott. Bridie watched as his eyes tightened with intense concentration, a thin uncertain hum coming from his lips as if he were learning a new melody and wasn't sure whether it was major or minor. Then all the color drained from his face.

"How?" was all he managed.

Scott wadded up the strip of his shirt and pressed it against Bridie's leg. "Hold," he said, and went back to tear another piece. "Does it matter? Am I lying?" A new cloth went around Bridie's thigh, tied off in seconds. The wound ached, but the pressure was slowing the bleeding.

Douglas's eyes looked wild and dark in his ashen face. "No. You're not lying."

Scott stood and faced the throne. "Do you see what I see, Douglas? Do you understand what it means?"

"I . . . I'm not sure."

"Lose your magic now and keep the hope of seeing Grandma McLaren again alive."

"I have to—"

"Think about it. Of course." Scott abruptly sat on the floor. It made Bridie realize how tired she was. *I wonder how long it's been since I slept.* She tried to sit cross-legged next to Scott, but it hurt her leg too much. She ended up sitting awkwardly in almost a sprinter's stretch, her wounded leg stretched out in front of her. *I hope Douglas doesn't decide to kill us after all. Because I'll never get up from this position.*

Douglas didn't look inclined to kill them. He looked sick. His face was pale and his eyes darted from Scott to the baby then down at the knife in his hand. In contrast, Scott looked calm in his lotus position. *Like the statue of the Buddha at the Pagoda,* Bridie thought. *Serene. Must be nice to know the future.*

"What's going to happen?" she whispered. "Is he going to listen?"

Shrugging, Scott said, "I don't know."

"Then how can you be so calm?"

"Because I do know that nothing we do or say in the next few minutes affects the outcome at all." He beamed a smile at her. "Unless of course you attack him again. That'd be bad."

Bridie gave a mirthless chuckle. "I'm not sure I'll ever stand up again." Scott began to speak, but Bridie interrupted, holding a hand up. "No, don't tell me. Let it be a surprise." Straightening her uninjured knee, she lay all the way back on the cool stone of the throne-room floor. "Wake me if he decides to let us live."

"And if he goes the other way?"

"Then let me keep sleeping."

But she didn't even have time to close her eyes.

"All right," Douglas said. "Can I even do it? Give up my magic? I mean, it's a skill I learned."

Before Scott could answer, one of the double doors to the throne room banged open, and Martes scampered in, stumpy legs pumping furiously. He looked none the worse for wear, despite a couple of arrows sticking into his cloak. They didn't appear to have penetrated his body.

"A little help here, guys?" he said just as the other door crashed wide and a dozen guards entered at a gallop. Seeing this, Douglas jumped to his feet.

"Hold!" he shouted. The guards froze. "Leave us." Turning sharply, they marched toward the door. "Wait!" They stopped. "Take the queen with you."

In quick order, four guards marched to the dais and lifted the queen—chair and all—between them. One of the guards still standing near the door asked, "Where shall we bring her, Sire?"

Douglas seemed to think about that for a moment. "Into the world and far away. I am sick of looking at her."

The speaker bowed and the four carrying the chair nodded their heads. Then they all marched out, four in front and four behind the queen, the guard who had spoken pausing to bow low once more. He shut the doors behind him.

Douglas sat back down. He looked tired. "Now we wait. I want her far away when my magic fades."

Scott shook his head. "Don't wait too long. You must be out of the castle before full dark."

"Why? Oh never mind." He looked down at his hands. Let the knife clatter to the floor. "Martes, come take this child to his uncle."

Martes was grinning from ear to ear as he crawled up onto the dais. Douglas dumped the infant into his arms. "Why are you smiling?" Douglas snapped.

Skipping off toward Scott, Martes said gaily, "Because I'm a thrice-damned genius, Boss. That's why!" He placed Fletcher carefully into Scott's outstretched arms, helping the blind man wrap him up. "I brought them here." He pointed at Bridie and Scott. "And have kept my bond. You and yours are safe again." Frowning, he went on, "At least you all will be soon, I hope."

"Well, we're all safe," Douglas said, "but if *you* piss me off before I'm powerless, I'll turn you into a newt." Douglas's face lit in an impish grin, and Bridie almost liked him again. "It wouldn't be a long trip."

"I don't doubt it, Boss," Martes said, still smiling. "Now, let's get this done and get your family home where they belong."

Douglas nodded. And began to sing.

I GUESS YOU don't need eyes, Scott thought, *to see magic.*

It was like a summer storm over the sea of possibilities. The notes rained down, multihued droplets of change. Beams of light burst through clouds of chance, skewering different futures and sending them skewing off in directions unreachable through natural law.

It was beautiful.

But something is wrong. Scott couldn't put his finger on it for a second, but something was missing.

Grandma McLaren! He couldn't see her anymore. Her future was gone.

"Wait!" he cried. "Douglas, stop!"

The rain stopped. The clouds vanished. Scott searched the distance for his grandmother.

"What is it, Scott?" Douglas asked.

Why did I stop him? Scott thought. *He would have been powerless. Bridie and Fletcher and I would have escaped. Douglas would have been killed, but hasn't he earned that?* But Scott wasn't sure he was capable of deceit anymore. He knew too much to lie. *Besides, I'd like to see the future where Grandma McLaren comes back.*

It was then he spotted her again. If anything, it was even more unlikely than before: Grandma McLaren and Douglas standing in a forest clearing surrounded by singing trees, talking quietly. Grandma McLaren in a housecoat and curlers; Douglas in stained tunic and breeches, a longbow hanging across his shoulder.

What did I miss before?

Scott traced it back, through the murk and mire, back to the room they stood in. Looked more carefully at how Douglas divested himself of his ingrained magic.

"You can't just lose your power, Douglas," he said.

"What? But you said—"

"You have to give it to someone," Scott said.

"But it's a skill. I had to learn—"

"That part—the craft of it—that you get to keep." Scott

frowned, trying to find the right words to convey what he had seen. "But the part that makes it real, the part that changes the world to fit your music, that's a part of you. It's in your blood, your bones. If you strip it out, it will come back." Scott was pacing. He didn't remember standing. "You need to give it to someone. Someone who can take it and use it. Keep it from returning to you. If you retain your power, you will continue to be Lord Douglas, Lord of the Realm. And Lord Douglas must cease to be so that Douglas, my brother, can live. And meet Grandma McLaren in a forest of singing trees some time in the future."

"Okay," Douglas said impatiently. "I'll give it to Martes. He's a musician."

"I don't think so, Boss," Martes said. "I think I know a little about how these things work. He said it's in your blood and bones. You'll have to give it to one of your family."

"But who? Bridie and Scott aren't musicians. They won't be able to— Oh."

Scott stopped walking and stood stroking Fletcher's soft cheek with his finger. Fletcher gurgled happily. "I'll need to get him some music lessons. But I'm sure he'll be a fast learner."

BRIDIE THOUGHT WATCHING an all-powerful mage get stripped of his magicks would be a little grander than it was. Scott said that from his point of view it was quite magnificent, but all she saw was Douglas singing softly to the baby. The tune was certainly interesting, but not exactly pleasant. Too discordant. And long. Douglas sang for what felt like an hour.

Could have been longer. I might have dozed off for a minute or two there.

And when it was over, neither Douglas or the baby really looked any different. Douglas was maybe not quite as thick and sturdy as he'd been, looking a little more like his old strung-out self, but maybe Bridie was imagining that. His eyes were the same odd black, anyway.

"Is that it?" Bridie asked. "Is it over?"

"Yes," Douglas said. "I'll need to go, now. Aine won't stay captive long."

"But didn't you *change* her?" Martes asked. "Like me?" He spoke without bitterness, which surprised Bridie. "She won't just change back when the magic fades."

"But she struggles constantly to change herself back. And she is quite powerful in her own way. She is also tied to this land. It helps her to loose her bonds." Douglas walked to the wall behind his throne and pushed on a spot just above his head. A hidden door popped open silently to reveal a small closet stuffed with armaments. "Without me to strengthen them . . ." Shrugging, he dug a bow and quiver from the closet. Strapped them on. "Anyway, full dark comes quickly. I have to go." A belt went around his waist, a sword into the scabbard that hung from it. A knife went into each boot.

Bridie blinked eyes that were suddenly teary. "Douglas, I—"

"No, Bridie. I don't want to talk. I don't want to think about the things I've done. I just want to go. Martes!" Douglas sprung onto the ledge of the window Bridie had broken coming in. "Get them home."

Martes leapt to attention, but it was Scott who spoke. "Bridie won't be going home quite yet."

Turning from the window, Douglas cocked his head. "Why not?"

The crone! I'd forgotten about her. "I have two days of service to fulfill to an old woman who helped me."

Douglas sighed. "I think I know which one. What will she have you doing?"

"Hunting," Bridie said. "Killing."

"I have a bad feeling about who you'll be after." Settling the bow more comfortably on his back, Douglas said, "Listen, Bridie. Don't try to cheat her. No matter your quarry, go after them with all your wiles and might. If you don't do your duty, you might never leave here." Then he smiled. "Like me!"

Then he jumped out the window.

"But why not?" Bridie yelled after him.

The answer came floating in, accompanied by a hearty chuckle. "You think I'll find a forest of singing trees in the real world?"

And Douglas was gone.

SCOTT DIDN'T SEE Douglas go. Neither did he see Bridie leave after receiving Martes's instructions on how to get back to the crone. But he could see their futures. And if they didn't look exactly rosy, there was nothing that he could do to change that now. Their fates were in their own hands. He had other worries. Like the ten pounds of hungry, bawling infant he cradled in one hand.

A child, Scott thought, *that is filled with enough power to light up the eastern seaboard.*

"Scott?" It was Martes speaking. "I think Douglas would want Fletcher to have this."

He pressed something into his free hand.

His guitar, Scott thought as his fingers brushed the strings, jangling them softly.

Hearing the sound, Fletcher stopped crying and reaching out, set one tiny hand on the cool wood of the guitar's body. Scott thought he could feel the instrument thrum in response.

"Take us home, please, Martes."

The dark was far from complete and the going was smooth. Douglas set himself a sharp pace through the tall grass surrounding Castle Douglas, heading for cover as quickly as possible. He wasn't near tired. He'd stripped himself of magic, but not of musculature. Scott hadn't objected, so he'd kept some of the "improvements" he'd made over time. Endurance, weapons skill, strength. Even kept the pinky tattoo. They weren't the important changes anyway. As he'd sung himself back to normal, he'd realized that the Lord Douglas he'd had to kill wasn't about looks or stamina. It was the interior changes that had made him what he was.

Wish I could have left the guilt behind.

Douglas could barely think about the countless acts of cruelty he'd performed as Lord Douglas. The thousands of fairies he'd killed. The *humans* he'd murdered. Changelings brought here as slave labor and slaughtered by him out of hand at the Battle for Calton Hill. He choked just thinking about it, and forced himself to turn his mind to other thoughts. Like digging through his memory for some hint of singing trees. He'd never heard of them, but there was plenty of Faerie he hadn't explored, content as he'd been to terrorize just his section of it. Sure, if there was an uprising in the outer reaches, he'd ride out and quell it. Maybe put a few hundred up on spikes to remind—

God, he thought, *I'm a monster.*

He almost missed the snap of a twig that alerted him to someone approaching.

And I'm going to be a dead monster if I don't start paying more attention to my surroundings.

Loosening his sword in its scabbard, he turned to face the intruder. Who was a lot smaller than he expected.

"Hiya, Boss!" Martes said cheerfully.

Douglas didn't smile back at him. "Come for your vengeance, baby stealer? Anger over the past will get you killed." *Or worse,* he thought. *Look what it did to me.* His hand tightened on his sword's hilt. "Well, I'm ready. Let's see which is faster: flute or blade."

But Martes didn't reach inside his cloak. With a pained look on his face, he said, "Douglas? Your magic is gone, not my word. I am to protect you and yours. There were no other provisions. There was no time limit." He smiled then. "Bran the Blessed's bursting bollucks, Boss! Don't be so quick to skewer your only ally out here. Besides, ye know you're bloody lost without me."

Douglas stared at Martes for another few seconds then let go of the sword's hilt. He smiled wide. "That's true. I learned a great deal from you. Most of which I never wanted to know." He turned to keep moving, half-expecting a blade in his back when he did. *But I'd rather get it over with now than spend the next ten nights sleepless and suspicious.*

But no blade came. Instead, he heard the familiar, "Up horse and hattock," and felt himself lifted into the air.

"It'll be faster this way," Martes said.

Douglas didn't answer. Looking out at the approaching horizon, he felt something he hadn't felt in a long time. Hadn't been capable of feeling. But now, through the guilt and remorse over the horrors he'd inflicted and the worry over his siblings and his son, he felt it.

Hope.

And it felt good.